ABOUT THE TYPE

This book was set in Bembo, a typeface based on an old-style Roman face that was used for Cardinal Bembo's tract *De Aetna* in 1495. Bembo was cut by Francisco Griffo in the early sixteenth century. The Lanston Monotype Machine Company of Philadelphia brought the well-proportioned letter forms of Bembo to the United States in the 1930s.

ALSO BY PEARL ABRAHAM

The Romance Reader

Giving Up America

The Seventh Beggar

american TALIBAN

american TALIBAN

A NOVEL

PEARL ABRAHAM

RANDOM HOUSE
NEW YORK

This is a work of fiction. All incidents and dialogue, and all characters with the exception of some well-known public figures, are products of the author's imagination and are not to be construed as real. Where real-life public figures appear, the situations, incidents, and dialogues concerning those persons are entirely fictional and are not intended to depict actual events or to change the entirely fictional nature of the work. In all other respects, any resemblance to persons living or dead is entirely coincidental.

Published in the United States by Random House, an imprint of The Random House Publishing Group, a division of Random House, Inc., New York.

RANDOM HOUSE and colophon are registered trademarks of Random House, Inc.

Grateful acknowledgment is made to the following for permission to reprint previously published material:
APA Publications GmbH & Co. Verlag KG, Singapore Branch: Excerpts from *Insight Guide Pakistan, 3rd Edition,* copyright © 2000 by APA Publications GmbH & Co. Verlag KG, Singapore Branch. Reprinted by permission.
Alfred A. Knopf, a division of Random House, Inc.: "Lay Back the Darkness" from *Lay Back the Darkness* by Edward Hirsch, copyright © 2003 by Edward Hirsch. Reprinted by permission of Alfred A. Knopf, a division of Random House, Inc.
Princeton University Press: Excerpt from *Alone with the Alone* by Henry Corbin, copyright © 1969 by Princeton University Press, 1998 6th pb. Printing and 1st Mythos edition with a new preface by Harold Bloom. Reprinted by permission of Princeton University Press.
The Royalty Network, Inc.: Excerpt from "Alice's Restaurant" by Arlo Guthrie, copyright © Appleseed Music, Inc. Reprinted by permission of The Royalty Network, Inc.
University of Massachusetts Press: Excerpt from "Don't Ask for That Love Again" from *The Rebel's Silhouette: Selected Poems* by Faiz Ahmed Faiz, copyright © 1991 by Agha Shahid Ali. Reprinted by permission of University of Massachusetts Press.

Library of Congress Cataloging-in-Publication Data
Abraham, Pearl.
American Taliban : a novel / Pearl Abraham.
p. cm.
ISBN 978-1-4000-6858-6
eBook ISBN 978-1-58836-978-9
1. Muslim converts—Fiction. 2. Americans—Pakistan—Fiction. 3. Americans—Afghanistan—Fiction. I. Title.
PS3551.B615A84 2010
813'.54—dc22 2009024403

Printed in the United States of America on acid-free paper

www.atrandom.com

9 8 7 6 5 4 3 2 1

First Edition

Book design by Christopher M. Zucker

For my mother,
Gitel Kohen-Brezeski Abraham,
in memoriam

They are only the last in a caravan of martyrs.

—King Hussein of Jordan

The Saint's fate yet hangs in suspense, but his martyrdom, if it shall be perfected, will make the gallows as glorious as the cross.

—Ralph Waldo Emerson

But you will exceed all of them. For you will sacrifice the man that clothes me.

—Gospel of Judas

OUTER BANKS (OBX), NORTH CAROLINA—AUGUST 2000

HE WAS LITTLE JOHN AT HOME, Gator John on wheels, John Jude on his birth certificate, Goofy-Foot John, or simply da kine to those in da know. He would also be Knowing John, or that's what he promised his mother. Thus he opened his *Tao* and read where he left off the day before—

> Knowing things makes you smart,
> But knowing yourself makes you wise.
> To rule others you must be powerful,
> To rule yourself you must be strong—

and stopped. He confined himself to one passage a day, one ounce of wisdom, so as to give it time and space, allow it play. Thus he was also Playful John.

So he linked to www.surfcheck.com to see the morning's surf, though swelling and curling and breaking just around the corner were the real waves.

The conditions today based on his digital view: swells that might develop into rideable waves at second tide. Which meant that business on the Outer Banks would be put on hold, lines at local supermarkets and stores would be long and slow, as everyone in checkout and bagging and restocking took the day off to catch and ride a wave. Which also meant lineups in the water so it would be harder to catch one.

In his inbox, seven new messages, from online buddies mostly, continuing chat-room conversations outside the chat room. But. It was August 8, his eighteenth birthday, and he and Katie & Co., his offline friends, were driving down to Hatteras to surf. In real time. He'd catch up on reading and virtual life later.

He reached for his baggy board shorts that according to the tall and tan and young and lovely at the surf shop had signs of aloha. She'd pegged him, she said, as a soul surfer as soon as he walked through the door. Crisped dry, along with his other salty shorts and tees, they clung to the clothesline he'd strung NW by SE of his room, an attic space retrofitted with dormers and skylights and portholes for plenty of sky and light and evening stars, as Barbara liked to say when she showed visitors around.

He pulled on a bleached shirt, grabbed his Thinsulate go-everywhere gray hoodie, and also the new Dylan biography he'd started, though it was unfortunately a hardback, which went against his own policy. He usually insisted on paperbacks, because they

a. presented no hard edges
b. slipped into his pocket
c. survived surf and sand as well as or better than the costlier version
d. and passed on without second thought to the next skate rat

Thus equipped, he scraped down the carpeted steps and heard Barbara on the telephone, per usual, since she lived and breathed on the phone. He tuned in to hear her inform the person at the other end that Bill Parish had also just this past weekend met a long-lost relative.

A long-lost relative? John queried short-term memory and recalled that his father had scheduled lunch last week with Great-aunt Lucy, one of the few Parish kin alive, since Bill had had the good fortune to be born into the most unregenerative family on earth. Barbara, John concluded, must be on the phone with someone who had truly met a long-lost relative but, as his dear, mad, competitive, generous, self-absorbed, self-important, loving mother was wont to do, she was busy topping that person's story instead of merely listening to it. If someone broke a leg, Barbaric Barbarella would have broken two legs, and perhaps an arm as well, and if the *Washington Post* had written about a friend or friend of a friend, then the *Washington Post* had also interviewed Barbara multiple times and had also misquoted her, or quoted her out of context, she knew exactly how it all worked, nothing was new to her, she couldn't be surprised or impressed by anything. She was Barbara Parish, wife of William Parish, lawyer to the powerful and famous, in other words homo importantus in his professional circles, and she, she herself, was also nothing to sneeze at, a Freudian psychoanalyst invited everywhere, who had her paws in everything Freudian, or at the very least wanted to and tried.

John stopped himself. It was way early in the day to allow his brain to go into petty überdrive; too soon to hand it over to busy Bar-barbarella's doings. But he'd gotten used to having the house to himself, and now it was the month of August, when Freudian barbarians take their vacations. Fortunately it was also the month for which East Coast surfers train all year, when the first good swells of the hurricane season arrive from the South, which makes for occasional overhead waves and stoke for everyone. He and Katie & Co. were practically living on the beach.

He poked his head into the open-style kitchen–slash–breakfast–slash–family room, noted that busybody Barbara was barefoot and bright in her pink and green shift, her beach uniform, she called it, which came, as did her entire Outer Banks wardrobe, from Life's a Beach: A Lilly Pulitzer Shop, on the boardwalk in nearby Duck. She made a point of stopping there once a week. While Bill relaxed in the pale yellow Adirondack chair at the store's open door and enjoyed the bliss of bay and ocean winds meeting across his sun-warmed face, Barbara would try on the latest arrivals and select another bright shift.

On this day, this early in the morning, Bill was most certainly hiding—meaning, most certainly painting in the nether region of the house, also known as his studio. John Jude waited for Barbara to feel his presence.

Happy birthday, darling.

He stooped to receive her warm lips on his cheek. A dozen of his favorite chocolate chocolate-chip muffins were cooling on the counter, and now she folded four of these ch-ch-chuffins into a cake box to go. She was a primo baker. She thought of such things and Katie & Co. appreciated it. The females in his life were mutual fans. Katie admired Barbara, and Barbara loved her. Barbara, John knew, was pleased he had friends she could meet. Too many of his friends, she worried, were virtual. Even their names, she said, were strangely biblically foreign: Josiah, Naim, Tajh, Ahmed, Jacques, Ibrahim.

People don't always use their real names online, John explained.

Of course, it's a mother's job to worry. She checked her copy of his summer reading list which she'd stuck on the fridge and noted that he was still on the books scheduled for the first two weeks of June: the *Tao*, the Whitman, Emerson, and Dylan.

At this rate, she said, your summer reading will take all year.

Which meant he wasn't keeping his end of the bargain. She and Bill had unwillingly agreed to let him defer Brown to allow him time to pursue his own interests, scholarship included. But it was summer and his birthday. He would catch up on his reading later.

So he gave her the finger—um, the sign, good-bye, later alligator, meaning he raised a fist, unfolded his pinky, then his thumb, and ducked out and away. Which never failed to amuse her.

Ha-ha-ha, she'd say as soon as she thought he was out of range. Isn't it wonderful that little John, who at near six foot tall is hardly little, feels perfectly comfortable talking to us as he would to his own friends.

John scooped up the Saab keys from the tray on the hallway console. His wax, leash, and sunscreen lived in the backseat. His skateboard leaned in its designated place beside the front door. Though the plan was for a day of surfing, he went nowhere without his skateboard. He made it a rule not to walk on terra firma. When he wasn't on water, he lived on wheels. He believed in continuous adaptation. The dinosaurs, he liked to tell Barbara, as if she were in danger of becoming one, died because they were too big and too slow. So he stomped on the heel of his skateboard, guided its nose over the threshold, opened the door, bumped down the first two steps, ollied onto the lip of Barbara's concrete planter, and finished with an air that gave him barely enough room for a ninety-degree flip before he landed in the driveway and rolled away. To practice a three-sixty, he needed a higher edge to grind on. If he explained the significance of the ollie to Barbara—that it was named for Alan "Ollie" Gelfand, the young skater who invented it—she would make it her day's project to find and purchase a concrete edge high enough for her son, her John Jude, who was surely as good as all the ollies in the world. She supported all ambition. She was a real-life incarnation of the genie in Aladdin's lamp, and John and Bill had learned to be careful what they wished for.

John popped his board up and guided it into the backseat. Then he went to retrieve his shorty and slipped it through the door at an angle, where it straddled the rear and passenger headrests and perched in perfect position to slice off his head. In the event of a sideswipe, Barbara liked to point out, he would be guillotined by surfboard.

Remember, she'd say, a hero who's alive benefits from his heroics.

There are worse ways to die, John informed her. Think wu-wei. Live as if you're already dead, unafraid. That's freedom, according to the *Tao*. Also Hegel.

He'd been meaning to read more Hegel if only so he could quote him at Barbara.

SO SOUTH ON 12 FROM SOUTHERN SHORES through Kitty Hawk into Kill Devil Hills out of Nags Head on to Whalebone and Bodie Island toward Oregon Inlet toward Rodanthe past Salvo past the residential developments of upper Hatteras, where traffic thins and land narrows, he and the girls drove and drove and drove, and finally water, water left and right, water straight ahead, they were driving toward water, water and sky and water and sky, finally. Spurts of dune grass barely holding on. In the washed-out area at Exe, hit by Hurricane Wye in July, bulldozers rumbled in the sun, building walls of sand, preparing for hurricane season starting in September. On the stereo, a double Dylan CD rather than the usual Bob Marley. The girls were trying to please him. For his birthday. To celebrate his first day, his beginning.

On December 8, 1981, Barbara pulled up to the stoplight at California and Eighteenth Streets and realized she was one month pregnant. So he was born August 8, 1982. So he is eighteen today. So he and Katie & Co. are celebrating. With this trip. With Dylan. Any other day, any other trip, they would have had the other Bob on, wailing Bob—oiyoiyoi-oiyoiyoiyoi-oiyoiyoiyoi-oiyoiyoiyoi—top man for wahines worldwide. John had yet to meet a wahine who agreed to differ. Not that he disliked Marley, but very little reggae soon fulfilled his need for reggae; therefore he was grateful to have Dylan along for the ride—Dylan the prophet. For his senior thesis in World Religion, he'd written on the mystical prophets of the great religions, proposing—not so originally, he now realized—that Emerson and Whitman and Dylan belonged on the same list. In class, they'd read excerpts of the Old and New Testaments, the Qur'an, Joseph Smith's Book of Mormon, as well as creation myths of the Middle East, Africa, and China, and he'd gotten interested in prophecy, which totally bothered Barbara.

Every great cause, she'd quoted, begins as a movement, becomes a business, and eventually degenerates into a racket.

I agree with you, John said, but that doesn't mean that the original vision was false.

Reading, he'd noticed that the same ideas recur in all mystical systems, in all time, even Barbara's. For example, the importance of love or aloha.

> Love, love, love,
> love is all you need.

The Beatles, he'd told her, or maybe just Lennon, could maybe also make the list.

The Sufi master Halki called the variations and differences between mystics numberless waves, all from the same sea.

So waves. John watched them, surfed them, and knew each one as unique, but also the same: another wave. So he read more Halki. And Sufism. Muhammed understood his own prophecy as an evolved rather than new truth, he read. Which shows integrity, John thought.

On the radio, Dylan asked whether Judas Iscariot had God on his side.

Did he? John asked the girls.

Was he the one who betrayed Jesus? Sylvie asked.

Yeah, Katie said. With a killer kiss.

They laughed. Well, Jilly drawled. Seeing as the kiss helped him become God, he might feel some gratitude. Wouldn't you agree to die if it meant you could live forever?

No, Katie said. Why should I care what I am after I'm dead, since I'm dead?

They continued toward Hatteras Point, a skinny bar of silence where sky and water meet, blue and blue with only a crayon line of sand between. In the slow sun the wide-angle windshield framed horizontal bands of water, sand, and sky.

This view, John announced, is as slung and slooping as ________, and initiated a road game of similes.

As my long board, Sylvie said.

As long and bleached as beach, Katie said.

As forever as this drive. Jilly sighed. I wish we would just stop. The surf here is looking really fine.

And suddenly, between breath and breath, they saw a perfect wave. John felt the communal gasp, pulled over, and stopped. They jumped out, shaded their eyes.

These were answers to prayers: lazy rolling things, heaving up and over in half time.

They looked at each other. Let's go, John urged.

They unloaded boards, they checked leashes, they slipped out of T-shirts, slipped into rash guards, kissed the crosses at their necks, lifted the boards onto their heads, walked down to the water, and the girls flung themselves in, paddling hard and fast, to the third, then fourth breaker, though from where he stood, John could see that the best waves were farther outside. He remained on the sand watching and counting. These inside waves were rideable, yes, but it would be the outside ones that would offer the real thrills, though riding outside waves in waters you didn't know took courage. Lines of prayer from Whitman came to his lips, his reward for reading:

> You sea! . . .
> Cushion me soft, rock me in billowy drowse.

The girls bobbed in the water, facing the waves, determined to ride. And then Jilly, whose strategy was to ride whatever came her way, popped up. And yes! The wave came, the wave carried her, she stood up to the sea, the tide, the forces of the universe.

She stayed on the lip of the wave, tictacing down the line, avoiding the drop until the end, when it turned over in lazy half time, and she stepped back in slow free fall. John applauded her performance.

She emerged two hundred yards down the beach and hiked back toward him. He was serving as her landmark, he knew, and stayed put. Katie and Sylvie, still afloat on their knees atop their boards, craning to see as much of Jilly's ride as they could, raised their hands to show joy in Jilly's joy. Then, determined to take what came, Sylvie popped up for the next wave. But it was choppy and closed out on her hard and fast. She went under; John held his breath until she landed on the gritty, bruising sand. Katie popped up and quickly bailed out, stepping off just in time. After which they convened onshore for a quick discussion.

The best sets are out there, beyond the fourth breaker, John pointed out.

True, Katie said, but look at the way they're breaking. There must be a reef or something.

Let's not scare ourselves, Jilly said. Let's just go.

This time John joined them, paddling hard, ducking under incoming swells. Katie and Sylvie stopped at the fourth breaker; Jilly, emboldened by her first success, kept going, and John went with her because someone had to. Katie and Sylvie watched, afraid for them. They were out here on their own, with no lifeguards, no help for miles, surfing in precisely the kind of conditions they'd promised their parents not to surf. But pushing beyond safe had always gotten them their best rides. When, minutes later, Jilly caught what looked like a double overheader and surfed for what felt like fifteen long minutes, Katie and Sylvie joined John at the fifth breaker. And each found bounty, brought to them by a confluence of winds and tides and ocean bottoms. The punishments, when they came, were also extreme. Each took a turn in raging water, thrashed against sand and rock. One minute John was Moses walking on water and showing off—Look, Ma, no hands—he performed a heelflip off the lip of the wave using the edge as if it were a concrete step, a maneuver he'd taken from skateboarding. But then the wave turned knifelike and closed out before he could land, and down he went, thrashing, and the force of the next wave came and held him down in the silent dark, the abyss of solitude, a place of no community. Underwater, he was free of communal life, free of Barbara and her social obligations. Here, in the dark, it was silent, and he was alone, with only himself, with only the deep and the dark and the infinite. Which invited his soul to stay and be. Alone. *Alone with the Alone,* one of the titles on his reading list. He should've read that book already. Note to self: Move the Corbin book to the top of the list. To do that, though, he needed air. He had to breathe.

He emerged with the skin on his shoulders raw. He emerged with a prayer on his lips, an invitation to his soul. He would become as he would become.

THEY STAYED for three hours, until tide, when the waves broke into choppy chaos. Fatigued, arms and legs scraped and jellied, they were prepared to call it quits, but then Jilly caught a lefthander and they stopped to watch.

She's scaring me today, Sylvie said.

It's like she's operating in another dimension, Katie said.

John agreed and wondered. What was it? Aloha, fortune, the gods?

They lost sight of her until she reemerged on the sand, a faraway exhausted speck.

Let's drive down to get her, Katie suggested.

They loaded their boards and drove and met Jilly trudging on rubber legs. She flopped into the Saab gratefully.

If only we could have such swells at the ESA Competition, she murmured. And closed her eyes and slept.

BARBARA HAD RESERVED TWO ROOMS at the Hatteras Motel: one for Sylvie and Jilly; another for Katie and John. They checked in and spent the afternoon taking showers and naps.

Early evening, hungry, anticipating the promised crab-bake dinner special, complete with buttered corn and margaritas, Katie nudged John awake with her sun-dried lips on his eyes and lips, with her long hair tickling his chest, with her untanned parts telling him what she wanted. So he awoke, and with long arms lifted and tucked her into his hips. Fully awake, he swung his leg over her and pinned her beneath him, the way she liked it, she said, and gave himself to her hard and fast, the way she liked it, after which he slowed down and slow and holding out and slower, until she could no longer stand to wait.

Katie dialed Jilly and Sylvie, to wake them. Meet us in the lobby in twenty.

In the lobby they compared burns and bruises. Sylvie, who bruised easily, had a huge black and blue on her thigh.

They drove to the nearby Harbor Resort, where Barbara and Bill were staying overnight and where they had reservations for dinner.

I could eat three crab-bake specials, Katie said.

Save room for the birthday cake, Barbara warned.

The girls reassured Barbara that they could eat all night and still have room for dessert.

So you think now, Barbara said, knowingly.

How was it? Bill asked.

John and the girls looked at one another. They hadn't discussed it yet; they'd been too exhausted and too awed, even frightened.

John spoke first. It was awesome, Dad. Scary.

Bill looked at his son, then at each of the girls, who merely nodded. He noted their faraway focus, as if they weren't quite here, at the table. Not a good sign, he thought, waiting to hear more.

There were some awesome double overheaders, John said. Jilly, especially, had the rides of her life. Probably her next life, too.

What do you mean, next life? doubting Barbara asked. And why was it only Jilly who experienced this?

Katie and Sylvie looked at each other, and at her. Because she went for it, Katie said.

But it was more than that, John thought. It was something else, he said, looking to Jilly for confirmation. I don't know what it was, but she had some extrasensory thing going today.

Jilly agreed. I don't know how it happened, she said. It was like I couldn't make a wrong move. My body sort of knew what to do on its own. I felt the wave like it was a live thing, and somehow my body knew what to do. I just shifted my weight to accommodate it. She shrugged. It was sooo eerie and totally cool.

Heaping platters of crab and corn on the cob arrived, and they set to cracking, picking, dipping, eating, cracking, picking, dipping, eating, cracking, picking, and the talk ceased. And though John loved crab feasts as much as the next person, and picked and licked the salty Old Bay seasoning which he liked as much as or more than the crabmeat itself, Jilly's words continued echoing in his head. I couldn't make a wrong move, she said. My body knew what to do, she said. Was it instinct? Or something more extraordinary?

He wouldn't ask her now, not in front of Barbara, who wouldn't appreciate the word extraordinary. But surely humans were endowed with imagination as well as intellect for a purpose, surely they were meant to rely on both. If there was anything wrong with modern man and woman, it was this: that in their attempt to grow beyond superstition, in their enlightened embrace of the rational, they'd abandoned knowledge of the extraordinary, the hidden, the transcendent, the whatever—call it by any name.

> If you can talk about it
>
> It isn't *Tao* . . .

Tao doesn't have a name.
Names are for ordinary things.

The cake arrived, revealing that Barbara had outdone herself. Only as a last resort could the three-tiered concoction be called a chocolate cake, because it went beyond chocolate and transcended cake. It was an absurd extravagant chocolate park, featuring every kind of chocolate—including M&M's, chocolate-covered graham crackers, Almond Joys, Goldenberg's Peanut Chews, chocolate rolls, chocolate twists, dark chocolate truffles, chocolate-covered raisins, chocolate pops, Kellogg's Cocoa Krispies, chocolate Ovaltine balls, chocolate-dipped strawberries, chocolate sprinkles, chocolate spread, Hershey's chocolate, Mounds, chocolate mints, chocolate nougat, chocolate crisps, chocolate gum balls, chocolate licorice, scoops of Ben & Jerry's chocolate brownie ice cream, and chocolate kisses—each one, Barbara explained, honors a phase in John's eighteen years of life, when that particular form of chocolate was his favorite. Where the central birthday candle would normally stand was a tiny carton of Hershey's chocolate milk, the one chocolate passion he'd never relinquished.

How'd you get it down here in one piece? Katie asked.

I packed the parts and put them together here, in the kitchen, Barbara said. I called in advance, and the staff agreed to give me a clean surface to work on.

The girls applied themselves to tasting each form, holding it up first for cataloging. Barbara remembered aloud the year or years in which each particular chocolate treat was *it.* Which made the girls laugh.

Wouldn't you say, Sylvie said, between giggles and tastings, that your son qualifies as a dangerously overcaffeinated chocoholic.

No wonder he's so skinny, Katie said. All that caffeine must keep his metabolism churning.

Bill agreed that John was surely a chocoholic and that Barbara was guilty of nurturing his chocoholism, but he corrected Katie on the source of John's metabolism. That, he said, is genetic, since I've always been thin and I don't favor chocolate. So don't get any ideas. Anyone else eating that much chocolate would gain weight.

Yes, Barbara confirmed. Chocolate hasn't worked for me. Clearly.

John, who was preoccupied with his gifts—a *Lawrence of Arabia* DVD from Sylvie and Jilly, a biography of Richard Burton from Katie, and, from Barbara and Bill, David Carson's *Trek,* an expensive design book filled with surfing references—looked up.

One small detail about my so-called chocoholism that hasn't been credited is how much of it, or, I should say, how little of it, I eat in any one sitting. I taste rather than eat chocolate, though I do taste frequently.

That's true, Barbara agreed. He has some God-given self-discipline.

Mom, John reminded, you don't believe in God. But I think I didn't develop neurotic tendencies because Barbara always let me have as much as I wanted. Most kids act as if they'll never see another chocolate bar.

Meaning, Katie said, turning toward Barbara, you've done something right.

THE EVENING'S ENTERTAINMENT, the girls announced, was a choreographed skateboard show, to take place on the area's best stretch of concrete, their own motel parking lot. Barbara and Bill followed the Saab back to the motel and settled on a stoop. John sprawled beside them, prepared to be entertained. In June, when he'd moved down to OBX, he'd taught first Katie, then Sylvie and Jilly, but he'd had to talk Katie into trying it, and now she was giving back, acknowledging the significance of his sport.

One board sport informs the other, he'd pointed out. You never know in which you'll make your mark. Christian Fletcher made the cover of *Surfer* with an aerial he had taken from skateboarding. Skater Todd Richards started snowboarding only to keep sane in northern winters, and he went on to the Winter Olympics.

Katie agreed that the three board sports shared a particular personality. Like you and me, she said. We're good together because we both ride side stance.

In Katie's opinion riding sideways made for a disposition that was other, that looked at and saw the world from an oblique angle. And surfing, she said, was better preparation for life because water and waves were always in flux, unlike the static street curbs on which skaters practiced.

But she agreed to try skateboarding and after stopping at Duck Village Outfitters for a six-point-seven-five-wide board, complete with trucks, wheels, and precision bearings, and also a helmet, knee and elbow pads, she started on pavement. John demonstrated correct foot placement, how to keep her front foot angled and on the front bolts, rear foot on the back bolts, perpendicular to the board. He demonstrated the push with the back foot, weight forward, feet pointed straight ahead, which she already knew from surfing. He reviewed the basics anyway, to make certain she knew right from wrong, and then, without a single fall or falter, she graduated to turns, quickly learning how to follow her shoulder into a semicircle. She especially liked tictacing, shifting her weight to her back foot and lifting the front wheels to the left and right, alternating between. Comfortable on a surfboard, she had no problem with balance on wheels. Within the first hour of her first skating lesson she was taking on skating's most necessary trick, the ollie.

Keep your back foot on the heel of the board, your front foot at center, he instructed. Lean forward, stomp on the heel, while at the same time or almost the same time pull up with your front foot, which will allow the board to ollie into an air.

It's cool how the skateboard appears glued to your shoes, she said, when he performed it for her in slo-mo.

She tried and tried, almost had it, then didn't, then almost again, and she was stoked.

I might change my mind about skating, she said. It's fun.

Then she fell on her back, and said, I take that back. She rubbed her tailbone and winced. I'd rather get tumbled and thrashed in the most extreme white-water washout, and go pearling in the sand. Anything is better than slamming on pavement.

But she got Sylvie and Jilly to try skating, and soon all three were practicing ollies, and now they wanted to celebrate it, or John, or the sport at large. In his honor. For his birthday. For stage lights, they used the headlights of both vehicles, engines running. For music, a boom box, of which John was in charge.

They started in semidark, to a song from *Dancer in the Dark,* and though the lyrics insisted on sight—I've seen it all, there is no more to see—the theme of blindness was odd. But hey, it wasn't Bob Marley.

They each took a turn performing an old surf move: Katie ducked and crouched as if she were entering a curl, Jilly hung ten, as if she were cruising a mellow Hawaiian wave on a nine-foot board, and Sylvie did some fancy stepping, crossovers, both forward and back, a trick old Kahanamoku made famous.

John laughed and clapped. They'd done their homework. Barbara and Bill cheered, too, though they didn't know the references. John explained.

I get it, Bill said. They're inside jokes.

Yes, John said. But also they're moves possible only on long, wide boards known as doors, impossible on today's lightweight small surfboards, and they're not exactly easy on a skateboard, not even a pig.

Introductions done, Katie came up for a series of tricks. She began by tictacing, ollied up on a block of concrete, slid along the edge on her front wheels, kicked her board into a kickflip on her way down, and landed—imperfectly, wobbly, but she stayed up.

John applauded. She had made real progress. She was strong, a powerful, muscular athlete.

Sylvie, who was as dark as Katie was blond, was up next. She was also longer and leaner, with limber rather than powerful muscles. And Jilly was always Jilly: freckled head to toe and funny.

Sylvie's specialty, John already knew, was speed, and she picked it up right from the start, ollied up, landed, delivered another air from a double kickflip, then ollied up again, slid on the rail the hardest way, between front and back trucks, landed, and kept going. Amazingly, she stayed fluid and following throughout, a Gumby. Speed and agility were Sylvie's defining attributes.

And then Jilly cruised up, performed a handstand on her board, and kickflipped her board with her hands, a parody of the real thing, and landed on her feet. She spun a three-sixty, popped an ollie, didn't quite land it, and then, as if to make up for the nonlanding, added an extra air, which turned into a somersault of sorts. She was a clown on wheels; she played; she entertained. She was extraordinary. Each of the girls was extraordinary in her own way.

They finished with a series of disco moves out of *Saturday Night Fever,* a skating train, then high kicks, New York Rockette style, references Barbara and Bill recognized and applauded. After which, they hugged the girls, hugged and triple kissed John, wished for many more birthdays to come, and said good night.

IN THEIR ROOMS, paid for by Barbara, her birthday gift to John, the girls collapsed, and, amounts of chocolate consumed notwithstanding, slept.

John turned the pages of *Trek.*

Your parents, Katie said, turning over with a groan, are so cool. For making this trip possible. For this book. For letting you stay at OBX all summer. You're lucky, Katie said, and pulled the sheet over her head.

John agrees. He is fortunate. He has Barbara and Bill, he has friends who share his passions. His world is wide open, or so it seems, he can take from it what he wants and needs, or so it seems, which makes deciding difficult. He knows what he does not want, but not the inverse. He knows that he will not dedicate himself to a life of earning and acquisition. He knows that to live fully is to avoid mere being, complacency.

Barbara, he knows, was eager to see him safely at Brown. She'd earmarked passages written by Brown alums, one by a female student. Radack, Jesselyn. Class of '91: On her own for the first time, she wrote: The only person I have to worry about is me, how unbelievably, amazingly selfish. What a gift!

She'd gone on to Yale and the Honor Program at the Justice Department. A total Goody-Two-Shoes.

Re: Brown, he said, yes. Eventually. But first he would take a year off. To learn and know. To remain eternally in process, to forever become though he doesn't yet know what. Therefore his policy is to pursue only what is of immediate personal interest, a commitment to the present. So he is fortunate. So he surfs the Atlantic. On December 8, 1981, a woman pulls up to the stoplight at California and Eighteenth Streets just as the radio announcer pauses to remember John Lennon. So she names her son John. On the radio, Hey Jude is playing, and she stays and listens all the way to the end, for seven long minutes. Despite its length, Hey Jude was number one for nine weeks straight, the longest spell at the top of the American charts for a Beatles single. So she names her son John Jude. So he skates the streets of Washington, D.C. So he graduates John Harlan High summa cum laude and defers Brown. He moves to the Outer Banks. Falls in love. Skates. Surfs. Turns the pages of *Trek*. He is fortunate. His world is wide open; he can take from it what he wants and needs, which makes deciding difficult. So he is committed to the daily minute, to living the present in the present tense, to finding the extraordinary in ordinary time, in the here and now. Thus he turns the pages of *Trek,* reads his daily *Tao,* reads his Whitman and Emerson and Dylan, and resolves to read more.

AUGUST 15, the day of the ESA Competition, and the morning was moist with saline. He could taste the salt on the membranes of his nose, mouth, and throat. On the radio, the National Weather Service announced the tide and trade wind conditions, the buoy report, the day's sunrise and sunset times, predicting possible head highs, which, if not mere wishful thinking, would give the girls an opportunity to show how good they were. Slowing for the stop sign at the end of East Dogwood, John licked his finger and felt the wind. On a scale of one to ten, the day was no more than a four. For surfers anyway. The winds were too calm for head highs, though that could change. For Katie's sake and for the sake of all wahines competing today, he sent up a prayer to the sea gods, to Lono, god of winds. If he could lash the seas with vines and swell the water, it might offer up surf-worthy waves. But would he? Did the gods care for wahines? Or for anyone for that matter? Philosophers didn't think so. Nor did Barbara and Bill, though that didn't prevent them from having him baptized. We did it for you, Barbara said when he asked, so that you wouldn't grow up feeling unprotected in some way. They'd also taken him to church when he was little. On Christmas Eve and Easter. And once to the blessing of the animals.

His own opinion: he was still undecided. It depended on how you thought of God. If God is nature, then God doesn't care, since nature doesn't. But if, as the mystics understood, God is the best of man and within man, then God cares, since man does.

John was eager to see Katie win. If she remained confident and centered, she could take home both a long and short board prize, she was that good. And she was favored for first place, but as anyone who follows these things knows, a favorite more often than not suffers an upset. He wondered whether she understood the challenge and, if she did, was it a case of knowing things or knowing herself.

He, John, already knew a few things. Numero uno: that he had no desire to follow his lawyer father into law and certainly not his pseudo-doctor mother into psychotherapy. He wouldn't be that kind of achiever, working eight to seven to pay the bills on the Adams Morgan town house and on their second home, the beach house in Southern Shores, which purchase he'd had a definite hand in, steering them away from Virginia Beach where they were looking, farther down the coast to the Outer Banks, where the best surf on the East Coast could be had.

The *outer* in Outer Banks was immediately attractive to his mother, who had a yen for adventure of the extreme and exclusive kind and declared as soon as they crossed Wright Memorial Bridge into Kitty Hawk that she had fallen in love with the place. After this first visit, she determined that to get them there and back they would require a sport-utility vehicle, and a week later left her signature with the local Mercedes dealer for a spanking-new black SUV. She planned to leave the old Saab at the house. All of which, both house and vehicle arrangement, John very much appreciated, though the ability to beget such things, or finance them, would not be his life's work. And it wasn't what Barbara and Bill wanted of him anyway. What they looked for from their son was originality and intellectuality and a lifestyle shaped by the liberal humanist ideas in which, as Barbara liked to point out, he had been immersed from the instant of his inception. They had provided him with the makings for a complete and perfect man, the faculties, talents, and privileges, both nature and nurture, and they expected him to fulfill such promise. And although the ways and means of fulfillment and how it would be measured had never been discussed, John understood, if only in a vague way, that proof of achievement would have to come from the media, with features in newspapers, magazines, radio, and television; in other words, what Barbara wanted for her son was the kind of hallowed celebrity a sophisticated parent could take pride in, meaning her son would do something highly remarkable, perhaps even original, but definitely not embarrassing.

At Jamba Juice, as first customer of the day, he paid for one of two

Sunshine Mornings with ice. He inserted the cups into their slots in the Saab and got under way, hopeful that he was early enough for a nearby spot. In the competitive nonsport of parking, in which the least evolved human with the most primitive aggression still intact wins, he found it more productive to simply select a corner on a particularly desirable street and stand idling, until someone came along, keys in hand, giving him enough time to get the car into position without engaging all his adrenaline merely to park. The means to any end should correspond in spirit to the get.

A spot on the corner of Byrd and Lindbergh opened, and minutes later, John was walking on the beach, sifting moon-cool sand between his toes. He went from tent to sponsored tent, from Quiksilver to Roxy to Hurley to Billabong, and finally found Katie & Co. gathered at Chickabiddy USA, a newly launched line of women's surfwear. He walked up behind Katie and placed the ice-cold cup on her bare back, which brought forth the expected shiver of delighted nondelight. She turned and sucked down her first long sip of Sunshine Morning, then passed the cup to Sylvie and offered John her saltandsand lips, which he liked despite or because of the grit, which was good, since they were rarely without it. She'd already been in the water.

Missed you last night, he said, inhaling her sun-warmed hair and skin, the coconut smell of Aloha sunscreen. It'd been their first separate night since the night before Hatteras, and he'd found it difficult falling asleep without her warm wriggling body tucked into his side. Though when he finally did sleep, he slept better and awoke rested.

The cup came back to Katie via Jilly and she took a second long sip.

Howz it look? he asked.

Inconsistent, she said. An interesting lefthander now and then, which could get better if the swells pick up, if tropical storm Sadie fulfills her promise. Our first heat begins in twenty minutes. We have to report on deck in ten. She shrugged. We're having fun, though. Check this out.

She loosened the drawstring of her cotton knapsack, reached inside, and withdrew a brand-new Chickabiddy rash guard. Without waiting to be asked, she pushed her head and arms through at once. And of course the rash guard was a snug fit, as was everything surf related for born-to-surf Katie.

They're sponsoring me today. If I win, they might be interested in sponsoring me for the year. Sylvie has the same deal with Billabong, and Jilly with Roxy. I went with Chickabiddy because I like their colors best.

Considering that Chickabiddy was only recently launched as a business, John wondered about the savviness of her decision. Women's surfing was said to be the fastest-growing sport in the country, maybe even the world, therefore the field was wide open, and what happened in this competition today could make the difference between corporate sponsorship and not, which could determine whether Katie's surfing would remain a passion or go on to become her profession. But it was a sign of character that she went for what she liked best.

Sylvie and Jilly slipped into their own rash guards, and John was treated to a fashion show put on by the three most promising female surfers on the Outer Banks.

Got yer eyes full? Jilly teased, turning and preening.

He was a lucky man, and he knew it. These neon colors, he said, wanting to say something, will make you infinitely visible.

And then they slipped out of their rash guards in synchronized performance, as if they'd rehearsed, and were once again in their string bikini tops and contrasting board pants, worn low on their hips, waistband rolled over so as to reveal the tops of their bikini bottoms, a style, the girls informed him, known as the Clinton-Lewinsky. It was late summer, and Katie's hair was sun bleached white, her skin was dark honey, and seeing her after their night apart, he couldn't help it, his penis stood erect. She was a total hottie, all muscle and energy, with nothing imperfect to forgive, though he liked to, or liked to think of himself as humanly forgiving. Surely this was love, he thought, which Barbara warned should make him very afraid.

Love, she said, quoting Nietzsche, is the state in which man sees things most of all as they are not.

But why should he be afraid of love? He would go where it led. He would go forth, and live and learn and become.

It was time to report on deck. Katie & Co. stood, brushed sand off their bums, and he walked with them toward the flags, where they received their competition jerseys, still wet from the previous heat. He gave Katie his best good-luck kiss, and Jilly and Sylvie each a hug.

Just be yourself and have fun, he said, sounding like Barbara.

KNOWING HOW SWELLS PERFORMED was a smart surfer's advantage, and though he wouldn't be in the water today, not for hours anyway, he walked as close as he could get and settled in to watch the sets, count the number of waves in a set, tracking at what point they started to increase in size, and when they started to diminish. Every set had a rhythm, a kind of natural internal clock that could tell you everything, if you knew what to look for. To Katie this knowledge came naturally, as involuntarily as she breathed. She fathomed the shape of the ocean floor by the shape of a swell, its heave, drop, and close, and since every surfer made contact with the ocean floor at some point, knowing where the rocks and reefs were could save your life. She thought of waves as personalities and got to know them as easily as she made friends. For her it was all innate intuition; she did no planning, lost no sleep. Nights, she sent up prayers to Lono, closed her eyes, and slept with the innocence of the heavenly cherubim.

The whistle sounded. The girls took off. Katie's first challenge, every surfer's first challenge, was to get under and past the white water with a minimum of energy. First to arrive got first place in the lineup, which made all the difference, especially in East Coast waters, where perfect waves were not plentiful.

All three charged with confidence. They leaped onto their boards, paddled hard and fast to the outside. From where he stood, it looked as if Katie and Jilly were in first and second place, with someone he didn't know in third. Sylvie was fourth. Behind Sylvie, two more competitors bobbed in line, altogether six wahines facing the depths, each waiting for the winning wave to come her way and bear her up and up and up to—

JOHN AWOKE, or he thought he was awake, and saw Barbara hovering, with Bill an inch behind her, which was usual, Bill was always hovering behind Barbara, but with fear in his face, which was not as usual. What were they afraid of? He smiled to reassure, lifted his hand to give them the sign, and discovered he couldn't: his right forearm was in a cast. He lifted his other hand and was relieved to see it intact, in its own skin. He made a fist, unfolded his pinky and thumb, and Barbara's fear dissolved, she smiled, became herself again, all busy bustle and chatter. She brushed his hair off his forehead and brought her warm lips to his skin, asked how he felt, while also concentrating on the conversation with the doctor, who was outlining John's arm and leg bones on film with his infrared pointer.

You can see the hairline crack in the wrist here, he said, pointing to a long faint line, and on the long bone of his leg here. But he's young. His bones should heal well and quickly. He was lucky, really. It could have been worse.

Could have been better, too, John said, and they turned toward him, surprised; they hadn't expected him to talk.

I mean, he explained, it could not have happened at all. He paused. What did happen, by the way? He remembered celebration, but for what and with whom?

How did I get here? he asked.

In skater terminology, the doctor responded, or the little I recall of it from my own skating days in the seventies: The car hit your skateboard while it was in the air, kickflipped it out from under you, and though you landed as planned, your wheels weren't there. That's one possible scenario. The facts are your board was smashed, and you are in one piece, more or less.

In other words, Barbara said, not caring much for skating or skating terminology just now, we're lucky you're alive. You also seem to have had something of a concussion. How's your head?

Thick, sort of, mmm, slow, John said.

That's probably the meds, the doctor said. We're doing our best to keep the swelling down.

What about my leg?

Not bad, actually, the doctor said. The X-ray indicates a fracture in the tibia. You may even, that is if your parents allow it, be on a skateboard again, in two or three months.

Two or three months! John roared. That was an eternity. What would he do without wheels for two or three months?

The doctor waited. You must've been riding right side forward since that's where the cracks are, which means you're a goofy-foot. So you're lucky because you'll have full use of your left arm.

He's a goofy-foot, Barbara confirmed.

If your own mother thinks you're goofy . . . The doctor shrugged, teasing. Your wrist should be ready to go in a few weeks.

John remembered dusk. He remembered grinding on curbs and benches and then turning back, he had been on his way back, to where Katie was toasting, being toasted, getting toasted. Then another edge presented itself and he flipped his board up and pulled his knees up, and—

WHO FOUND ME?

The driver called 911, Bill explained. An ambulance took you to the emergency room. The EMS guy found your ID card and called. We arrived soon after you did. The driver was here, too. He said it was dark and he didn't see you until it was too late. You were leaping off a bench or a curb or something. He thought at first that he'd hit you. Miraculously, it was only your skateboard.

Rational, legal Bill was talking miracles? He must have been scared.

John wondered but didn't want to ask what Katie knew.

I called Katie this morning, just before we left, Barbara said, reading his mind. She was still asleep, but her mother said she'd tell her as soon as she awoke.

Two hours later they left with promises to bring his MP3 player, his Dylan and *Tao*, his Burton biography, and some Power Bars, though he was getting out the next morning. Still, John said. It might be a long night.

When they left, he settled into recall. Katie must have won since she'd been celebrating, but there'd been some question or doubt about her placing first, some unpleasantness. Someone had challenged the numbers or her performance, and now he wasn't quite certain whose side he was on. Did she win fair and square? What exactly had happened?

He remembered an interference penalty. Against Jilly. But there was some debate over this call because no one could say for sure who had right of way, in other words, who was closer to the curl. He knew both girls and their styles and even he couldn't tell whose wave it was. But the judges somehow determined that Katie was first in the lineup, and they charged a 2.5 penalty against Jilly, which she wanted to contest but was advised not to. If she showed poor sportsmanship the judges wouldn't recommend her for the all-star team. Frustrated, unable to undo the false charge, she started to cry, and John found himself taking her side. If Jilly had miscalculated or misstepped, it was due simply to enthusiasm and high spirits, which didn't deserve punishment.

When she realized what the judges had done, Katie came forward and did the right thing: she filed a request that the penalty not be charged on her behalf. It had been an irregular wave that looked as if it would close out, she explained, and then it curled at the last minute. Predictably, this made the judges like Katie more, which was to her benefit, since the rules called for subjective judging with extra points awarded for innovation and difficulty, for style, power, and speed in the most critical phases of the wave.

Finally, under advice, Jilly submitted a written note to the judges explaining that if she had interfered it had not been intentional and that she had apologized to her fellow competitor, and now wanted to apologize to the judges. The head judge accepted the apology, and wished her a smoother event next year, but John wondered whether Jilly would ever compete again.

Of the maneuvers, he remembered several fantastic airs, one of them by Katie. Though she sometimes had trouble landing her ollie on wheels, she had performed it perfectly in the water. She'd nosed up above the lip of a wave, stomped down on the heel of her thruster, raised her other leg, leaped, and turned herself and her board around in the air, using the old shove-it he'd taught her, and amazingly, she'd stuck the landing, and then, as if this was all in a regular day's work, rode down the face of the wave, coolly stoked. She'd grinded on water, and it had been awesome to behold. On the beach, spectators cheered, and he had joined them, proudly. It was a super-athletic maneuver, performed with impressive power and style.

Inspired, Jilly and Sylvie each followed with their own awesome stunts, each performing to her own strengths. They were an awesome threesome, and it was clear to everyone that they were having fun out there, raising the bar with each maneuver. The crowd whooped, the judges concentrated hard, trying to catch every detail, to distinguish fine points, and there was much exulting on the beach, a kind of hush between whoops. These girls, John overheard the head judge saying, have got it goin' on.

When the heat sheets were tabulated, Sylvie and Katie came in tied, and unable to break the tie on paper, or maybe simply because they were such fun to watch and the crowd was demanding more, more, more, the judges sent them back for a ten-minute surf-off in which Katie somehow advanced by a fraction of a point. John didn't catch the how and why of that fractional gain, because he was distracted with Jilly standing beside him, watching, swabbing her nose and eyes. At first, this annoyed him. Then her grief moved him. He put his long arm around her. She should have been in the water, too. Of the three wahines, she'd proven herself most courageous. At Hatteras she'd surfed like the best of pros. He felt her disappointment keenly, and grew angry. He wanted to shake the judges.

For the rest of the evening, John felt himself drawn to Jilly rather than Katie, and this appalled him. He had an unreasonable attraction for the underdog. He hugged her, the triangles of her bikini wet his chest. When the awards were announced and the trophies distributed, she did her best not to cry. He watched as she air kissed both Sylvie and Katie. After which she split. She loaded her board on the roof of her dad's car, threw leashes–lotions–rash guard in the backseat, and left quickly.

When the numbers were posted, Katie threw her arms up in a V for victory, which didn't sit well with John given how equivocal a win this was. But he was being unfair, he knew. Uncomfortable in his disloyalty, disturbed at his fickleness, at how quickly his passions could shift, he wondered at the meaning of a love that was so changeable and turned away. Mr. Dodd, Katie's dad, brought out a cooler full of strawberry wine coolers, and the celebrating began. It was nearing dusk, and while Katie was fully engaged in happy-winner mode, all of which made her the picture-perfect candidate for the ESA, hence suddenly, disturbingly less attractive to him, he thought he wouldn't be missed if he went for a ride.

HE CHAFED. He wanted to scratch under his cast. Three long months of immobility translated to twelve weeks of house arrest. This was not what he had bargained for. This could not be his year off. What would he do? It was mid-August, the fifteenth or sixteenth, or was it already the seventeenth, he wasn't sure now, but the next three months in a cast would be three months of forever. He would miss an entire fall of his life, September, October, and part of November, when the best waves came east. Unable to surf, he couldn't stay on at OBX as planned, which would make Barbara happy. There's a time for everything, she liked to say, and September is the time to go back to school and books and the fall season. She overvalued art and culture in an unknowing aimless way, he thought. She purchased the books on best-seller lists; she booked series tickets in music, theater, and dance for herself and Bill, and now and then included a third ticket for John. To broaden his mind, she said.

It's good for you, she said, to have the occasional experience of civilized adult life.

She liked seeing him in a suit, his hair combed, appearing in public as a mensch, one of several New York words she dropped, though she wasn't really from New York.

So Barbara would have him where she wanted him, in D.C. The general election was coming up in November, she was planning to host her usual fund-raiser at their Adams Morgan house, and she would try to engage him in various tasks, his contribution to the cause, she would call it. And he would be stuck at home on crutches, without wheels. He could hear her voice in his head. Even if your body isn't fully operational, you have your mind. She lived in his head, and without wheels, there'd be no escape. He had to get away from D.C. and Barbara.

HE WAS EMERGING from sleep when Barbara and Bill arrived, bearing his MP3 player, his laptop, the *Tao*, the Dylan, the Burton biography, Zone bars, and Katie trailing behind. John welcomed the company, but he was especially happy to have his music and his books for later, for when he would be alone again. He dreaded this long night in this place of the sick and the dying, but, he reminded himself, it was only one night and now he had his music, and, for the next hour, his parents and Katie.

Checkout is scheduled for 9:00 a.m. tomorrow, Barbara reminded him. I'll be here, she promised, with a wheelchair at 8:30.

A wheelchair, John protested. What's wrong with crutches?

The doctor, Bill explained, doesn't want you to put any weight on your broken arm, at least not yet. In a week or two, when the fracture is on its way to healing, he'll prescribe crutches.

You're on hydrocodone, so you're not feeling pain, Barbara pointed out. But that'll change when you come off it. Give it a rest, and you'll be as good as new in a few months. Deal?

Barbara's bustling eased over his initial discomforts. Katie's natural sociability and teasing took care of the rest, and in a matter of seconds, following a hug and glad you're okay, she engaged him in the usual banter, a kind of tacking, the zig and zag of skateboarding.

If you'd been in water instead of on concrete, she teased, you might have gotten worked, but you'd still be walking.

Yeah, John agreed, drowning is preferable to broken limbs because then I might still be afloat, at least until I washed up on some shore somewhere.

Please stop, Barbara said. Both sports are extreme, and you're both either fortunate or not to have parents who are willing to live with risk.

John gave Katie the sign, which she returned; they touched pinkies, a truce. She settled in at the foot of the bed, and Barbara and Bill left them alone, to make wheelchair arrangements and sign papers, they said.

What now? John asked, and Katie understood that he was asking about her future plans, about how winning would affect them.

She shrugged, making light of it, for which John liked her.

Same old, she said. I guess I'll keep working at Jamba Juice, maybe take a class at NCCC, though I can't figure out in what. My dad wants me to take business. And I'll keep practicing whenever I can. As first-place winner, I qualify for the Championship Surf-Off and I need to stay in good form for that. Sylvie's parents want her to go to a four-year school, but she wants to stay on and practice.

And Jilly?

I don't know, Katie said. She won't talk to me, which is too weird. Her mom says she's too upset to talk. I feel bad, but I don't know what else I could've done. One of us had to place third. But still, I'm sorry for her.

John wasn't sure what Katie could have done. Refuse the prize, perhaps. Or better yet refuse to continue without Jilly in the water. In the heat of the moment it would have been hard to predict how things would turn out, and Katie couldn't have known that she'd place first. So it really wasn't her fault. So what was he holding against her? Perhaps she didn't have to celebrate quite so victoriously, given what happened.

Why? Katie asked, watching his face. Do you think I should have done more?

John shrugged. He didn't know, he wasn't sure, but this was a good example of what was wrong with competition, judged as it was by a collective, awarding not the best, but the face that best served its image. He didn't know how Katie could have helped being that face, or how she could have prevented Jilly's penalty, but having seen Jilly surf, they both knew there was something less than truth involved in Katie's win. He didn't want to, shouldn't have to say it, but Katie wouldn't let him off. She stood facing him, hand on hip.

You have to answer the question, she said, in a bossy teacher's voice.

John felt cornered, badgered. He shrugged. He looked away, opened the Dylan book, but Katie waited.

Only you really know, he finally said.

After which Katie became quiet; he could tell she wanted to leave. Seeing her unhappy, he regretted what he'd said, tried to take it back, but it was too late. Katie excused herself to find a restroom. She returned ten minutes later to say that Sylvie was picking her up out front in a few minutes. She gave John a whisper of a hug, and hours later he was still wrestling with his own bad conscience. He had made her feel bad. For no good reason. He should have apologized right away. He had wanted to apologize. She had done nothing wrong.

UNABLE TO SLEEP, he plugged his laptop into the hospital's DSL and went online. He might as well catch up on the latest chat-room conversations, which he'd missed. He might as well catch up on his lapsed correspondence.

Josiah had forwarded a chat session on the similarities of the stories of Genesis and those of the Qur'an. Thought you'd be interested in this one, he wrote.

John was interested. He'd started participating in this chat room in April, when he was reading fast and hard for World Religion, but he hadn't kept up with the conversations or his research or his summer reading. He had not even gotten to Pagels' *Gnostic Gospels,* scheduled for the end of his second week in June. He was way far behind.

He opened the file. Josiah and Naim and Ahmed and Ibrahim had participated, and also someone new named Noor. It started with Naim criticizing Genesis' version of the Ishmael story, and Naim, John knew, really knew this stuff.

I read a convincing argument, Naim wrote, that it was Ishmael not Isaac Abraham went to sacrifice. According to this scholar, Isaac wasn't even born yet. But Genesis gets chronology wrong all the time. As proof, this scholar offered the fact that God's blessing to multiply as the sand came true for Arabs not Jews. There are 100 million Arabs in the world and only 10 million Jews.

John paused. The proof seemed sort of unkosher, backward reasoning. But the idea that it was Ishmael not Isaac who was the intended victim made a lot of sense plotwise. At least from what he knew about the plot of Genesis. He wondered what Mr. G would say about this. They'd read the Binding of Isaac in class, discussed how awful it would have been for Isaac; also for Abraham, someone added.

Exactly, Mr. G had said. A lot of readers and critics found the story difficult and wrote about it, including the Danish philosopher Kierkegaard. So if you're still in the market for your senior topic, I recommend his famous problemata, published in *Fear and Trembling.* Before settling on his own topic, John had considered Kierkegaard.

Naim went on to criticize Sarah's infamous treatment of Hagar and, in response, Ahmed cited the orthodox explanation that God made Sarah do it because he wanted to test Abraham's faith. Sounds like rationalization, I know, Ahmed wrote, but Abraham's journey into the desert took him to Mecca and the Ka'ba, so there was a reason for the abuse.

But you know, Noor interrupted, the details and especially the chronology are only important if you interpret the stories literally. I think of them as ancient myths that are useful to explain why we do things, sort of like fairy tales. Hagar's quest for water, for example, is now part of the hajj ritual. My mom says that the reenactment of her desperate search celebrates Islamic motherhood.

No one responded to Noor's comment, perhaps because she was new and they didn't know her yet. Noor dropped out, the conversation drifted to other things, but John wished she'd stayed, and that the discussion had gone further. It intrigued him. He'd have to pursue it on his own. Maybe add Kierkegaard to his reading list. He sent a poke to Noor, introducing himself as Attar, student of Arab literature, got no response, looked at the bedside clock, and guessed that it was too late for her. So he opened his Summer-Reading-List, a file saved on his laptop. He reviewed the books on the list and regretted having read so little. He'd never updated the list, never got to the Corbin. So Barbara was right. He'd slacked off, and now it was mid-August. He would have to make up for June and July. Renew his commitment to reading and knowing. Revise the list. So he settled in to work. He added the Qur'an. He added Kierkegaard. He was pretty sure Barbara's copy of the book was still on the shelves in D.C. He would read it. He would become Knowing John. As promised.

STUDENT: John Jude Parish
Session Hours: Mon–Fri 7:00–8:40 a.m.
10-week syllabus
REVISED 08/16/2000

Course Title: **MY Summer Reading**
I AM GOING TO START LIVING LIKE A MYSTIC

Course Description: Today I am pulling on a green wool sweater/ and walking across the park in a dusky snowfall./ The trees stand like twenty-seven prophets in a field,/ each a station in a pilgrimage—silent, pondering./ Blue flakes of light falling across their bodies/ are the ciphers of a secret, an occultation./ I will examine their leaves as pages in a text/ and consider the bookish pigeons, students of winter./ I will kneel on the track of a vanquished squirrel/ and stare in to a blank pond for the figure of Sophia./ I shall begin scouring the sky for signs/ as if my whole future were constellated upon it./ I will walk home alone with the deep alone,/ a disciple of shadows, in praise of the mysteries. —Edward Hirsch from *Lay Back the Darkness*

Week I. Today I am pulling on a green wool sweater
Text: *Tao.*
Song of Myself. Whitman, Walt.
Transcendentalism. Emerson, Ralph Waldo.

Week II. The trees stand like twenty-seven prophets in a field
Text: *Bob Dylan: An Intimate Biography.* Scaduto, Anthony.
The Gnostic Gospels. Pagels, Elaine.

Week III. The ciphers of a secret, an occultation
Text: *The Sufis.* Shah, Idries.

Week IV. I will examine their leaves as pages in a text
Text: *The Qur'an.* Muhammed.

Week V. Consider the bookish pigeons, students of winter
Text: *The Arabs: A Short History.* Hitti, Philip K.

Week VI. I will kneel on the track of a vanquished squirrel
Text: *The Gift.* Hafiz.

Week VII. Stare into a blank pond for the figure of Sophia
Text: *Stations of Desire.* Ibn 'Arabi.

Week VIII. I shall begin scouring the sky for signs
Text: *Aesop Without Morals.*

Week IX. I will walk home alone with the deep alone
Text: *Alone with the Alone: Creative Imagination in the Sufism of Ibn 'Arabi.* Corbin, Henry.

Week X. A disciple of shadows, in praise of the mysteries
Text: *Fear and Trembling,* Kierkegaard.

SHE WAS A FORCE, a hurricane. Somehow, between hospital visits and daily life and sleep, she'd also cleaned his room, unhooked his clothesline, put away his clothes, arranged his books in neat piles on a bench at the foot of his bed, and purchased a long stainless-steel tray table on wheels. Most impressively, she'd had a temporary ramp installed over the stairs that led up to his room. In a day.

Awesome redecorating, Mom.

Barbara took his appreciation in stride. This room needed it. You'll probably spend more hours here in the next few weeks than you have all summer. But, she continued matter-of-factly, it doesn't have to be all work. The general outline of our schedule will, at least for the next few weeks, give shape to yours. Mornings, when your father paints, you can read and work. I might be in the garden or out running errands. If you want anything in particular from the shops in Duck or Kitty Hawk, let me know the night before. We'll eat a light lunch together at noon. Afternoons you can travel with us, if you like. We might have drinks with friends, or go to the beach, or play tennis—I hope you'll want to join us for some of this, even if only as a spectator. And, of course, Katie and the girls will visit.

Today we're playing doubles with the Winograds at four, she said, and I've proposed you as scorekeeper since it seems we're all either in our menopausal moment or experiencing early Alzheimer's. So we're counting on you.

John understood that this was Barbara's way of keeping him socially engaged, despite his immobility. He rolled his eyes, as was expected of him. He'd please her this once, keep score, after which he'd have to reassert his independence. He was eighteen, and he wouldn't spend his evenings watching his parents play.

Before he could settle in, Barbara announced lunch on the screened porch. Bill steered the wheelchair down the ramp and through the house to the porch, moved John's regular chair out of the way, and the wheelchair into its place. Then he followed Barbara to the kitchen.

With no choice but to sit, John sat. And felt the ocean breeze. He gave his attention to the canopy of quivering leaves, to the shadows parting and departing on the sunlit patio outside, and recalled endless hallowed summers, but why were they no longer so endless? Slow and silent had departed with childhood. For the first time all summer, he dropped into reverie, a laptop at rest until called forth again with the brush of a hand. He'd had a busy summer. That's why summers were no longer slow. And now he had two weeks left to recapture slowness, unless he allowed Barbara's planning to get in the way.

She came in bearing a tray of sandwiches, clicking him out of his reverie. Behind her was Bill with plates, chips, pickles, and mustard. He set them down and went back for the jug of lemon iced tea and glasses. Barbara pulled cloth napkins and picnic cutlery from the covered basket on the buffet, set the table, and then they were all seated, the sandwiches were named—cucumber with cream cheese, ham and cheese, tomato basil. John took a bite of each, to rate them. On a scale of most to least satisfying, the ham and cheese came in number one; the beefy tomato basil second.

You suffer, Bill said, the twenty-first-century mania for rating things. We grew up with *Consumer Reports,* which helped rational shoppers make informed decisions. Which was useful. But your generation is encouraged to rate everything.

Barbara blamed it on the online phenomenon, with stores like Amazon encouraging readers to rate every book and product. Consumer interaction is capitalism's latest frontier. Reality television's success is based in the popular vote. We're raising a generation for whom opinion is a kind of knowingness, which is a parody of knowledge.

If you just listen to yourselves, John said, you'll notice that you're sounding like your parents and grandparents. Every generation gets criticized by its elders.

It's possible, Barbara conceded, that this late in human development, knowing too much about everything, we're all mere parodies, acting on images of who we supposedly are, or images we've conjured up for ourselves as acceptable.

It's been said before, Bill said. All the world's a stage—dot dot dot.

John pushed his plate away and retired to his room, to reacquaint himself with himself, and plan the next weeks.

Out of habit, he went to www.surfcheck.com and watched the virtual waves, their virtual heave and crash. They were head high, the promise of yesterday's hurricane had materialized, and Katie and Sylvie were out there somewhere. About Jilly, he didn't know; she might be home moping, though the best thing she could do was get out there, practice, push against limitations, against what did or didn't happen, and prove how good she was. Katie was right. Jilly had as good a chance at championship as anyone else. After Hatteras, he would have put his money on her, but personal doubt and general negativity could hold her back. So he writes a poke: If you seek safety, it is on the shore. Warning: E-mail cannot be unsent. So he postpones sending it. So he Googles the word transcendent, reads the original, medieval, philosophical, and colloquial definitions, understands only the last one, links to links, moving through pages on American Transcendentalism, medieval transcendence, Emerson and Whitman, whose sources were Buddhist—

> I am the poet of the body
> And I am the poet of the soul . . .
>
> I think I will do nothing for a long time but listen,
> And accrue what I hear into myself . . . and let sounds
> contribute toward me.

He'd been meaning to do this ever since he handed in his senior thesis. He'd been meaning to read and continue his chat-room conversations. He'd learned a lot from some well-informed correspondents. John checked to see whether Noor had participated in the chat room again. She hadn't. But in his inbox he found her response to his poke.

I live in Brooklyn and study at NYU, Noor wrote. I was named after the queen of Jordan, who in case you don't know started out as just a daughter in a Syrian-Scottish-Swedish American family, named Lisa Halaby. But she graduated from Princeton with a degree in architecture and urban planning and met King Hussein when she was working on the design of the International Airport in Amman. Before marrying King Hussein, she accepted Islam and took the name Noor, meaning light. And she's very beautiful.

Noor from Brooklyn seemed to him exquisitely sensitive, lonely, sublime somehow, though he was largely making her up, imagining her, as he'd made himself up for her, introducing himself as a reader of Arab literature, which he had yet to read.

I love Arabic poetry, she wrote in response. Isn't the trilateral root system of classical Arabic awesome? she asked. I love how it allows the poem to mean more only if you know more vocabulary. Sort of a reward for knowing. The Sufis, who wrote in code to stay safe, really knew and used this root system. My dad says it's impossible to understand the depths of Sufi ideas without a grounding in classical Arabic.

She was writing to him as an insider, John noted, assuming that he read in classical Arabic, though even Arabs, he'd read, often don't understand the Qur'an.

Curious, John Googled the trilateral root system and read about the variety of conjugations possible on one three-letter root, about near and far meanings. It became clear to him that though his research may have been good enough for high school, he knew next to nothing. But he would begin knowing. He would take this inadvertent time-out to learn. He would read his Hafiz. He would read the Ibn 'Arabi. Become a student of Arab literature. He would write Noor. Write Jilly. So he toggles back to his poke. He hesitates. Fact: The first letter in the first modern novel (*Don Quixote*), which borrowed or stole from Sufi work, his tenth-grade English teacher lectured, was never delivered. So he delays. Links to pages on Islamic spirituality. Finds a Sufi center in Los Angeles. Finds Madonna's Kabbalah Center. He should call Katie, whom he loves. He should answer Noor's e-mail. He rereads her long and intriguing response to his poke.

She presented herself in an organized manner, first introducing herself as the daughter of an Arab American family who lives in Brooklyn, was named for Queen Noor, reads poetry, attends NYU. Then she answered his query about the Qur'an as an evolved variation. Muhammed, she wrote, came into contact with the ancient mystics of the Middle East, including the Essenes, a Gnostic sect that was also a source for Jewish and Christian mysticism. This makes sense to John, considering that the stories of the Qur'an feature the characters of the

Torah, which stories also serve as source code for the New Testament, which, and which, and which, on and on, just as, so too, because.

My dad, Noor wrote, likes to say that the denial of relationship and influence and cause and effect is driven by political interests. For which John doesn't much care, having no ambitions in that direction. His policy, he decides, will be Whitmanian all-embrace. He would be all-knowing, omnivorous, omniscient, omnificent; what Barbara would call an omnium-gatherum. He opens his reading journal and inscribes Whitman's words:

> I understand the large hearts of heroes,
>   The courage of present times and all times;

So he Googles the word Islam, the fastest-growing religion of the twenty-first century. One in five people in the world, he reads, considers himself Muslim. Fewer than 15 percent of Muslims are Arabs. The majority of the populations in fifty-one countries are Islamic. There are between 1.4 and 1.6 billion Muslims in the world, and this number is increasing at a rate of 2.9 percent. Which inspires him. So he reads his Rumi:

> Start a huge, foolish project like Noah.
> It doesn't matter what people think of you.

So he determines to expand his project, though he is way behind. He determines to become a student of Arab literature. He links to powells.com and orders *Beginning and Intermediate Arabic* and also a Penguin Classics edition of the Qur'an.

AT TENNIS, John sat in the shade of the white gazebo and half listened to the off rhythm of the bazooka ball, called the score when it stopped, love–thirty, love–forty. Barbara and Bill were losing fast, fulfilling his expectations. Since social life, not tennis, was what they were after, they weren't good at tennis. Socially they were managing fine.

While the ball bopped to and fro to nonglory, he threw his head back to see the tops of the towering trees surrounding the tennis court like tall toy soldiers playing siege. They were loblolly pine, the tallest, straightest pines of the South, their canopies all at the top, one hundred fifty feet away. Loblollies. He liked them for their lanky height, their straightness, being of similar build. At age fifteen when he'd shot tall and grown his coarse hair out to big hair, someone had called him a loblolly, and though the name hadn't stuck, too many syllables, he'd developed a kinship with this tree. Its essence might be his essence. It had the advantage of height, as he did. Though rooted at the base, it reached high. And rooted at the base as he, too, was for now, immobilized by his double casts, he could still think himself up to their highest points and float aloft in their upper breezes, near the heavens.

From: Noor Bint-Khan NoorK@earthlink.net
To: Attar attar7@adelphia.net
Date: August 21, 2000
RE: Middle Ages

Salaam Attar,
I'm sorry to hear about your double injuries, but if it means you have more time to read, then maybe it's for the best, as my mom likes to say of anything bad even when there's nothing good about it, like when my Cairo grandfather had a stroke and we all went to Egypt.

I've been mostly at home in Brooklyn this summer except when I'm at the library or at work, where I wait tables at a café on Mott called Gitane. Do you know it? It's really really popular. On weekends, the line wraps around the block. The food's Middle Eastern, so hummus and couscous and yogurt dishes, and stews with raisins and cumin and lemon, the kind of food I eat at home, too, so it's a good thing I like it.

My dad thinks working in a café will corrupt me, but I really wanted to do this, and my mom finally said do it without telling him. When he asks, she tells him I'm at NYU, taking a summer class in order to graduate sooner, which is a little true I guess since I'm at the library trying to get a head start on my reading for comp lit. which is like a double major in history and literature, with a focus on Arab and Mid-East culture. My adviser suggested I hit the books right away.

Anyway, it's interesting to me that you're not Muslim though your name is Attar and you're a student of Arab literature in translation. I grew up with Arabic, but I no longer use it so much, and though I can totally read and understand it, it becomes harder to speak it. My mom says I'm just rusty because my brother and I speak Een-zhlee-zee-yah at home, which helps my mom learn it, which is, I guess, a good thing, but makes my dad unhappy because it also helps my brother and me forget. My dad took English classes when he moved here since he had to prove his knowledge in order to drive a cab, his first job in America, but he's really old-fashioned and anti-assimilationist though he's also an immigrant lawyer who helps Arabs get their green card and become U.S. citizens, which really is a contradiction of sorts, as I try to tell him.

Which school are you going to in the fall and what will you study? Noor

From: Jilly Jilly24@comcast.net
To: GoofyFootJohn GoofyFootJohn@adelphia.net
Date: August 22, 2000
RE: overhead waves

Hi JJ,
I'm not calling not because I don't like you anymore or because I don't wanna talk to you or because I blame you. I'm just feeling bad. My mom says give it a week and it'll go away. She says I'll wake up one day and care less. Anyway I'm so so sorry to hear you're off your wheels AND board—I can imagine, well, I know how terrible that is so I totally completely sympathize.

I've been skateboarding. My dad helped me build a ramp—a homemade job—but it works, and I want to tell you how glad I am I learned to skate, and you deserve all the credit, and I agree it totally makes a difference in my surfing too. But you already know all that.

Later. Jillyxoxo

Ps I'll visit soon as I can.

From: Noor Bint-Khan NoorK@earthlink.net
To: Attar attar7@adelphia.net
Date: August 23, 2000
RE: John a.k.a. Attar

So am I the only one using my real name in the chatroom? That's so embarrassing.

From: Katie KatieOBX101@NCoptonline.net
To: GoofyFootJohn GoofyFootJohn@adelphia.net
Date: August 23, 2000
RE: visit

Dear JJ,
I saw your Mom in Duck and she said just stop by whenever. Is whenever all right?

xxxxxxxooooooKatie

From: Noor Bint-Khan NoorK@earthlink.net
To: Attar attar7@adelphia.net
Date: August 23, 2000
RE: Middle Ages

Ooops, I just realized I never really responded to your question about Islam seeming more open during the Middle Ages because the poetry is full of references to wine and love.

You're right that it's stricter now, but it's complicated to explain why. My mom says that in some ways she grew up with more freedom than I have here in America, in Brooklyn. I don't see how that's possible but she says I can't know that I'm not free because I never experienced anything else. At my age, she says, she and her friends were striving to become worthy souls. Her family is strictly Muslim, but still she claims there's more individuality there. Here, she says, everyone's the same, clones of each other. Americans, she says, all strive to earn lots of money, become millionaires, and so on. I don't know. I can't say that I entirely buy this.

ps: The Sharia school in Brooklyn offers classes in classical Arabic. I know some of the students and it's only a few blocks from my house.

From: Naim Naim24@optonline.net
To: Attar attar7@adelphia.net
Date: August 24, 2000
RE: middle ages

I want to respond to your statement in the chatroom that all religions and all prophets are really one because they share the same sources and influences. This idea is so typically American and so inclusively idiotic as to make everything meaningless. Although the three religions met and exchanged ideas in the 12c, they weren't exactly friends. Nor were they accepting of each other. It's more like they stole from each other. Jews stole the forms and structures of Muslim poetry. Christians stole Muslim tales and Muslim technology and Muslim architecture and presented it as their own. And Islam isn't pure either. It got its aesthetics and sophistication from Persia, which it occupied for 1400 years. But occupation and assimilation are never harmonious. Stealing isn't friendly or innocent. Even though Spanish Muslims and Jews were equally persecuted, and despite their supposed kinship and languages that come from the same Semitic family of languages, they will never be the same.

And anyway where are you trying to go with these sentimental ideas? It seems to me it can only be towards nonbelief. Believing in everything equals belief in nothing. Even if you aren't looking at all of this from a purely religious point of view, even if you're taking an academic approach, you're going at it the wrong way. In academia especially, one doesn't become a student of everything, because that's impossible. One must choose to become a knower of one thing, and with specialized knowledge one then has the ability to understand other things. If as you say you're a student of mysticism and Arab literature who wants to learn to read the works in their original language, then you must take the time to immerse yourself in Arab language and culture, which means moving to an Arab country, eating and dressing like an Arab, and learning the language the only way language can be learned: through daily use. But please take my advice only if you're serious about your interests and not merely a poseur.

From: Fawal bin Sina <FBS@ShariaSchool.com>
To: Attar attar7@adelphia.net
Date: August 25, 2000
RE: Arabic classes

Salaam Attar,
We are grateful for your interest in the Brooklyn branch of the Sharia School of Classical Arabic. Classes for the semester have begun in July and will continue through to the end of January. If as you say you are already studying the language, you may be able to join the group belatedly. In the beginner's course, the alphabet and some grammar are some of the first areas covered. If you've already mastered these, you will most likely be ahead. Perhaps it's best to come in and take a placement exam. For the cultural and historical lessons missed, your instructor can assign you supplemental readings.

You may register via our website or alternatively when you visit the school in person.

May Allah be with you,
Fawal bin Sina

From: Abdul abdul310@optonline.net
To: Attar attar7@adelphia.net
Date: August 25, 2000
RE: middle ages

I am responding to Naim's comments. His take on what you wrote is really really really narrow-minded; he sounds like someone's fundamentalist grandmother, may Allah protect him. It's super ridiculous to study with a narrow mind.

Attar, in my opinion, you should feel free to approach your scholarship from any and all angles, and what better way than with an open mind toward all religion and all prophets and all cultures. Follow the words of our great sheikh Ibn Arabi: I am capable of every form.

We are all born of Adam, or, if you're into science, we're all evolved from apes, whatever, it's the same one source, therefore why shouldn't all innate human wisdom hark back to one source, be it Sufism, Buddhism, Zen, Abrahamic Kabbalah, the Masons, the Coalmen, the American Odd Fellows, New Age, the Zoroastrians, or whatever name spirituality happens to be going under. I agree with you that it's all trying for the same thing, even when taking different paths to get there.

Scholars wiser than Naim have pointed out that believing in infinity or zero, which by the way was discovered by Arab mathematicians, is a form of skepticism that leads to self-knowledge. Certainty, on the other hand, leads only to mean narrow-mindedness and evil, like the Spanish Inquisition.

THEY CAME THE NEXT DAY, post tide, with salt and sand and stoke and coconut aloha. They tumbled into his room, talking all at once: The surf has been beastly, Sylvie said. Totally bruising, Jilly said. Awesome, Katie finished. She was as blond and tan as ever, legs long and lean and strong. And her eyes, they were see-through blue, he was looking into her soul. They hugged, making room for his awkward double casts.

When did Jilly return, John asked, happy to see their threesome existence restored.

This morning—Katie shrugged—when I drove up to her house and stayed on my horn until she came out.

My mom worried about the neighbors and made me go out, Jilly said.

What made you do it? John asked, looking at Katie. He felt capable of falling in love with her all over again, as if he weren't already.

I woke up and I just wanted her in the water with us. We've been surfing buddies since fifth grade and it seemed too silly to stop now. Besides we were coming to see you after, and I knew she'd want to visit.

We're saving money for Hawaii, Sylvie said. You should come with us.

Definitely, Katie said. Your casts will be off by then.

But, John said, I've been thinking of moving to Brooklyn. To study Arabic.

Arabic, Katie echoed.

Difficult choice, Jilly said, sarcastically. She cupped her palms, making them a scale. Which will it be: Arabic, Hawaii, Arabic, Hawaii, Arabic—

Barbara came in bearing a tray of cups and saucers and a pot of hot chocolate. She returned with muffins.

Not much surfing in Brooklyn, Sylvie said, with a full mouth.

Yeah, John drawled. Brooklyn is definitely not Hawaii.

What's this about? Barbara asked.

Hawaii, she echoed when the girls told her. Do your parents know? The waves are dangerous.

That's why it's called extreme surfing, Mrs. Parish, Jilly said.

For how long? Barbara asked.

Katie shrugged. For as long as we're having fun. We'll have to get jobs down there, but I figure one Jamba Juice's as good as another. Or we'll wait tables at night, live on tourist tips.

But what about college? Shouldn't you be thinking about your education?

Well, Sylvie said, John's thinking about Brooklyn and Arabic.

Barbara turned to John. Brooklyn? Arabic?

It's a pretty new idea.

Aren't there Arabic classes in D.C.?

Not classical Arabic, John said. And this school comes highly recommended. I haven't made up my mind yet, but the course is designed in three-semester sequences so if I don't start this fall, I'll have to wait till next year, but by then I'll be at Brown.

Hmmm, Barbara said, thinking quickly. I like it, I mean, I think structure would be good for you. Let's see what Dad thinks.

She gathered up the tray and cups, and left, John knew, to start the discussion.

Your mom's thrilled to have you anywhere but Hawaii, Katie observed when Barbara left.

John agreed. Barbara was easy to see through. Though she loved Katie & Co., she worried about their intellectuality or lack of it. Even graduating from the local community college wasn't a sure thing for Katie.

Brooklyn, John explained, means school, which is where she thinks I ought to be. It's not Brown or Yale, but it's school.

The girls didn't give up. You can go to Brooklyn in the fall, and still come down for Christmas, Sylvie pointed out.

I'll think about it.

Sylvie and Jilly left for work and Katie stayed. They had to have it out, John knew, and first thing, he apologized.

I had no reason to blame you. I overreacted to the way things turned out. I was feeling badly for Jilly, who didn't deserve what she got. I tend to root for the underdog—it's just the way I am, I guess. I'm sorry.

Katie nodded. Yeah, I kind of know that about you. And I asked myself what I could've done differently, and honestly, I don't think I could've done anything. I didn't even know right away that the decision had gone against her, since I was still in the water. And even when it was posted, I didn't know how it would influence the final score. Jilly could still have overtaken me, us. I mean, you know how good she is.

John nodded. She was right. In the heat of the moment, she couldn't have known. So they hugged, so they made up, so they were cool again. But summer was over, he was moving back to D.C., though he had to get out of D.C. She was going to Hawaii. And they were only eighteen, too young, Barbara would say, to commit to each other, and after all this, especially after all this, he couldn't disagree.

BROOKLYN, NEW YORK—SEPTEMBER 2000

THEY SAW THREE APARTMENTS. The first was a furnished flat on the ground floor of a brownstone, with a backyard patio, which John especially liked. Then they drove downtown, took the freight elevator to the third floor of an old factory renovated for residential living, and followed the Realtor into a large light-filled space with industrial-sized windows, high ceilings, revealed ducts and pipes. Best of all, John noted: it had concrete floors, which was awesome. He could grind at home. When his cast came off. Which was awesome. But the concrete didn't thrill Barbara. She thought the place too hard and too cold. Not a place I'd call home, she said.

She liked the third place, a luxuriously furnished large one-bedroom in a doorman building on Brooklyn Heights' promenade with views of lower Manhattan.

No way, John said. This is just too, way too over the top.

He saw himself—his new self—best in the ground-floor brownstone apartment, which was furnished, offered easy access with no stairs, and was located conveniently near Atlantic Avenue and only blocks from the school.

You don't think it's molelike? Barbara asked.

John weighed the mole description and liked it. Reading and studying is molelike. It's a good fit, he said. Besides when I'm not reading and studying, I'll be out doing things. Like skating the Brooklyn Banks as soon as this comes off.

All right, then, Barbara said, and the Realtor produced the paperwork for the brownstone apartment.

AT THE SHARIA SCHOOL on Montague, their next stop, ten wide brownstone steps slowed John down. Barbara took one of his crutches to allow him the use of the handrail and walked beside him patiently as he lifted up his casted leg one clumsy step at a time.

Inside, she admired the high carved dome, the circular entry hall, and the stained-glass windows. I'm very glad when visitors take pleasure in the architecture, the headmaster said, materializing suddenly out of nowhere.

He introduced himself as the Sharia's maulana, put his palms together to greet Barbara, then shook John's hand.

This was once a synagogue, he explained. Now it's our own beautiful and spiritual setting for learning.

His skin was dark tan, he had a black beard, and he was dressed in almost all white: white tunic, white pants, and a white turban, but with a long buttoned black Nehru jacket and black dress shoes. Barbara, John saw, was finding the getup super attractive. She was all smile and nod. She was entirely charmed.

The maulana gave them a brief tour of the school, opened doors to classrooms, ushered them in, and they stood for a few minutes, listening. On one blackboard, John noted what looked like conjugations. The students were studying Arabic grammar. In another classroom, students were taking turns reading aloud, in what sounded to him like good accents. Barbara, he noticed, wasn't paying much attention to the scholarship; she was noticing cultural things. Is this an all-boys school? she asked when they stepped into the maulana's office. I haven't seen any women.

Our late-afternoon and evening classes do have some female students, the maulana said, but the formal study of this language seems to attract more men than women. Perhaps because women are good with language and tend to learn their mother tongue at home, he finished, totally flattering Barbara.

There was a knock on the door.

Excellent, the maulana said, clapping his hands together. John, the maulana said. I want to introduce you to one of your new colleagues. Khaled has agreed to help you out your first weeks.

John stood on one crutch and shook hands with Khaled, who sized him up and smiled. They were about the same height, but compared with Khaled's dark hair and skin, John seemed pale though he'd spent most of the summer in the sun.

They exchanged e-mail addresses. Just let me know when you'll be here, Khaled said.

THEY TOOK A CAB back to Manhattan, to NoHo, to the little café where Noor worked. The taxi pulled up to a blue-and-white-tiled entrance on a busy sunny sidewalk crowded with people smoking, gesticulating, waiting in line. John watched from the window, delaying, until Barbara nudged him out.

Come on, she said, and led the way. A waitress, a girl with wavy dark hair, side parted and bobby pinned, listened to Barbara's inquiry, looked up, saw John, and smiled.

You must be John's mother, she said, and wiped her hand on her apron before offering it to Barbara. I'm Noor. And you're the real-life John, she said.

As real as I get, John said.

Noor glanced behind her, at the tables. Let me see what I can do. Give me a minute.

Barbara turned to John. Pretty, she mouthed.

A smoker, seeing John on crutches, offered his perch on the little bench out front, and before John could decline, Barbara intervened. He'll take it, she said. Thank you.

It's a lovely spot, Barbara said, and wandered away to look at the shopwindow next door.

John leaned back, felt the sun on his face, a warm September glow reflected in the red brick across the street.

Noor returned and perched beside him. How are you?

He moved to give her space. Don't, she said. I can't stay. Did you find an apartment?

John nodded. On Nevins, on the ground floor, which is necessary until I get this thing off, he said, pointing to his fat dirty white leg scrawled with colorful Katie & Co. signatures. He wished now that he'd waited to meet her without it. On wheels, she would have known him as he was and wanted to be known.

I'm sorry about this, he said, but it's coming off in a few weeks.

But that's how I knew it was you, she said.

She smelled of apple or rose or currants, but intermingled with garlic and something else.

And then Barbara appeared, carrying a tiny bouquet of almost black hothouse roses. I had to have these, she said. They're exquisite. The entire shop's exquisite, including the girl behind the counter.

Nathalie, Noor agreed. She looked over her shoulder into the café. Your table's ready.

They followed her to a tiny corner near the window. It's a little quieter here, she said, handing them menus. Can I bring you a pot of Moroccan tea?

Yes, for me, Barbara said. John, a hot cocoa?

John nodded without taking his eyes off Noor, off her thin face, her prominent nose, her wide dark eyes. Her skin, he thought, was light cocoa, cocoa with plenty of milk. Desert skin and hair, desert Bedouin eyes, with the depths of sand and caves. He was thinking like a book, in clichés, and he was ashamed of it, but he couldn't help himself. Noor was as deep and brown as Katie was clear and blond. And somehow, though he was only one man, the same man, he found both beautiful.

When Noor stepped away to place their order, John exhaled and stretched his good leg, glad to watch from a distance, relieved to have her probing black eyes and inquiring brow, which sent him into meltdown, preoccupied elsewhere. He looked up to see Barbara smiling into her menu, looking too pleased.

She decided on the stew. John asked about desserts.

I'll bring you something, Noor promised, and soon returned with a Persian bird's nest, made with honey, apricot, and pistachios, she explained. In truth it goes best with tea. I'll bring an extra cup.

John broke off a piece and tasted. Not bad, he said. Though it's not chocolate.

Barbara tried it. Not a bad start to a romance.

Mom, John said. We're chat-room buddies. I thought you liked Katie.

Barbara nodded, but she made no effort to hide her smile, and John wished she weren't there, or that he were anywhere but here, that he had waited until his cast was off and come alone. Who in his right mind brings his mother to a first meeting with a girl?

BACK HOME IN D.C., Barbara took to self-dramatizing. On the phone, in the street, at the supermarket, in the diner, gym, wherever she met someone who had the misfortune to ask how she was. In response, she would plunge into a run-on:

John Jude is moving to Brooklyn, and though I love New York, and it really isn't so far away, and this move will give us more reason to spend weekends away, still, Barbara lamented, my baby's leaving home and he's only eighteen, and he's not fully mobile.

He's perfectly self-sufficient, Bill pointed out. He was fine this summer.

She nodded, she agreed, he had been fine, but still she went on. It was the end of an era: they had raised a son, and now he was moving out, into the world, into the lives of other men and women. Would they love and protect him as she had?

If this is the end of a phase, Bill soothed, it's also a beginning. John survived the skirmish with Katie, or whatever it was. He's a resilient, smart boy. He'll make you proud. He's already making you proud. Look at all the scholarship he's taking on.

Oh, I know, Barbara mourned, and laughed, and laughed at herself for mourning and laughing. He's wonderful and wonderfully smart. My baby.

BETWEEN THE THREE OF THEM, even with John on crutches, and with Barbara serving as the lightweight brigade, they worked quickly, passing one another in the corridor, carrying on a conversation in passing: Barbara carried John's laptop and Harman/Kardon sticks; the pillows and quilts; she left the box of books and the suitcase of clothes for Bill; she picked up a still-unopened white box, noted its nonheft and return address, wondered aloud as to its contents, and pronounced the strange name—Al-ma-Ha-laat, John corrected, meaning the store, he explained. I ordered some books and a dervish CD.

Dervishes, Barbara thought. Long-haired gurus'd had their moment in the sixties and seventies, when she was coming of age, but were they making a comeback now, in this new millennium, this moneyed age in which Republicans were actually, unbelievably, looking good again to American voters? Perhaps it was just John being

John, reacting in counterpoint. He found her socially conventional, he once said, and convention is an enemy to art and love.

According to whom? she'd asked.

According to—um—I don't remember.

Wait until you're my age, Barbara said, and judge me then. At your age your dad and I were revolutionaries. In '67, we traveled down to D.C. together. We marched.

Bill brought in the cooler of drinks and food, opened a Coke, and stepped out the back door onto the patio. Not bad, he said.

The doorbell rang. John's first visitor: Noor, with a brown pita wrapped in paper and tied with bakery string. From her book bag, she withdrew a small bag of coarse salt.

It's a Middle Eastern custom, she explained. Bread and salt, for a new home.

Lovely, Bill said, introducing himself.

Barbara found a pretty dish to use as a saltcellar. From the cooler, she brought out cheese and a bottle of champagne and went to find glasses.

I can't stay, Noor said. But I wanted to ask you, John, when's your first class?

Monday afternoon.

Shall I meet you at the Sharia after? We can go to a little place I know nearby.

WHEN HE ARRIVED for his first day of classes, Khaled was waiting for him out front, smoking a cigarette.

I appreciate this, John said.

Khaled shrugged and squashed his cigarette with the toe of his black Pumas. He wore Levi's and a bomber jacket, but his shirt was a tunic, Pakistani style.

He took one of John's crutches, and they made their way up the stairs slowly.

The letters carved into the stone above our heads, Khaled explained, taking the tone of tour guide, spell the Ten Commandments in Hebrew: I AM GOD, DON'T STEAL, DON'T LIE, DON'T FORNICATE, and so on. Jews it seems need their codes carved in stone. The rest of us just remember them.

Khaled had a weird way of drawing out his words, as if he didn't care that much whether he said them or not, which John found interesting, though the bit of anti-Semitism was not. But maybe this was the usual thing people say about each other, and he was just overreacting in an overly politically correct American way.

There were fourteen kids in his class, all male, between about seventeen and twenty-one, he guessed. Most of them wore some sort of head covering, in white or color. John wasn't sure whether it was for religion or style. And though they all spoke English and appeared American, they also didn't seem fully American; they were like some kind of hybrid. Maybe it had something to do with Brooklyn. They were urban, but not D.C.-style urban.

They eyed him warily and kept their distance in an obvious way intended to make him feel it. When he took a seat in the desk nearest Khaled, several nearby already seated students abandoned their desks quickly for ones a row or two away. One student named Fawal intentionally dropped his pencil in front of John's desk, and instead of bending down to retrieve it, he made an elaborate effort to keep his distance by kicking at the pencil with the point of his shoe. The others laughed, and John understood that Fawal's performance was a statement or a hazing of some sort, which succeeded because he got his laughs.

John didn't catch what Khaled said to Fawal, but he heard the reply, which referred to him as a saa-eH, meaning tourist, and he understood that he'd have to prove himself a serious, nontransient student.

In session, John listened hard, kept his attention on the instruction, but he also observed his colleagues who were very unlike the kids at John Harlan High. He wondered whether the difference was cultural, religious, or something else.

Don't mind, Khaled said, when he asked. They're being totally uncool.

Is it because I'm not Arab?

No, Khaled explained. Muslims accept Muslims of any race. But they can tell you haven't submitted to Allah.

How do they know?

Easy, Khaled said. By the way you walk, stand, speak, dress. A man who prays doesn't stand so tall.

What about you?

I like difference, Khaled said.

Though Khaled's hair and skin were dark, his eyes were light, or lighter than the others. And he was taller; still, in his height and lank, he resembled John, and this sameness somehow encouraged their friendship. John wondered whether Khaled's drawl was some kind of regional accent; without it, he would sound like an American kid, more or less. Maybe it was just something he was trying on for style.

Were you born here? John asked.

Yes, but I spent almost every summer in Pakistan.

The students here are mostly Arab Americans, Khaled informed him. Their parents are assimilated or in a mixed marriage.

Khaled, who spoke Pashto and English, was studying classical Arabic because he planned to study abroad the following year, at Islamia College in Peshawar, where his mother's family lived and where his cousins attended classes. And he wanted to visit Egypt and Saudi Arabia.

Living in and with a language, he declared solemnly, as if he were reciting a sentence he'd read somewhere, is the only way to truly learn it. The school recommends a year abroad for everyone. You should come with me.

Right, John said. Think how welcome I'd be there.

It would be different, Khaled said. There you'll be their guest. Here you're an intruder.

So if Fawal suddenly started attending John Harlan High, John understood, they might have been friends. But here, at the Sharia, he wasn't welcome because he was invading the one place in Brooklyn, or in America, that was all theirs.

AS PROMISED, Noor was on the steps in front of the school, in a cluster of students, all talking at once it seemed to John. This was a scene, a kind of post-class ritual, and he was grateful to Noor for this early initiation. It was her way of granting him insidership.

Some of the men smoked, but the women did not, he noted. Noor was talking to a girl named Samina who turned out to be Khaled's girlfriend. John introduced Noor to Khaled and was introduced to Samina, a student at Barnard, then Khaled and Samina hurried off to his brother's house, where they were expected for dinner. The others also soon dispersed, and Noor led the way to the promised café.

It's really not far, she said.

As long as you don't mind my snail's pace.

He inhaled deeply, energized by the night, the new friendships, his first formal lesson in Arabic. Even the nonwelcome, which would take working through. He had the feeling that this was the beginning of his life. He was finally fully free of the prison of childhood, of well-meaning Barbara and her version of adult life.

The café was tiny, with only a four-foot bar. Noor secured one of the small tiled tables outside, pulled out a chair for John, and went to order havaj.

On her return, she took her seat, and though she slipped out of her red coat, she rewrapped the thin pink scarf around her neck. Her lips, fuller than any lips he'd kissed before, appeared sort of sulky, and he liked that. But did Muslim girls kiss? What would she do if he leaned forward and did it? And what about Katie? Couldn't he meet a girl and just be friends? He forced his eyes away from her lips.

She had on a girl's pale blouse with a peter pan collar, a cardigan, and jeans, held in place by a glitter cowboy belt. Her shoes were red velvet Chinese slippers with a thin band at the ankle and embroidery at the toes. She was delicate and serious at once, both girl and woman, and it seemed he couldn't help himself. It didn't matter what his mind advised; his eyes returned to her lips. And sitting with her here, alone for the first time, he wished to be past this awkward newness, onto something deeper. Then he stopped himself. He had a tendency to rush the best parts of life.

He took a breath and started slowly.

How are your classes? he asked. I never got to ask.

So far I think I like literature better than history, but that's probably because the reading is better. For history I have to read Gibbon, or I should say parts of Gibbon, and for my class on the Middle East, Hitti.

Short or long? John asked.

Short, Noor said. I don't think any professor could get away with assigning the long one. Isn't it like nine hundred pages?

I just started it, and I'm liking it, which makes me think I might want to read the longer one. I don't know. It was on my reading list forever, but once I got started, it moved fast. It's not at all like the boring textbooks I read for high school.

Noor agreed to give Hitti a second chance. Really, I should like it, since it's for a course in my concentration.

Sounds like you know what you want to do after graduation.

Journalism, Noor said. I want to be a foreign correspondent in the Middle East.

The havaj arrived, and Noor took up her spoon and stirred. John picked up his cup, but Noor reached across the table and guided it back to the saucer. You want the mud settled before you start drinking, she said. And you?

Um, John said, and released his cup. I guess you could say scholarship, but I don't have a, like a career plan. That's why I deferred college. So I can figure it out.

Noor smiled, but only slightly. She wasn't a girl who laughed needlessly.

So what are you reading besides Hitti? she asked.

Poetry. I'm into this Sufi poet, Ibn 'Arabi.

Noor reached into her green schoolbag, brought up a thin black notebook, opened the flap, and recited,

> My heart is capable of every form
> It is a meadow for gazelles and a monastery for
> Christian monks . . .

John joined her, though he stumbled here and there for the next word. Their translations differed. John's had a camel in it, Noor's a caravan. Still, they finished together.

> Love is my religion and my faith.

Noor's lips were slightly parted now, and John brought his fingertips to his own, then reached across the table to hers. And they were warm, they were yielding. So he lifted himself up on the arms of his chair and touched her lips with his.

That's for knowing it. I hoped you would.

She drew her black eyelashes down, obscuring her eyes, and said nothing, but out of the corners of her eyes, she glanced right then left, without moving her head. To see if anyone had seen? John looked. It didn't seem to matter to anyone. Seated at this tiny table in the growing bluedark, they were as good as alone.

He told her about his new CD, recorded in Morocco. I got it in the mail last week. It has a rendition of the poem, in French. Mon coeur est devenu capable. I'll play it for you.

I'd like that. She picked up her cup. You can taste now, she said.

Cinnamon, he said, sipping. And nutmeg. And something else.

Cardamom, Noor said. Good?

John sipped again. Surprisingly, he said.

I'm glad you like it, Noor said, because I love it. The secret spice that no one guesses is a pinch of white pepper, not black, white, which is different. She reached into her backpack again and brought out a small glass vial sealed with a cork stopper. My own mix, she said, and removed the stopper, and passed the vial under her nose.

John leaned forward to sniff.

Careful, Noor warned, holding back. If you inhale or exhale hard, the cinnamon powder will rise up and choke you. Just let the fragrance come to you, kind of on its own. John leaned back. Ready? she asked. And passed the vial under his nose in an arc.

She was right. The smell arrived, in time.

He wondered whether she'd had boyfriends, whether she'd had sex. Did Muslim girls make love? She'd sort of allowed him to kiss her, though she'd also worried about being kissed, or being seen kissing. Islam, he knew, was against premarital sex, but so were Christianity and Judaism, all traditional faiths. He looked at her. She was most likely a virgin, he thought, and for now, with the cast on his leg, she found him safe. Maybe. With Noor, unlike Katie, he wasn't certain of anything.

I read somewhere, he said, that Muslims read poetry more than they read the Qur'an, which is amazing. In the United States, where supposedly church and state are separate, and freedom of choice is law, the New Testament is the most read book. According to statistics.

It's complicated, though, Noor said. In Arab culture, poets are sort of like spokesmen or journalists or even oracles, like the Prophet. They write about politics, and if they take a stand against a leader or an issue or something, they have a huge influence. Even the Bedouins honored poetry. It's why the caliphs and clerics always want to cut off the poet's tongue.

They honor poets by cutting out their tongues? John asked.

Noor laughed. It's an expression. It means subsidizing the poet as a way to avoid his bite; it's kind of a bribe.

He wondered about her background, her parents. Khaled seemed modern, Noor less so. Or maybe it had something to do with her being female.

Eye-na al-Hahm-maam? John asked.

Noor pointed him toward the back of the café. When he returned, she insisted on walking him home.

His apartment was only a few blocks away, and they walked slowly. After a short silence, John asked whether she would go with him to the Brooklyn Banks to watch the skating. After my cast is off.

Sure, she said.

Great. You'll get a better idea of who I am when I'm not crippled.

You're not crippled, Noor said, just temporarily challenged.

They laughed.

John invited her in, but Noor declined.

LATER THAT NIGHT, pausing for the nth time on the same sentence, replaying every moment of the evening in his head, John realized that if he had asked Noor out for tomorrow night instead of Saturday he would not have had to wait so long. At the very least he could have suggested that she meet him again after classes on Wednesday and walk back with him to hear the CD. She might think I don't like her, he thought. But when he pulled his laptop into his lap and checked his e-mail, he found one from her, wishing him good night, and felt better.

He wrote back: miss you already. can't wait until saturday. how about tomorrow? and also wednesday, after class. john

He waited ten minutes. When there was no reply, he decided that she might be asleep already, or in bed, reading. In his inbox, there was a message from Katie, and though he hesitated over the feeling that the double pleasure of e-mail from both girls on the same night might be a double infidelity, disloyal to both Noor and Katie at once, blue-eyed, white-blond, born-to-surf Katie, his first love, whom he still loved, he finally couldn't hold out and opened Katie's letter, too.

From: Katie KatieOBX101@NCoptonline.net
To: GoofyFootJohn GoofyFootJohn@adelphia.net
Date: September 29, 2000
RE: overheads

Hey JJ,
Just want you to know you are missing really truly awesome surf. Hurricane Ida hovering over the Caribbean brought walls of water, but unlike what we got at Cape Hatteras, these were nasty, and closed out on us like fiends. They crested and came down so hard and fast, we had no space at all, and we ate it. A lot. Even Jilly. We all came away with bad cuts and bruises, and Sylvie got a black and blue that's now ugly yellow, but no broken bones, so we're lucky. We're all three working extra hours to save for Hawaii. We want to make extreme wave surfing also a woman's sport. I think Jilly and Sylvie have become like dangerous addicts, so it's my job to remain practical and keep us safe because someone has to. If you were coming along, I wouldn't have to, which I would really appreciate so I hope you're planning for Hawaii in the winter.

Have you been to Brooklyn Banks yet? And when are you visiting OBX again?

XOXOKatie

HIS ARABIC LANGUAGE BOOK provided stickers with words printed on them. For this morning's vocabulary lesson, he was required to paste eleven new words to their corresponding items in his apartment and learn them. On crutches, he made his way to his ah-ree-ka, where he spent a good part of the day reading, said the word aloud, ah-ree-ka, rolling his *r*'s like a Mexican, and pasted the label on the sofa's arm where he would see it. Then he attached the label miss-baaH to the lamp beside his ah-ree-ka. On the other side of the miss-baaH was a koor-see for the occasional guest, though now and then he, too, sat in it. Covering the square of floor space outlined by his ah-ree-ka, miss-baaH, koor-see, and taa-we-la, on which he kept his books, laptop, and glass of water, was a small sahzh-zheh-da, a kind of cowhide thing, not the Persian carpet the word evoked. On the door to the patio he stuck the label baab. On the clock in the kitchen, a saa-ra, on the telephone, a teh-lee-foon, and on the picture hanging in the hallway, a ssoo-ra. On the tiny window in his bathroom, he stuck a neh-fee-da, and on the shower curtain, a see-taa-ra, though it was surely meant for a regular window curtain. After which he hobbled from object to object and named each one aloud, as if it was for this that he was here, in order to say: ah-ree-ka, miss-baaH, koor-see, taa-we-la, sahzh-zheh-da, baab, teh-lee-foon, saa-ra, see-taa-ra, ssoo-ra, neh-fee-da, ka-na-ba, haa-tif, to say these things and forever name them.

Tired, he relinquished his crutches and leaned back on his ah-ree-ka.

He had been able to pick up other vocabulary on his own. He knew, for example, that his ees-me was John Jude Parish, that he was a talib who had signed on for da-ra-sa at a ma-dra-sa, that he was taking dars with a moo-dar-rees, but learning to read and write in Arabic script presented a greater challenge. For one thing he hadn't learned a new alphabet since he was a child. And Arabic letters changed according to their place within the word, with variations on the form for initial, medial, or final placement, which meant learning to recognize three variations on each of the twenty-eight letters, a sum of eighty-four different calligraphic shapes. He had gotten the hang of reading right to left quickly enough, but writing the letters from right to left was more difficult, and he found himself etching them backward, from left to right, which Noor said was like writing the word cat on a page starting with the *t*.

You're avoiding the difficulty, his moo-dar-rees suggested. It's a matter of habit, he explained, and though habit is difficult to break and reform, sometimes requires hundreds of repetitions to reform, it is possible with some effort and attention, and ultimately rewarding.

This argument rang true, John could think of other habits he'd had to break in order to make progress, like unlearning a bad skating tic in order to master a new maneuver.

Thus he practiced daily. He got out his yellow lined pad, and slowly, it was painstakingly slow work, he looped up and out calligraphically. A quill or fine paintbrush rather than a number 2 pencil would be a more appropriate tool for making these detailed shapes, he thought. It was super close work, with dots and dashes and lines and curves, and every filled page of etchings a calligraphic artwork worth framing or, at the very least, mounting with a magnet on his mother's fridge.

He covered a long yellow page with Arabic alphabet. He stood and stretched. And on crutches, he made his way to the kitchen to pin his fresh page of *ah to ee* on the refrigerator door, using the English *A* and *Z*. The pages accumulated. He was on his sixth page, filling two a day. He stood in front of them, read them back, aspirating the *H* in the back of his throat to extinguish a candle, gargling the *kh,* and kawing the *q*. He practiced the short stop for a glottal pause, a silent musical beat. Then he hopped back on crutches to his ah-ree-ka, rolling the *r,* ah-rrrrrree-ka, and sat down to fill another page, this time from memory, attempting to force memory.

LATE AFTERNOON, HIS CELL PHONE RANG. Noor. He heard cups clattering, steam hissing, voices, and wished himself there, at a table, watching her.

I got your e-mail, she said, but I shouldn't go out again tonight. Instead, would you like to eat with us? My dad won't be home, so it's only my mom, my brother, and I.

John wrote down the address on the pad near the teh-lee-foon and promised to be there before seven. He hung up. This was perfect. He had put in a good day's work, and now he could enjoy his reward. He would read for another hour, then shower, then make his way to Noor's house, exploring the streets on his way while there was still light. He probably ought to bring something, a small gift. He would ask Barbara.

I'm so glad you called, she said. How was Dr. Kluge?

John told her about his new removable lime-green cast.

I'm not convinced that your doctor made the right decision, Barbara said in the way she had of questioning all authority, with the exception of her own. I worry that you won't wear it all the time.

John demurred. I, he declared, taking Barbara's tone, am one hundred percent certain that the decision was a good one since it has improved my mobility by about fifty percent. I can bathe with less trouble and scrub off dead skin cells. You should have seen how scaly my skin was when the old one came off. Plus it stank.

As long as you don't do any more damage, Barbara said.

Okay, Mom. Don't get teary on me. I called to ask you for gift ideas. I'm invited to dinner at Noor's house. What should I bring?

How lovely, Barbara said. They might not drink alcohol so a bottle of wine won't do. How about dessert? There must be a bakery on Atlantic. Why not stop on your way, and ask them to fill a cake box with an assortment of fancy cookies?

Cookies? I don't know. That's not especially Middle Eastern.

I know, Barbara interrupted. Halvah. Pick up a block or two. You can also look around; there are sure to be other special deli items. Olives, or a pretty spice. Stick to an edible. And take along your backpack, so you'll have your hands free for your crutches. How far a walk is it?

Mom, John warned. I'll be fine. Thank you. How's Dad?

Oh, he's well. Working hard, as always. He promised to read a draft of my paper, and though I'll be delivering this Saturday, he still hasn't gotten to it. Would you like to read it?

Not really. What's the subject?

It's for that conference on the nonvoting American; students are one of the major culprits, by the way. They tend toward apathy until they're conscripted for war. My paper is on the complacency that peace and prosperity engender. By the way, it just occurred to me that you'll have to cast an absentee ballot, since you're not registered in New York. I'll forward one to you.

HE TURNED RIGHT on Atlantic, as Noor had instructed, walked slowly, stopping at the open vats of olives and pickles and spices, inhaling the fragrance of ground herbs. What were they? Parsley, sage, rosemary, and thyme, and then he couldn't get the song out of his head.

At the next store, he purchased a half pound each of vanilla and chocolate halvah. He watched the counterman wrap them up efficiently, first in wax paper, then brown paper and string.

He paid for the halvah, leaned his crutches on the counter to slip off his backpack, but the man stopped him.

Not necessary, he said. He tucked the two packages into John's backpack while it was still on his back, zipped it up snugly, and clapped his hands.

A good evening to you, young man, he said. With good appetite. Im'sh'allah.

NOOR OPENED THE DOOR, and several feet behind her was her mother, looking him up and down, taking in his lime-green cast and crutches. She wiped her hands on a dish towel, but not, it turned out, in order to shake his hand because she didn't offer it. She merely bowed her head to acknowledge the introduction. The rest of her remained quiet, unmoving.

Ta-shar-rahf-naa, John said, showing off what he'd practiced. Noor's mother smiled. Only her lips moved. Her eyes, her head, her shoulders, and arms remained still. She moved only what was necessary, unlike Barbara. She moved, John decided, like a kung fu guru.

Marhaba, she said, and led the way in.

He followed them into a kind of living room, but an unusual one, with low velvet cushions and bolsters, a brass tray in the center holding a teapot and tiny glasses. John thought this might be an indoor version of a Bedouin majlis.

Noor's mother spoke to Noor, in Arabic. Noor translated. My mom suggests unsweetened mint tea before dinner.

John seated himself with some difficulty, laying down first one crutch, then the other.

I'm sorry, Noor said. Can I help? She offered her arm, but John declined, and managed alone, clumsily.

This will be harder in reverse, he said.

You have a new cast, Noor said.

Yes, removable and lighter, but still clumsy, as you can see. The doctor promises to take it off entirely in two weeks.

Im'sh'allah, Noor said, palming her hands, looking very much like her beautiful mother. Her beauty, John reflected, wasn't yet fully developed, but it would deepen with age. For him, though, for now, at least, these early hints were enough.

On her knees, Noor poured tea into two glasses and served first John, then herself. She sat with her legs tucked under her and held the glass cupped with both hands, warming herself as if she were cold.

Only two more weeks, she said. You should get it covered with signatures before it comes off. Here, I'll start. She handed him her glass, sprang up, and went to get a marker. After which she sat, chewing on the plastic tip, thinking. Then abruptly uncapped the marker, and signed in Arabic with a calligraphic flourish.

John tried but couldn't read it. He thought there was a my to start with, then was lost. I'll have to decipher it when I get home, he said.

Noor nodded. Good practice, she said.

She sipped her tea. Before dinner the tea is unsweetened; after it's sweet.

Speaking of sweets, John said, and reached for his backpack on the floor at his feet. He unzipped the bag and brought out the parcels, one at a time.

Noor sniffed. Mmmm, halvah. How'd you know?

My mom's idea, John admitted.

It's Ali's favorite dessert, but he has to stop eating it, he's getting fat. Here he comes now. He tends to announce himself with slammed doors.

A stocky little boy came in, stopped, and stared.

Go back into the hallway, take off your coat and shoes, come back, and I'll introduce you, Noor instructed.

Ali stepped out, Noor and John could hear his clumsy movements in the hallway, the thud of a heavy book bag, the slam of a sliding door, then muffled steps.

John, this is my brother Ali. Ali, this is my friend John.

Pleased to meet you, John said, and pushing himself up with one arm, reached out with the other.

Ali's small hand slipped into his. I understand, John said, that even without knowing you, I managed to bring your favorite dessert for dessert.

Halvah? Ali asked, then saw the wrapped parcels beside Noor. Chocolate?

Both, John said. Though I'm partial to chocolate, too.

Noor handed Ali the parcels. Take them directly to Oom, she said. Don't even think of opening them.

He has his shoes on, Ali pointed out to Noor, and ambled out, swinging a parcel in each hand. Noor and John laughed.

He's not fat, John said.

Pudgy, Noor said, like American kids.

Baby fat, John said. Which he'll lose within a year, guaranteed.

I hope so. She stood. Let me help you up, she said.

Shouldn't I take off my shoes, or shoe? I'm setting a bad example.

Nah, Noor said. It's hard enough for you to get around as is.

She offered both her hands to help him up, but John pushed up against the bolster with his arms, keeping most of his weight on his good leg.

Ali came in. Oom says to say dinner's ready.

We're on our way, Noor said. She handed John his crutches. Careful on the rugs, she said. They can slip.

Ali pulled out a chair for John, and he sat at a Western-style dining table with regular chairs: though they lounged like Bedouins, the Bint-Khans dined Western style.

Mrs. Bint-Khan put her palms together, bowed her head, recited, clapped her hands, and finished with an Im'sh'allah.

Noor lifted the heavy lid of the casserole and announced, Tajine of chicken with lemon and cracked green olives.

John inhaled. Lemon, olives, cinnamon, and ginger maybe.

Ty-yee-ba wehzh-ba, he wished the others, as his book advised.

It was a strange combination, but deliciously strange. The couscous infused with stew was awesome. Delicious, he said.

Andak kam sana? Noor's mother asked him, then looked at Noor to translate, but John didn't wait. He recognized the question from his workbook.

Andi 'as-hara sana min tha-maa-nee-ya, he said, meaning, I'm ten years older than eight years.

Noor laughed. Her mother smiled and said in English, Good answer. Who learned you?

Taught, Mom, Ali corrected. Who taught you.

John responded. Ana hina lee dirasa al-r-ra-be-ya. Ana talib.

Mrs. Bint-Khan's face crinkled. Hoo-wa 'aa-il? she asked Noor. Hoo-wa Kaatib eye-dahn?

He doesn't know yet, Noor answered. But a journalist is a good idea. My mom thinks you could be a journalist, too, since you're so good at languages. It does kind of suit you, I think.

John shrugged. For now, I'm a reader. He put another olive in his mouth. I love these.

FOR DESSERT they returned to the living room. Noor poured sweet tea. Ali brought in the halvah on a platter, and Mrs. Bint-Khan came in with a tray of cups.

Mahalabiyya, Mrs. Bint-Khan said.

I love these, Noor said. I can eat three cups in three minutes. And proving it, she finished her first cup and reached for a second.

They heard the front door and Ali jumped up to greet his father, whom he led into the room moments later, as if pulling a pull toy.

John attempted to get up.

Sit, sit, Mr. Bint-Khan said, and lowered his hand toward John.

Noor stood on tiptoe to kiss her father. After which he settled on the cushion beside his wife and brought her hand to his lips.

Watching this intimate family scene, formally ritualistic but also private somehow, John was both enchanted and embarrassed. He should probably have left earlier. Perhaps there'd been a signal and he'd missed it.

Noor held out a small deep dish. Libb, she announced, and Mr. Bint-Khan reached in and came away with a handful of sunflower seeds.

Want to try them? she asked John. My father eats them as a kind of digestive.

Thanks, John said, declining, I really should go. Noor helped him up, handed him his crutches. I'll get my coat and walk you, she said, and hurried out.

John thanked Mrs. Bint-Khan for having him as a guest in her home, for making him welcome, for a wonderful and beautiful dinner. He stopped, self-consciously, not accustomed to saying so much, having run out of things to say.

Noor's father sprang up and walked John to the door. He was wiry, medium height, with dark skin and wavy steely hair. And he dressed part Arab, part Western. Like the Sharia's maulana, he wore the white Arab tunic and floppy white pants, but with a Western pin-striped jacket thrown over it, and with the dash of a Hollywood movie star, which both attracted and intimidated John. Sharia students mixed it up, too—Khaled wore the tunic over jeans and sometimes the knitted cap—but not with so much style. Still, John decided, mixing it up was the way to wear these clothes. One or two items at a time.

In the hallway, Mr. Bint-Khan took John's hand in both of his, as if to read it, and said, You are new to Brooklyn and new to the Arabic language and culture, both of which are old, laden with history and tradition. And you are no Muslim.

Noor reappeared, buttoning her coat, and Mr. Bint-Khan released John's hand. Well, good night to you, he said, and withdrew.

John welcomed the cooling air on his face, on his red cheeks, which were aflame. It wasn't his imagination. Mr. Bint-Khan thought him intrusive. But Noor was talking, and John tuned in to listen.

Did my dad say something to you? she finally asked. You shouldn't mind him. He thinks every new person, every new thing even, is a threat to the family. He'll get used to you, but it'll take him a while.

John couldn't really disagree with Mr. Bint-Khan, and yet, he wanted to. I'm different, he wanted to argue, not an everyday American, not a mere tourist. But what, he asked himself, really made him different?

You're quiet, Noor said.

You have a wonderful family, John said. And you're very beautiful. And I, I feel as if I've stumbled into a fairy tale as a bumbling fool and emerged with a donkey's head. Maybe it's the food, the ginger and cardamom.

No, Noor said. You've just read too much of *Arabian Nights.*

John laughed.

At his door, she hesitated, then nodded, and came in.

For only a few minutes, she said. Or else—

Or else your father—she was right behind him, he could feel her warmth, and he didn't want to move. They were just inside, in his long hallway entrance, the door still open.

He turned and found her lips with his, and kissed them ever so lightly, their second kiss, but this time his lips traveled to her nose and eyes and back to her lips and down to her throat.

Your coat, he said, and reached to help her out of it.

She shook her head. Better not, she said. And she put her chin on his shoulder.

Then we'll stay right here. All night. Our Arabian night in Brooklyn. Or is it a Brooklyn night in Arabia.

Yes, she said. You're jinned. Hair ah-la toos-beh-hoo-na. See you after class tomorrow.

I miss you already, he said.

She backed out through the still open door, blew him a kiss off her open palm, and hurried away.

Inside, John dropped onto his ah-ree-ka and stayed there. He touched his lips, remembering her chapped lips on his. She chewed them, he'd noted. Whenever she was the least bit anxious. He would have to remind her to coat her lips to protect them. That is, if he ever saw her again, if her father allowed it. He hoped to see her tomorrow. After class. She would wait for him on the steps after class. Or he would never see her again.

He stood at the mirror in his bathroom and looked at himself. You arrre no Moosleem, he quoted and, on crutches, stopped to press PLAY on his minidisk. He removed his cast, propped the leg up on the tah-wi-lah, leaned back, and listened.

> Wherever turn
> His camels, Love is still my creed and faith.

For Ibn 'Arabi, for himself, and for Noor, love might be enough. Mr. Bint-Khan clearly felt otherwise. And Barbara, he was quite certain, would agree with Mr. Bint-Khan. He pulled his laptop into his lap.

From: Uniform Source Maryam@Al-ma-Ha-laat.com
To: Attar attar7@adelphia.net
Date: October 3, 2000
RE: Muslim suit

Dear Mr. Attar:
We have the Muslim tunic and djellabah pants, about which you inquired, in white. Based on the information you provided, you will need a size Extra-Long. The cost of this suit is $75, plus tax. The qoob-ba or skully is $10.

The cost of overnight shipping will be $19.95. We accept all major credit cards. Please remember to provide a mailing address.

Thank you,
Maryam
Sales assistant at Al-ma-Ha-laat.com

FOR HIS FIRST THERAPY SESSION at NYU Medical, John arrived early and unrealistically optimistic, though Barbara had warned him not to expect miracles, that healing takes time. Still, he hoped to walk out of the place without crutches, freed.

After a fifteen-minute wait, a girl named Sarah introduced herself as his therapist. She had a narrow face, long lank hair, a girl way too ordinary for miracles, John thought.

She looked at his chart. We will begin with mild exercise, she said in the singsong of routine. Your doctor doesn't want you to put too much weight on the leg, which means we will be working in a seated position.

I feel more than ready to get on it, John protested.

She looked at him. She didn't know how to smile, he decided. Next week, perhaps, we'll do more. She led him to a reclining chair, and he heaved himself into it.

John pulled up the leg of his pants, and undid the Velcro holding his cast, which Sarah took from him, pausing to notice Noor's squiggles, signs, and signature. Pretty, she said. What does it say?

Kaththar allah kheirkum, John said, then translated. May God increase your bounty.

She took a tube of Bengay from the taboret beside her, squeezed some onto his leg, and massaged. His skin tingled.

To warm up your muscles, she said. They've been fallow for so long, we want to stimulate them.

Now, she said, I'm going to push against your foot, and I want you to push back gently, but steadily, in other words keep a gentle but firm pressure on, nothing sudden. And keep your knee bent. In fact, here. She reached behind her and brought out a soft block. Place this under your knee.

Ready? she asked, and put her right palm against the sole of his foot.

John nodded, and felt her gentle pressure pushing his leg back toward him. He returned the pressure, maintaining the distance between his leg and himself, and pinpricks like electrical impulses shot up his leg.

Good, she said. How does it feel?

As if my leg has been aching to do that.

Yes, your bones want and need weight on them in order to maintain their strength. She paused. I'm going to bring it up a notch. If at any point the sensation becomes unpleasant, if it feels at all like glass breaking, stop the pressure right away.

John felt her push harder, and he pushed back just enough, matching pressure with pressure.

She held it for a few moments, then released it. Good, she said. And again.

Let's give your knee a workout. She stood, lifting his leg. Just relax, she said. Give me your leg. More, she said. Give it up. Allow me to do the work. Don't try to do anything now.

She cupped his ankle with one hand and held his calf, just below his knee, with the other, bent and unbent the leg, then moved it side to side, then in small circles. Okay, she said, pushing his knee toward his chest. You may push back gently. Try to straighten it, but don't lock.

John pushed, she pushed back, and they remained suspended for long seconds.

This is going well. Let's take a quick X-ray, and if it looks good, and your doctor gives us the go-ahead, we can try putting some weight on it.

BILL HAD A MEETING in New York City, and he offered to take John to an early dinner at Nobu Next Door, Barbara's recommendation. She had seen Chef Nobu on the *Today* show, and seeing him work, she said, you just know the food will be amazing.

105 Hudson, between Franklin and North Moore, John e-mailed Bill, and they agreed to meet at 5:30.

It was early, and the wait was short. Seated, they studied the menu.

John was torn. He wanted a taste of the cooked dishes, but he also couldn't pass up sushi rolls. Not here, in sushi heaven.

Order two starters, one cold and one hot, and then a sushi roll, Bill recommended. He ordered sake, the ceviche Nobu style as an appetizer, and the broiled black cod with miso as his entrée.

After considering the fish and chips Nobu style, the sashimi tacos, the lobster tempura, John finally settled on the salmon skin salad, the eggplant with miso, and the bigeye and bluefin toro scallion roll.

Bill asked about classes and Sharia students. Have they been welcoming?

Some, John said. Others are wary and critical. I'm told it's because I'm not Muslim.

I can understand that, Bill said. You're taking on their texts without adhering to their tenets.

I think it's also a sort of territorial thing—

The first course arrived, and for the next five minutes they gave all their attention to the compositions in front of them, drops and dabs and garnishes placed with the precision of an ink painting.

Weird but good, John said, tasting the salmon skin. He offered Bill a taste.

As an American, he continued, I think I threaten them when I enter their school, the one place they can think of as totally theirs. Does that make sense?

Sure, Bill said. Especially since you also bring with you American-style freedom.

John nodded. With his chopsticks, he reached for another mouthful of his salad, but paused midair.

Um—Dad. De Niro just walked in.

Well, he owns the place, Bill said.

John waited.

De Niro nodded greeting and moved toward the bar lined with illuminated sake bottles. The bartender poured him a cup, and he sipped, and the liquid, John thought, somehow expanded the man, and he filled the entire space. Sake cup in hand, he was suddenly at their table, asking how's everything. He shook Bill's hand.

Truly excellent, Bill said.

Awesome, John said.

Good, good. Enjoy, De Niro said, and moved to another table.

John returned to his salmon salad; Bill to his ceviche and sake.

What else are you reading, Bill asked.

Sufi poetry. Sufi books. One by Idries Shah. He mentions this wine allegory from the thirteenth century by a Sufi poet, Suhrawardi. It goes something like this:

The seed of Sufism was sown in the time of Adam, germed in the time of Noah, budded in the time of Abraham, began to develop in the time of Moses, reached maturity in the time of Jesus, and produced pure wine in the time of Muhammed. It's cool because it connects everything. Prophets, humans, religions, time.

The entrées arrived with a flourish. Bill tried his black cod with miso and leaned back to savor it.

John tasted. It's the miso. It's awesome.

You're interested in thinkers and thinking, Bill said. You might want to try philosophy at Brown.

JOHN WAS PLEASED to find Khaled in his usual pose, leaning on the stair railing and smoking, exuding his particular not-quite-American nonchalance, which revealed itself in the way he held his cigarette between thumb and index finger, as if he were smoking a joint; in the way his shoulders hunched around his cigarette; the way he stretched his words out, which didn't quite go with the way he stood a little too close, with no sense of the airspace Americans allow each other.

When Khaled saw John, he stopped short, and John felt himself taken in, his lime-green cast, his new white shalwar kameez, his old navy peacoat worn casually unbuttoned over them, the Black Watch tartan scarf hanging from his neck, and his favorite checkered Van sneaker on one foot. He'd dressed for effect, and it wasn't going unnoticed.

Khaled smiled, appreciatively. Salaam, he said. Islam looks good on you.

Aleikum a salaam, John responded.

I printed the brochure for you, Khaled said, reaching into his pocket.

What brochure? John asked, trying to recall a conversation about a brochure.

Of Islamia College, Khaled reminded him. So you can apply for the summer semester, when I'll be there.

The summer semester? John echoed.

The Sharia recommends it highly, our version of junior year abroad.

John stopped at the foot of the old synagogue's first step. He could smell Khaled's breath. Though he liked him well enough, such close physical proximity to another male was new to him. He shifted to the right, and adjusted his left crutch in order to free his left hand and receive the brochure.

The pictures were in color and depicted what looked like countryside, a mountainous region identified by the caption as the blue Margalla Hills. John mouthed the words. Blue. Margalla. And found them attractive. The school's main building was pale stone done in Moghul style. The classically laid out long stone walks and arches and fountains were tree lined and immaculate. In the background, powder-blue sky with the Margalla Hills in a blue haze in the far distance. The brochure also featured a photo of Islamia's president in turban and white tunic, with an old-style Dickensian coat over it.

You should go online to find out more, Khaled said, throwing his head back to blow his smoke away from John. He put out his cigarette, relieved John of one of his crutches, and they walked up the steps.

You have a new cast, Khaled said, pointing with his chin toward John's leg.

Yes. And in two weeks, I'll no longer need it.

Excellent, Khaled said. Then we can do things.

John nodded. He'd like that. He wondered what sorts of things Khaled did in his off time. He worked, John already knew, at a video store in downtown Brooklyn, and he also helped out an older brother in some kind of moving business. He would have no interest, John knew without asking, in the skaters at Brooklyn Banks. He was somehow too grown up or too elegant for grinding.

IN CLASS, John worked hard to respond in full sentences to questions put to him in al-r-ra-be-ya, and though he managed only with difficulty, with long pauses and multiple ums, Mr. Sami complimented him and threatened the others: If you don't do something about it, this new all-American talib will soon surpass you.

After class, Fawal walked up to John and asked him what he thought he was up to. John looked at him.

What do you mean? John said, careful not to match hostility with hostility.

The student pointed at John's clothes. Either you're Muslim or you're not. You can't pick and choose parts.

Khaled stepped up. He's American, he said in Arabic. Let him be.

He steered John toward the door. Outside they found Noor and Samina already in conversation.

Noor stepped back and stared at John. Why are you dressed like that?

John shrugged. Asked that way, the question was unanswerable.

Why? Samina asked, ending the uncomfortable silence. Don't you think it suits him?

Khaled agreed. It does somehow suit him, even with his cast and crutches.

That's not the point, Noor said. I just don't understand why.

Why not? Khaled said.

John swallowed an uncomfortable lump in his throat. He was grateful to Khaled for backing him up.

Do we have time for tea together? Samina asked.

Khaled looked at his watch. I have an hour before my shift. Can we go somewhere nearby?

There's the corner bistro, Samina suggested.

Does your mom know about this? Noor asked when they were seated.

John shook his head. My mom would laugh and call it a phase.

The tea arrived. I wonder, Samina said, why you mind. They're only clothes.

He's not Muslim, Noor said. So it's kind of like a lie.

What if looking Muslim helps him become one? Khaled inquired. Would that make you feel better?

Noor leaned her head on her arm. It's just that it's not who he really is.

But students in America do things like this all the time, Samina said. My friend Alice is doing the seventies this year. Last year, she did grunge, which her parents hated, but her boyfriend was into it.

John was relieved when the conversation finally drifted away from him. Samina, he learned, was a second-year, full-scholarship, French-literature major at Barnard, making the long trip from Brooklyn to Morningside Heights every day.

Next year, she said, I want to live on campus. Or I might do junior year in Paris. Khaled will be in Pakistan anyway.

I wanted to live at school, too, Noor seconded, but NYU is so close, and my mom and little brother would be too sad if I moved out.

Khaled had to get going, and Samina went with him.

See you tomorrow, Khaled said. They'd paired up for a class assignment. Working together, Mr. Sami suggested, can make it more fun and productive.

Noor and John walked toward Atlantic Avenue. Noor was silent, and finally John said, If you hate me in these clothes I won't wear them again.

No, she said. It just came as a surprise.

They were at his corner, and Noor paused.

Do you want to stop at my place? John asked.

I can't, she said, and stood on tiptoe to kiss him, right-left-right, whispered good-bye, and walked off.

John stood on the sidewalk, puzzled, watching her retreating red coat. She definitely didn't like him in Muslim clothes. She'd welcomed his not being Muslim, he understood now. Maybe because her father objected to it. She was complicated, this was complicated, more than he knew what to do with, and it wasn't even really about him. He turned toward home.

Inside, still in his jacket, he stood in front of the mirror. It's certainly not because these clothes are unattractive, he decided. The white definitely went with his dark brown hair. And his dark jacket made the thin cotton seasonally appropriate. He looked like a traveler, a great adventurer. Sir John Parish, at your service, he introduced himself to himself, and bowed.

THEIR ASSIGNMENT—a short essay on a verse from the Qur'an, written in al-r-ra-be-ya—required real thinking rather than mere memorization, and John found himself looking forward to it. He'd read Corbin on Ibn 'Arabi's interpretation of Jacob Wrestling with the Angel, on the angel's identity and the story's meaning, and now he thought it might be cool to write about it. He would wait for Khaled, who might have other ideas.

In the meantime, he read more of Corbin, practiced the alphabet, then went to shower, which still took twice as long as it should, but half as long as it had the week before. After which he was hungry. He planned to make a quick sandwich, then he remembered that he had eaten his last slice of bread the day before. And he also had no milk or juice left, nor much else. He would have to find a supermarket. He'd passed corner delis, but no supermarket. He hoped Khaled could help.

Khaled arrived twenty minutes late. John was just finishing the last of the frozen meals his mother had stacked in his freezer.

Coffee, he told Khaled, pouring water into the electric drip machine on the counter, is all I can offer. Where's the nearest supermarket?

Khaled thought about it. It's really too far for you to walk. Besides, how're you gonna carry your groceries home? Can you wait until tomorrow? I'll try to borrow my brother's car.

John nodded. I'll stop at a local deli in the meantime. Or order in.

He showed Khaled the apartment. Roor-fa ah-noum hoo-naa, he said, and opened the door to his bedroom. Khaled followed him into the kitchen, which John introduced as his math-bahk, then outside to al Ha-dee-qa.

This is all for you? Khaled asked. And you don't even have a keT-Ta or kelb.

They laughed. We used to have a cat, when I was little.

THAT'S THE JEWISH VERSION, Khaled said when John mentioned Jacob Wrestling with the Angel.

Genesis, John said. So?

The point is it's not in al-r-ra-be-ya, Khaled said, stretching out the vowels for emphasis. And this assignment is intended as an exercise in language. Is it all right to smoke? he asked, patting his pockets for a pack.

And you don't think it will be exercising me enough to write in al-r-ra-be-ya? John asked. And no, you can't smoke in here. But you can in al Ha-dee-qa.

They stepped out to the garden, and Khaled lit a cigarette. He inhaled, found the fence to lean on, then spoke.

We have a similar story by the way. The angel Gabriel visits the Prophet in the cave and commands him to recite. The Prophet resists at first, saying, I can't read. How shall I recite? The angel Gabriel grabs him and repeats the command, Recite. Three times this happens. Finally, the Prophet submits and recites.

Let's work here, John said pointing to the sofa.

Khaled noticed the label marking the sofa an ah-ree-ka. He looked up with a smile and saw the mis-baH and ta-we-la. You're a very serious student, he said.

My mom calls it either focused or baroque, depending on whether she's trying to be complimentary or not.

Did you check out Islamia's website?

As a matter of fact, I did, John said. You realize that it's a Muslim school for Muslims?

So, Khaled said nonchalantly. You'll make al shahada. Im'sh'allah. I'll introduce you to the brother in charge at our masjid.

I need to think about it, John said, and realized that he had been thinking about it. To taste is to know, Sufis believed, and he had been looking to know. As Burton had known. After studying the Kabbalah, the dervishes, Buddhism, and more, Burton chose Sufism. And translated Arabic literature, submitted to Islam, practiced the salaat, fasted, read, meditated, danced with dervishes, hung in a well, went to Mecca, and encountered the extraordinary. Burton had lived the life of a nineteenth-century adventurer, but he'd also penetrated the ancient wisdom of secret worlds. Which John wanted. Both the physical and spiritual experiences. So he would study and know. So he would practice. Plan. Im'sh'allah.

HE STARTED by typing the passage from Genesis in English, then, with Khaled's help, he cited in al-r-ra-be-ya the Sufic idea that the man is Jacob's own ego, his inner enemy, whom he vanquished, then recognized as his other I, or his thou, a God, and prostrated himself and asked for a blessing. When Jacob asked to know the man's name, it was not revealed, because, the Sufis say, it would have unveiled a difficult truth: the inseparable unity of man and God, not an I or a thou, but a One. According to the Sufis, then—and also the American Transcendentalist Ralph Waldo Emerson, John added in parentheses—man is God and God is man.

Khaled introduced the story of the Prophet's first revelation and submission in complex Arabic sentences way beyond John's ability. Together they managed to write something close to what they were attempting to say. They finished with several sentences on the difference between struggle and submission, which they compared to performance versus grace, made the point that both ways ended in triumph, Muhammed founded Islam, while Jacob became the father of a nation, but Jacob suffered damage to his physical self while Muhammed did not.

You know I'm really really really digging this, John said. This way of reading and interpreting. This way of understanding people, and life. Struggle and submission as character defining. It's way cool.

There's a sort of proverb, Khaled said, and recited: There is no difference in the destination, the difference is in the journey.

That's good, John said. Let's use *Same Destination, Different Journeys* as our title.

They reread, edited, read again, and agreed the essay was good enough.

John printed two copies and handed one to Khaled.

The doorbell rang. John picked up his crutches. He returned with a priority mail envelope from Barbara.

It's just from my mom, John explained. My absentee ballot. To make sure I vote.

Who you voting for? Khaled asked.

Gore, of course, John said. Aren't you?

No. Bush is a better man because he believes. Muslims are voting for Bush.

That's strange, John said, because I can guarantee you that Democrats are better friends to Muslims, certainly better friends than Republicans will ever be.

We judge a person by his ideals, Khaled said. And a man who believes in something higher is more trustworthy.

I don't disagree with you in principle, but it isn't true of most Republican politicians, and it's certainly not true of George W. Bush. I know, John said. I live in D.C.

Khaled merely shrugged, a gesture John was coming to admire. It seemed to him usefully inflected with various meanings. Khaled shrugged either to end discussions or further them, to project attitude, purchase persona, capture comedy, a variation on the American I-don't-care, or I-don't-want-to-disagree-with-you, or to-each-his-own, or it's-not-worth-mentioning, or a mere go-on. One thing Khaled didn't do is stop to explain. Already, he was stretching his legs, getting ready to leave. He stood, shouldered his backpack. I have to go now, he said. I'll ask my brother for his car and e-mail you. And I'll see you in class Thursday. He put his palms together and bowed his head ever so slightly. Massak allah bilkheir, he said, backing out of the room.

John followed Khaled down the hallway.

Kathar allah kheirkum, John said at the door, and they both laughed.

You're good, Khaled said.

IN HIS INBOX were three e-mails, one each from Katie, Sylvie, and Jilly, each informing him of a skating special on Tony Alva on HBO. In a p.s., Katie also mentioned that their trip to Hawaii was definitely scheduled for January, and that she still hoped he would join them. He paused to imagine himself in Hawaii for the winter months, a return to sun and surf and aloha, to body over mind. He wished he didn't have to choose. He had embraced the physical for a summer, and now he was giving himself to mind. Broken bones had initiated this return to scholarship, and he couldn't just stop. Some days, he thought of the accident as his sign: to choose mind over body, spiritual over the physical. He couldn't put Arabic on hold and surfing back in play; surfing, so right for last summer, would now be a cop-out. He would stay put and make progress in his studies, his readings, his language skills. And he would continue the friendships he'd started. But he would skate. He turned on the television, found the HBO channel, located the special on his electronic guide. It was scheduled to begin at eight, and he wondered whether Noor would want to join him to watch. He considered calling her. He paused to wonder at the inevitable infidelities of life: though the alert had come from Katie, he wanted to watch it with Noor. Barbara would merely smile. He paced forward and back on crutches, shrugged, and dialed Noor at work.

You'll get to see this other side of me, he said.

That might be useful, Noor said, since I'm kind of wondering who you are. But I can't. I already told my mom I'd be home for dinner. Can you record it for me?

AFTER HIS THERAPY SESSION with Sarah, he hailed a taxi and gave the address on Mott. He would visit Noor and get something to eat at the same time. In his backpack, he had the tape for her. He opened the window and gave himself up to this brief, stop-and-go tour of lower Manhattan.

The café was quiet and sunny, but Noor wasn't there.

I think she usually arrives about one, the waitress informed him.

He ordered the cucumber hummus plate and a hot chocolate. It was early, only 11:30, which was why it was quiet. He sipped his hot chocolate and sank into a sun-induced reverie. Red brick spun to gold on the garden wall across the street. Should he leave the tape for her, so she'd know he'd stopped in? Would she meet him after class tomorrow night? He'd forgotten to ask, and now he was at the bottom of his cup, swallowing bitter mud.

He left the tape, paid for lunch, and walked west on Prince. He would try to see a bit of SoHo.

Crossing Broadway, the jostle and push scared him. He had to concentrate. Keep his crutches from snagging on a crack in the sidewalk or a pedestrian's toe. People passed on his right, and people passed on his left, as if he were a slow wide load in traffic. Then a grom on a board snaked around him, using him as a found street obstacle, and John recovered his humor.

ON HIS MACHINE at home was a message from Khaled. I'll pick you up at 3:30. I have to be at work by 5:30, so we'll have to shop fast.

A dusty white van pulled up and beeped once. John emerged on crutches and heaved himself up into the van.

I'm taking you to Costco so you can shop in bulk.

In the store, Khaled pushed the large cart from aisle to aisle, and John had only to point at something and it would make its way into the cart. When they'd covered every aisle, they pulled up at the register with three six-packs of Hungry-Man-size turkey dinners, a jumbo family-sized Cheerios, packs of waffles. A full cardboard tray of Campbell's tomato soup. Another tray of Chicken of the Sea tuna. A case of Coke and a large can of Hershey's cocoa. A double pack of

Thomas' English muffins with raisins. A jumbo jar of Smucker's natural peanut butter. Entenmann's All Butter Loaf Cake.

I hope you have enough money, Khaled said.

I'll put it on my parents' card, John said and produced the new AmEx that Barbara had given him.

This should last all the way through January, John said. You're welcome to stop by and help me eat through this.

Khaled laughed. I'll keep that in mind.

The groceries on his side of the cart were more basic. A sack of rice, a sack of lentils, a sack of chickpeas, a sack of onions. A family-pack size of chicken quarters. Lemons. He led the way back to the van and loaded the bags. When they were buckled in, Khaled looked at his watch.

Good, he said. We have time for a quick stop at the masjid. I want to introduce you to the brother.

Khaled turned off the Gowanus, took a left on Atlantic and a left on Flatbush Avenue, and kept going until John wondered where they were. Finally, Khaled stopped in front of a small nondescript square white structure.

This is your mosque?

It was a small factory at one time, Khaled explained, and still looks it, at least on the outside.

Inside, every inch of wall and floor was sheathed and muffled in thick Turkish rugs, like an ABC Carpet department. Khaled took off his shoes at the entrance. John took off his one sneaker, then, making a quick decision, pulled back the Velcro straps holding his green cast in place, slipped off the cast along with the special fat shoe he'd been wearing. In stocking feet and on crutches, he followed Khaled in, the tap-tap of his wooden crutches muffled by the thick rugs. At the room's center, Khaled kneeled and prostrated himself and remained that way for several long minutes, whispering. John stood by silently. He hadn't seen Khaled this way before, in prayer, and yes, it changed something, changed Khaled into someone impassioned, even spiritual, which was weird, unlike him, unlike his usual cool, drawling self. John was seeing a different side of Khaled, his spiritual aspect, and liked it. He caught what he thought was an illaha, and understood that Khaled was mouthing the words of the shahada, la illaha il'allah et Muhammed rasulu. Some of the mystics, John had read, repeated the phrase five hundred times an hour in order to achieve an altered, exalted state. Khaled stopped after about ten repetitions, then unbowed his body and sat back on his heels. He held his hands together, palm to palm, and recited one more time, slowly—heatedly, John thought—la illaha il'allah et Muhammed rasulu. And suddenly, silently, a man dressed in spotless white appeared and gave his hands to Khaled.

Khaled greeted the brother, then turned to John. This is my remarkable friend I told you about, John Parish. He's studying at the school as well as reading on his own.

Since John's hands weren't quite free for a handshake, Brother Gabirol placed his hand on John's shoulder, not as an overzealous clap but as a gentle encouraging caress.

Give me a moment. Brother Gabirol disappeared behind a rug on the wall at the far end, as if it were a door, and returned with a pamphlet.

Take this home and read it at your leisure, the brother said. He had a Pakistani accent, John thought. He pronounced the word leisure the British way.

This literature, Gabirol continued, explains the salaat in some depth and provides an excellent grounding in the meaning and purpose of prayer. If you like, come back and we'll discuss it, perhaps you'll have questions, which I can try to answer.

John accepted the pamphlet. Shukran, he said. I'll read it and try to understand.

DURING THE QUESTION SESSION following the delivery of their paper, Fawal stood to speak, addressing himself to John.

If you are a faithful man, he said, you can't possibly think that man, including Jacob, since he was only a man, could struggle with and vanquish God.

Let me explain, John said, pausing momentarily at hearing himself identified as faithful, at having to speak as a man of faith. Fawal knew he hadn't submitted to Islam.

I'll try in Een-zhlee-zee-yah, he said, and got a smile from some students, but not from his challenger, who only glared. John took a breath. Jacob is fighting himself not God, at least that's how I understand the story. He's fighting against his own limitations, and I think what I'm trying to say is that every person who seeks that kind of self-fulfillment must fight this fight against his own limitations. The Sufis go further. They say that Jacob's imagination created the enemy in the first place, and so he had to struggle with this apparition because it was his own inner enemy, created in his own mind, but still real enough to prevent Jacob from achieving his full potential. After vanquishing his own self-created, imagined enemy, Jacob comes to understand himself as a theophany of God; in other words, he achieves full self-knowledge, or Emersonian divinity. This is what the morning light reveals.

Another student asked John whether this was how he had broken his leg, fighting himself, and a low rumble of laughter began as a wave, rippled wide, and finally included John and Khaled.

That, John said, is the best explanation I've heard yet.

Mr. Sami ended the questioning. He put his hand on John's shoulder. Well done. Our brother here may be on his way to becoming a Sufi Gnostic.

After class, Fawal walked up to him and said, Our greatest sheikhs were first good Muslims, then Sufis.

John nodded. Good point. I'll work on it.

Outside, they found Noor and Samina waiting. How did it go? Noor asked.

John and Khaled looked at each other and laughed. The students, Khaled told them, want John to submit to Islam.

One student, John said. And I'm not sure he wants me to be Muslim. He may just want me out of his face.

AT HOME, John looked for and found the pamphlet Brother Gabirol had given him. Was it true? Were the great Sufis first good Muslims? He read and ruminated on the description of a man in private, of meditative prayer as the imam of a man's own microcosm, of the ritual of private prayer as an act of creation. Prayer as creative, with the creative imagination concentrated, visualizing your highest form, a way of knowing your own highest potential. The condition of this personal revelation, John read, is that it be privately contemplative, solitary, so that the act of prayer itself becomes the fulfillment of one's highest capacity, one's divine potential, the possibility of an epiphany. Which he has been wanting. He has been looking to know the extraordinary, he has been wanting to experience his own highest capacity. Jilly had found hers in the sea, on a wave. Maybe for him, the extraordinary will arrive in meditative, creative prayer.

He studied the steps of the salaat as described in the brochure and tried it, though with the cast on his leg he couldn't take the full position on both knees. He removed the cast and tried again, gingerly. But he would have to memorize the seven verses of the Qur'an, so that he could recite the tasbeeh, the tamheed, and the tahleel with his head down, eyes closed. He tried the head turns, first right, then left, while pronouncing the illaha il'allah. In solitude, in the privacy of his apartment, he would attempt prayer, but he wondered whether Noor would disapprove. And did praying the Muslim way make him Muslim?

The brochure also discussed the zakat, the third pillar of Islam, which was easy enough to commit to. He would set aside 2.5 percent of his monthly allowance for charity, which came to twelve dollars and fifty cents a month, not much. He took thirteen dollars from his wallet and sealed it in an envelope, which he addressed to Brother Gabirol. He would let the brother determine which charity should get it. The fourth pillar, the pilgrimage, he decided, would be his reward: a travel adventure, starting with a summer in Pakistan.

THE X-RAY SHOWED John's tibia healed, and Sarah went to work. She started by inserting his leg, from the knee down, in a whirlpool-like vat of heated silicone particles that bubbled and pushed and warmed up long-unused muscles. The sensation was weird, John thought, silicone rather than water therapy, but it did seem to work. His muscles were less stiff. After which, Sarah used her weight to push against his leg, instructed him to push back hard, and harder, until she could no longer hold up against him.

Okay, she said. Since that didn't hurt, let's try the leg in standing position, using your own weight.

John stood. Took a light step forward and felt nerve endings rushing up and down his leg, reconnecting. He had tried it once at home and scared himself. But here, in front of Sarah, he was more confident, and he transferred more weight onto the leg, then stepped forward with his good leg and shifted his weight again. He looked at Sarah, delighted.

I'm walking, he said.

Congratulations, she said. Are you game for more?

John nodded and kept going. When he turned, he pivoted on his good leg.

Careful, Sarah warned.

He walked back toward her, a toddler showing off his first steps. I'm ready to go.

It would seem so, but you'll tire easily at first. Your muscles will need building up.

She took him to a stationary bicycle and helped him on. This way we can control the resistance and exercise your muscles without putting your full weight on the bone. One thing: Don't push on the pedal, pull up instead, and the force of that will bring the pedal round. Got it?

Afterward, John hailed a cab. He had an idea. In the long corridor entrance, where his renovated board was parked, he removed his cast without stopping to take off his coat, stomped on the heel of the board with his good leg, to turn it, and stepped on, and YES. If he kept his weight on his left foot, and used his vulnerable right only for light steering, he could be on wheels sooner rather than later. He rolled slowly up and down the corridor, pausing at the end to steer about. So long as he stuck to the basics, no grinding, no fancy maneuvers, his wheels would help rather than hurt. He could skate to school and back, but he couldn't skate circles around Noor, at least not yet. Still, he was stoked.

He continued practicing, moving from room to room, from kitchen to living room, on wheels rather than crutches. The hardest part was getting on and off the board, but if he was careful to favor his right leg, keeping it in the lead, he could manage. His left leg, which had gotten a workout these last months, was stronger than before.

The phone rang and he skated toward it, picking up after the first ring, and Barbara was immediately suspicious.

Were you waiting by the phone?

I happened to be near it.

How are you and Noor getting along? she inquired. John knew that no matter what he said, Barbara would suspect him of pining.

Mom, I had my second therapy session today and I was able to walk.

So that's what you're up to, Barbara said, catching on quickly. You're walking without your cast.

Well, not quite, but I am getting around a lot faster.

John, Barbara said, in a stern voice. I shouldn't have to say this. You know better. You've been in a cast for three months. You don't want to put yourself back in a cast foolishly. What's another week or two?

Mom, my leg's healed. The X-ray shows no sign of the fracture. My therapist put me on a stationary bike today, exercising my muscles. It's a matter of getting my muscles up to speed now.

Okay, Barbara said. That's great news. Your arm certainly seems to have healed well. Remember to send in your ballot.

I already have, John said. Last week. Does Gore have a chance? What's the word in D.C.?

A lot of waffling, which means voters are uncertain about Gore. Clearly he just isn't convincing enough people. And though I completely understand why he did it, I'm not persuaded that distancing himself from Clinton was the wisest decision.

Well, he's got my vote, John said.

Good. My next patient's here, so we'll talk later. Be careful. And also, Dad suggests you visit us this weekend, for the fund-raiser. There's a chance one of Gore's daughters will attend. She's about your age. Think about it? I'll call you tomorrow.

John hung up and cruised up and down his hallway. D.C. for the weekend? All the more reason to be rid of his cast and crutches. Also, a weekend with his parents would give him an opportunity to mention the possibility of a year in Pakistan. They wouldn't like it. They'd mind that he was deferring Brown again. But if he broached the subject correctly, if the credits could transfer to Brown, they'd eventually approve. Barbara, he knew, was a great believer in educational travel.

HE WENT TO CLASS ON WHEELS, backpack on his back and, under his arm, his crutches, in case of emergency. Khaled was already there waiting and smoking, as usual. John cruised up at full speed and executed a sudden full stop in front of him. Startled, Khaled dropped his cigarette, cursed, grabbed John by his upper arm, as if to keep him upright.

Are you for real?

John was pleased to have startled Khaled.

Look, he said, demonstrating. I'm actually keeping my weight off the bad leg.

Anyone else know about this? Khaled asked. Like your doctor?

Nope. I'm hoping Noor shows tonight, because I want to surprise her. Is there a back-door exit in this building?

Khaled smiled. There is, he said. We'll exit into the alley, and you can come around the block on the sidewalk, pull up in front of her, and make her heart stop. After which she'll be fully in love with you, if she isn't already.

NOOR SHRIEKED. Which only encouraged John, and he skated slow circles around her, which was more than he'd intended to do. He held back on the finish, avoided the flourish of an ollie or grind, grateful to be on wheels at all, grateful to inhabit his body again, to have full use of his limbs. He felt reborn.

Noor put her hands on his shoulders, to stop him, and laughed. You're amazing and insane at once, she said. When did you get your cast off? I don't know how anyone can go from crutches to a skateboard in a day.

I still need my crutches, John said, and pointed toward Khaled, who wasn't just carrying but using them, hopping two-footed, amusing Samina.

It's like they've switched places, she said.

They hurt my underarms, Khaled said, pausing. I don't know how you could do it for so long.

Precisely, John said. Which is why I'm happier without them.

Doing without them, though, doesn't have to mean going directly to skating, does it? Noor said. You could try walking, like the rest of us.

Watch, John explained, getting on the board again. Wheels don't require me to put much weight on my broken leg. Though nonintuitive, this actually helps.

They laughed. Well, we can go places faster now, Noor said.

Rumbling on wheels beside Noor, who was on foot, John noted with pleasure that she was more talkative tonight. She liked him again, though he was wearing the white tunic over his regular jeans.

Ali would love it, she said, but I'm afraid to let him see you. He will immediately want to try it.

I'm happy to teach him, but he'll need permission from your parents. They've seen me so they know what can happen, but I could teach him the simple stuff, no tricks.

Do you want to stop at my house to show him? Noor asked.

Now? he asked, surprised. He hadn't expected another invitation so soon. He wondered but didn't ask whether her father was home. He'd find out.

Here, let me carry these, she said, taking the crutches from him.

At their building, Noor rang the buzzer. Oom, she said. Send Ali down. I want to show him something.

Ali came racing out. Mr. and Mrs. Bint-Khan, John noted, stood at an upstairs window. He waved. Then he skated down the sidewalk, turned, came back, keeping it all low and slow and very safe. On his second loop, Ali skipped beside him.

I want to try it, he said. Please?

You'll need your parents' permission, John said.

Ali lifted his arms toward the heavens, though his parents were only on the second floor, put his palms together, beseeching. Noor looked up, saw her father nod. Her mother, however, had her hand over her mouth.

Is it possible to slow the wheels down even more? Noor asked John. My mother looks afraid.

Okay. If you hold his hand, I'll hold his other hand. I'll need one of my crutches and I'll try to stay in front of the board, to slow it down.

But Ali wouldn't hold their hands. He'd seen kids on boards, and he already knew where to place the heel of his right foot, and how to use the other foot on the sidewalk to get the wheels moving. Whoa, John said, putting the point of his crutch in front of the board, to stop it. I can't keep up with you, if you go so fast. And it's your first time. You don't even know how to stop.

Listen, Ali, Noor said. You can only try it if you do exactly what John says. If you fall, Oom'll never let you do it again, so you'd better hold my hand.

Noor and John led Ali down the sidewalk. For his return, John instructed him. If you want to take it back by yourself, just remember to step off the board when you get to the steps. Got it?

Ali nodded. They started him off, then let him go and held their breath and watched Ali bend his knees and struggle for balance, but he stayed on and, when the sidewalk came to an end, hopped off coolly and scooped up the board.

Noor and John clapped. Above them, Ali's parents clapped and waved. Do you want to come upstairs for tea? Noor asked.

John agreed and they made their way up the stoop and into the elevator. Mrs. Bint-Khan welcomed John. Mr. Bint-Khan shook John's hands with more warmth than he'd expected and led the way into the living room.

Noor tells me, Mr. Bint-Khan said, you have an interest in Sufism. As it happens, we have a scholar coming to lecture on the topic. Would you like to attend?

John nodded. Very much.

Very well, Mr. Bint-Khan said, clapping his hands together. Noor will bring you.

Noor grimaced. I have so much homework, and I'm already in lecture like five times a week, but if you really really want to, I'll go.

Noor doesn't yet believe that all learning leads to the same place, Mr. Bint-Khan said.

Let's put it this way, Noor said. If I don't attend classes and write assigned papers, I won't graduate.

WHEN HE EMERGED through the double doors of Union Station on wheels, Barbara was already there, waiting in her black Mercedes. He cruised up to the vehicle, deposited board and bag in the backseat, himself in the passenger seat, and kissed his mother, who was shaking her head.

I knew you'd be on wheels, Barbara said. Did your therapist approve this, too?

Kind of. She said yesterday that I was definitely walking.

But she didn't recommend skating.

That's my own insight. I realized that on the board, I could keep eighty percent of my weight on the back leg, and use the front leg only for steering. Which is perfect, considering. Obviously, no tricks for a while.

I'm glad to hear it, Barbara said, drily. I'm very pleased to hear that my son has a percentage of good sense, however slight it is.

John put his hand on her shoulder. Mom, it's nice to see you, too.

She pulled up in front of TipTops. I'll be a moment, she said.

John grabbed his board and got out. To grind again on Connecticut. He hadn't done it since June, when he'd moved down to the Outer Banks, and now, newly back on wheels, he couldn't get enough of it. Besides he knew every seam of this sidewalk, every lip and crack, every metal plate. He could skate Connecticut Avenue in the dark, in his sleep. His experience of being grounded for ten weeks, he could now admit, had been terrible, and though he'd accomplished much, read and learned, he'd lived only half a life, the life of the mind, but disconnected from the body, which isn't full life. It was doable, he'd done it, but life without the physical was life without joy. Physical play makes for intellectual play. Thus he feels deliriously alive, impatient to range wide, to explore new things, new places. Thus he can't wait. Thus, before Barbara turns the ignition to restart the engine, he blurts it all out:

Mom, he said. I want to study abroad, starting this June. At Islamia College in Pakistan. Khaled's going.

Pakistan? Barbara echoed. What about Brown?

I checked out Brown's Middle Eastern studies concentration, which requires extensive language credits and a year abroad in the region, so I'm pretty sure my credits from Islamia will transfer. It's Pakistan's most prestigious college, known for the best classical Arabic teaching.

Sounds like an adventure, Barbara said, but is it safe?

It's in the countryside, in the hills. They have a website you can check out.

But you'll miss a summer of surfing and the girls.

True, John said. But there's plenty of white concrete for grinding.

Let's talk about this at dinner with Dad. We have a reservation at Dish. There's lunch meat for a sandwich in the fridge. I have two more patients to see today. What will you do this afternoon?

I want to get out on the street, reengage.

She shook her head. Be careful. She pulled up at the house to let him off.

BILL DIDN'T THINK Pakistan or Islamia such a brilliant idea. Especially after that recent attack on the USS *Cole,* he said.

But that was in Yemen, John said.

If you wanted to study abroad in England or Ireland, for example, or anywhere else, I'd have no objections, but that region is a violent place right now.

Unfortunately, Barbara said, Ireland doesn't offer immersion in Arabic.

It'll be hot in the summer, Bill warned, and I don't think they'll be offering air-conditioning.

I'll get used to it, John said. The pics show a beautiful campus. The main building is supposed to be an important example of Moghul architecture. But a simple life will be part of the experience. I'll live in the dorms, and they're probably not that different from college dorms in the U.S., minus cable and DSL.

True, Bill said, and John felt he'd been persuasive enough, at least for now. After which, they moved on to other things: John's healing bones, his therapist, Noor, the Bint-Khans, the surprise of the polls, which showed W. running alongside Gore.

Muslim Americans, John said, are voting for Bush. According to Khaled. I guess they're more comfortable with religious people.

Orthodox Jews, Barbara said, feel the same way. It's a tragic mistake. But we're doing what we can. I had your jacket dry-cleaned. You'll find several pressed shirts in your closet. And please, for once, would you wear a tie?

JOHN ENJOYED THE BUSY WEEKEND, his mother's attention, his father's objections, and then he was relieved to get on the Sunday evening train back to New York, to the quiet of his apartment in Brooklyn, where his daily schedule and activities were entirely determined by his own interests and needs. He would see them again on Thanksgiving.

On the train, he practiced the seven Qur'anic verses he was committing to memory. Then he reread the pamphlet on prayer. It wasn't as if he'd never prayed before. He had, but informally, stepping onto a wave, or ollying up for a particular grind. Now he wanted to experience what the pamphlet called creative prayer, but did that mean he had to accept God as his God? Because that's what the prayer declared: There is no God but God, and Muhammed is his prophet. But what did that mean exactly? Of course God is God. Who else would he be? He brooded and doodled. On the back cover of the pamphlet, he sketched the black Ka'ba at Mecca, a closed box, then erased a small opening at the top of the box for the column that jutted out, Ibn 'Arabi's great secret, the symbol that directed him back to himself because it was the only entrance to the temple and to the black stone within it. The column, 'Arabi understood, represented the individual, the angel of the self. And the secret of divinity, the divine itself was within the self, his I. John noted that the column could be perceived as an I and drew it that way, and then understood this as his own revelation, an original one. Which pleased him. No matter what Barbara said, John was convinced that the idea of private prayer as an opportunity to achieve one's highest potential was not a lot of talk about nothing. Still, he would find out for sure, he would learn it and try it and prove for himself whether it was a nothing or a something. He would revisit the masjid and ask the brother to teach him how to perform the salaat. He would know what there is to know. He would find out whether for him, personally, God amounted to an absence or a presence or a nothing. If only he could concentrate all the powers of his heart, as Corbin wrote. If only he could achieve the kind of prayer that serves as an act of creation. He prayed to achieve it.

THE LECTURE, TITLED ORTHODOXY: An End to Prophecy, started with the claim that dogmatic religion brought prophetism to an end, meaning the end of individual excellence. Prophecy, the professor explained, is a personal, self-generated calling, independent of church, community, and group thinking. When the church placed the incarnation in a particular moment in historical time with no possibility of its recurring in the present or future, it rejected the second-century Montanist prophets and brought prophecy to an end. What is history but a fable agreed upon, he quoted Emerson quoting Napoleon; Emerson concluded that there is properly no history, only biography. In other words, the church availed itself of history in a play for power, and falseness and lies arrive as soon as the law of community is given precedence over the needs of the individual. In Islam, as in the Christian incarnation, the divine manifests itself in human form, but not on earth, and significantly not in a historic past, but recurrently, in the middle world, the world of the imagination also known as Hurqalya, and this is why, so long as there are humans with active imaginations capable of experiencing Hurqalya, the sophistry of the phrase God is dead doesn't exist in Islam. You have not and will not hear anyone write or say that Allah is dead. But unfortunately Islam, which never should have a church or authoritative council, is also guilty of corruption, the scholar finished.

Mr. Bint-Khan introduced John as his daughter's new, scholarly friend and asked whether he had any questions for the professor.

John thought a moment. Yes, he said. I would ask why Islam calls itself the seal of prophecy if recurrent incarnation is at its heart. Also, doesn't the professor believe that we are turning back toward prophecy and individual excellence, especially here in America, where personal achievement is so highly valued? You might almost be able to argue that achievement is the American religion.

The professor demurred. Your good questions require another lecture.

NOOR HAD AN ESSAY due the next morning, on the subject of genre, the memoir versus the autobiographical novel, or the personal essay versus the reported, fact-driven piece. She complained that there wasn't that much to say on the subject, that it seemed to her that fabrication didn't belong in journalism, case closed.

John disagreed. It's basically on the question of fiction as truth, on whether the imagination can inform fact, and therefore might help journalism. For example the professor's ideas on prophecy.

I don't see how prophecy could inform the subject of genres in literature and journalism, Noor said.

John wondered how she couldn't see it. Think of prophecy itself as a genre. The prophet believes in his vision the way any artist does, so he thinks he's prophesying the truth. And it is true for him because it comes out of his own head, his Hurqalya—I love that word, hurqalya, because it makes everything possible. This is really cool stuff to write about.

I don't know if I can figure it all out for this paper, but I'll think about it.

When they said good night, Noor stood on her toes for the left-right-left kiss, though he was wearing his white tunic again, and he walked home wondering whether she no longer objected to his dressing as a Muslim. And was dressing as a Muslim the beginning of becoming one? He asked himself whether this was what he wanted, whether his interest in Arabic literature and Sufism required that he accept the face of Islam, whether immersion had to include, as it did for Richard Burton, submission. John asked himself whether he was prepared to bear witness. Faith, he understood by now, was not a simple act of belief; faith was active prayer, and prayer was creative, an invitation to his divine self, to the fulfillment of his own highest capacity. With Brother Gabirol's help, he'd learned and was practicing the salaat, with its recitals of the tasbeeh, the tamheed, and the tahleel, rehearsing the head turns, first right, then left, pronouncing the illaha il'allah. In solitude, in the privacy of his apartment, he was praying daily, but he worried that Noor would disapprove.

He also didn't tell her that he'd committed to zakat. And now Ramadan was only three weeks away, and he hadn't yet decided whether to fast. He would discuss it with Brother Gabirol, who would ask whether John was ready for the shahada, and John didn't know. If he could commit only to prophecy, reject dogma, all repression and restriction and politics, then yes, he could declare himself ready to submit to Islam. That, it seemed to him, was the professor's choice; and that was what he, too, would choose: prophecy, vision, divine potential without dogma, law, and the restrictions of orthodoxy.

The professor, Khaled assured him, is Muslim. Islam is the least dogmatic of the three religions, though there are people who're trying to change that. In fact, it's the only religion that's interpreted legally, by lawyers. That's why religious persecution like the heresy trials of the Spanish Inquisition could never happen in Islam, not legally anyway.

So, John kept asking himself, was he prepared to submit?

He said the word shahada, practicing the sound of the Arabic *h,* which was formed deeper in the throat than the English one. It had some gargle in it, a sound that didn't exist in the English language. The professor articulated beautifully, with perfect stops between syllables, a space of sound represented on the page by the apostrophe. It was a beat, a hesitation, a stutter. At school, the students seemed to swallow that silent note, to hurry on to the next one or forget to leave the opening, but hearing it in the professor's Arabic, John felt it was as necessary a beat as silent beats are in music because it made the Arabic musical, and correct. Mr. Bint-Khan also made time for this silence; Noor, John noticed, only did it when she was reciting or quoting. Attempting it, John found he waited too long, he fell behind, lost the rhythm of the phrase and sentence. The timing wasn't all that easy. He would have to live the language along with the life in order to learn it. Done right, it sounded a bit like a click.

THEY FINALLY GOT AROUND to visiting the red brick plaza bordered by Franklin Street to the south, Pearl Street to the east, Park Row to the west, and Police Plaza to the north, known to skateboarders everywhere as the Brooklyn Banks.

With Noor on foot and John on wheels, they crossed a municipal parking lot and a housing project and made their way to the sloping walls under the shadow of the bridge. The sound of so many wheels grinding on concrete made his heart pump.

This is weird, Noor said. I've lived here forever and I never heard of this place. But who'd think of a park under the bridge. And it doesn't exactly look like a park anyway.

John filled her in on the Banks' history. It's legendary for skateboarding. The most awesome skaters have grinded here.

But it's like a rundown dump, Noor said.

Skaters don't mind rundown, John said. Watch what they do and you'll understand why. Here, watch this guy.

They watched a kid ollie his skateboard onto a rail, slide down, land, and roll away. That was an ollie to a feeble to a backside grind, John explained. Watch again. He's good. He lands buttery, pops out of his feeble, and continues grinding as if it's all nothing.

Can you do that? Noor asked.

Yeah, but this guy is good.

He took Noor's hand and led her to another spot, so she could see from a different angle.

This trick, he said, is known as the heelflip. It's so fast, it's hard to see what he's doing. I'll show it to you in slow motion, or I'll explain it to you without actually doing it. I'm sworn off tricks for another month. But watch. He's doing it again. His front foot's in the middle, toes hanging off the side. His back foot's on the tail, ball of the foot on the corner. He bends his knees, he's balanced over his heels. He's starting his jump. Now. His toe smacks down on the tail. Now he's dragging his front foot up toward the nose, kicks off the corner of the nose. Flips the board. I can't say it quickly enough to keep up. Watch again. He stops the board from overflipping. Now he's landed, balanced himself, and he rolls away.

You lost me, Noor said, but I can see how easily you could break an arm and a leg. How did your mother ever let you get into this?

It's not as bad as it looks, John said. Besides, it's great for kids. It gives them something to focus on. And you don't practice these tricks until you're really balanced on wheels, and can skate and ollie in your sleep.

What's an ollie?

One of the most basic maneuvers. It made grinding on streets possible. And it's the basis for all other tricks.

This was the Brooklyn Banks, and John wanted to perform. For himself, or for Noor, he didn't know which, but he wanted to.

Here, he said, watch this low one, in slow motion. He popped his board up, jumped, bent his knees, dragged his front leg, then replaced his feet on the board, landed, and rolled away.

You make it look super easy.

I'll teach you, John said, but first you have to learn to roll.

Noor shook her head. Not for me.

He looked at her and understood that, unlike Katie, Noor had no desire and no need to test herself this way. Though she would support his ambitions, she herself would avoid physical risk. He paused to feel how much he missed Katie's enthusiasm for the new, her fearless embrace of the difficult, her risk taking for the sheer thrill of it. With Katie, he could share the thrill, and he could expect her to compete against him, top his stunts, his experiences.

Seeing his disappointment, Noor offered her little brother. You can teach Ali, she said.

Okay, John said. That is if your parents okay it. We'll have to get him a kid's size board. We can take him to Five Borough Boards.

John took Noor's hand and led her to another group. Watch closely, John said. They're practicing backside one-eighty ollies.

How many tricks are there?

Six basic ones: the manual, the ollie, the backside ollie, the pop-shove-it, the frontside pop-shove-it, and the heelflip.

Noor was due to begin work in half an hour, and they walked up to Prince and Mott. She went into the café, came out with two hot chocolates, and they sat on the curb in a patch of afternoon light, blowing into their cups to cool the milk.

Before he left, she touched his cheek, right left right left, then breathed words into his ear, which left him in ecstasy.

Skateboarder-scholar, she whispered. I can't believe I even know you.

MUHAMMED, FAIWAL, JAMAL, OR KAMEL. These were the Muslim names Brother Gabirol recommended to John, but after standing in front of the mirror and trying each one, he found they didn't work for him, and he determined to stick with Attar or remain John.

Gabirol suggested that Khaled serve as first witness. As second witness, John considered Mr. Bint-Khan, Noor's father, since as a woman Noor couldn't perform this service. Barbara, he knew, would criticize such gender inequality, but feminism was new, and these were ancient traditions. When he asked Noor how Muslim women felt about feminism, she explained that ideas of equality weren't as black and white as Americans believed. Besides, she said, Islam only seems discriminatory to a Westerner used to Western freedoms. Behind closed doors, Muslim women are powerful. Samina agreed with Noor.

The Prophet's wives, Samina explained, determined on the veil as a way of heightening their stature, something Americans seem unable to get.

Western-style feminism, Noor said, at least in Islam, would require our women to relinquish their special place in Muslim life. It's true they might gain something, but they'd lose more. At least that's how my mom explains it, but then she believes that Muslim life offers more freedom than anyone will ever have in America. Me, I'm in between.

He found himself going back and forth on his idea of Noor's father as second witness so often, he finally discussed it with Brother Gabirol, who thought about it, then advised against Mr. Bint-Khan.

If it were the right thing to do, you wouldn't have doubts, he said. And it's probably not a good idea to involve the father of a girl with whom you have a fledgling relationship. This is too important, a life-changing decision.

John objected to the word fledgling. It's more than that, he said. I've come to really really like her.

All the more reason to remain independent then, Gabirol said. If this relationship does continue to develop, and should you come to marry the girl, you might appreciate the fact that her family had not participated in your deepest beliefs. The decision to make the shahada is a deeply personal one, not based in earthly love of a woman, but rather in a more celestial, higher love.

Brother Gabirol suggested a devout Muslim entirely unknown to John as second witness, someone Gabirol would approach for the service, and John agreed. With Gabirol watching, he rehearsed the movements and recitals of the salaat, including the seven Qur'anic verses that he'd committed to memory. Gabirol declared himself impressed and offered John two possible dates: one, the following Friday, when the entire congregation would be gathered for prayers; the second, a weekday evening, in a private, small ceremony performed in the small chamber, off the main hall of the masjid.

John opted for the private ceremony, with only the two witnesses and Gabirol. Privacy, he knew, would make him less self-conscious, more focused on meaning rather than performance. Sufism and Islam had come to him largely privately—he hadn't participated in congregational services so far—and he would keep it that way. At least for now. Also, for a public initiation, he would have to invite the Bint-Khans, and if he invited them, he'd have to also invite his parents, which meant he'd have to tell his parents, but he'd decided to tell them about it only after the fact. This would be his decision alone; he would deal with their response to his decision after. Besides, he knew that Bill wouldn't relish the ceremony. He'd question his son's motivations and integrity, and worry about the future. Barbara also would hate the idea of her son submitting to anything or anyone, but she'd think of the event as an experience, an opportunity to observe another culture and religion. That is, if she were allowed to attend. It occurred to him that as a woman, she might not have full access to the ceremony, and Noor's explanations wouldn't satisfy her.

With the date set for the following Wednesday, John found himself moved to urgent prayer and meditation. He reread Corbin on creative, concentrated prayer, studied his Arabic, and repeated the la illaha il'al-lah hundreds of times a day, until he felt himself in a kind of trance, eyes straight ahead and staring, unseeing. He dropped off his tunic and pants at a local Chinese laundry. Wednesday evening, he would attend class as usual. And after class, Khaled would drive him downtown to the masjid.

NOT WANTING TO RISK dirtying his freshly cleaned white clothes, John brought them with him in his backpack, still wrapped in brown paper. So he enters the small bathroom at the masjid. He washes his hands and face, changes into his clothes. So he emerges minutes later, hair glistening, face shining, garments spotless, barefoot. He is ready. Thus Brother Gabirol introduces John to his second witness, a distinguished elderly man named Maulana Ismail. Thus they shake hands. Thus he kneels on a prayer rug. Gabirol kneels in front of him and places his right palm, thumb to thumb, against John's right palm. The maulana and Khaled kneel on either side of him. Thus they form a protective circle around him, a ring of safety, and he feels good, he feels safe, he feels this private ceremony is right. Brother Gabirol looks at him inquiringly. He is ready. He nods. Thus Brother Gabirol closes his eyes. Thus John recites. He articulates the verses, with pauses for the apostrophes. He tries for the throaty *h,* the correct number of breaths. He gets it right only sometimes. He uses his closed fist on his chest to mark the breaths. Subhan allah wal-hamdu. La illaha il'allah et Muhammed rasulu. He brings his forehead to the floor and repeats la illaha il'allah, he breathes, he repeats, he hears behind his own words and breaths and beats Gabirol's words and breaths and beats. Thus he keeps going, thus he recites five hundred times. Thus he feels himself transported, afloat. Thus he isn't here on his knees. He is elsewhere. He is in another place and another time. An ancient place, an older time. He is with Ibn 'Arabi in Mecca, and he feels older than himself. He is on wheels, grinding, circling the Ka'ba, perambulating, chanting, shouting with great joy, la illaha il'allah, la illaha il'allah, la illaha il'allah. Thus he understands that this is what it's for. JOY. Self-celebration. He is with Ibn 'Arabi. He feels rather than hears Brother Gabirol rock back on his heels, and reluctantly he returns from far away to his place on the rug, to his prostrated, perspiring body. He is in Brooklyn now. The room is overheated. A trickling moist sheen covers his skin. He smells an odor he doesn't recognize, something herbal or medicinal, but burnt, burnt parsley. He begins his five hundred first recitation, and Gabirol, who is keeping count, nods. John raises his head, turns toward his right, toward the maulana, and greets him with as salaamu aleykum, then to his left, toward Khaled, who replies wa aleykum as salaam. Gabirol stands. Gabirol places an embroidered white mantle over John's shoulders. Allahu ak-bhar, Gabirol announces, and they repeat after him, Allahu ak-bhar, Allahu ak-bhar, Allahu ak-bhar. Thus John believes. Allahu ak-bhar.

PESHAWAR, PAKISTAN—MAY 2001

THEY WERE FLYING BRITISH AIRWAYS, New York–London, London–Islamabad. Pakistan's newest, most modern city would be John's first view of this world. More than sixty languages, his guidebook informed him, are spoken in Pakistan, but English is the official one, used in business, government, legal, and public discourse.

You'll have no problem, Khaled said. Even at Islamia, lectures open to the public are in English.

At Barbara's last fund-raiser, a young Pakistani writer working at his country's embassy described Islamabad as an Islamized version of D.C. air-dropped into the foothills of the Himalayas. Be sure to visit Mr. Books, he'd said, Islamabad's best bookshop.

On the plane beside Khaled, John read about Islamabad's Zero Point from which all distances are measured.

Zero Point. A film of the universe's history run in reverse would show the universe contracting to a dot, eventually disappearing back to the beginning, before time and space, to a primal zero, the birthplace of the universe, when the big bang banged and burst forth a fury of galaxies, stars, planets, our nonstop cosmos. In the beginning was the point. In the beginning, some 15 billion years ago, before time was timed, on day zero of the world.

He would grind to Zero Point, a sacred spot, and begin again in the womb of the world. He would join an ongoing race of scholar-adventurers, men who have surrendered themselves to the life movement of the universe. He would be this century's Richard Burton, Sir Richard Burton, speaker of twenty-nine languages, translator of the *Kama Sutra,* editor of *A Thousand and One Nights*; Sir Richard Burton, explorer of wild Sind, of Baluchistan and the Punjab; fearless Richard Burton, first European to make the famous pilgrimage to Mecca; the great Sir Richard Burton who described the mystical fana al-fana as a merging of the creature with the creator; Lieutenant Burton, secret service agent in western India; Captain Richard Burton, Sufi initiate; Murshid Burton, who could move the name of Allah through his body; Gnostic Burton, dervish and wandering holy man; Devil Burton, amateur barbarian and frequenter of brothels. All of which would make Barbara both proud and unhappy at once. But she would come around. She and Bill were cool parents, and John was determined to prove himself. In his own way.

He circled Zero Point on the map to mark it. From there, he would set out with his backpack, his skateboard, and guidebook and, for the rest of life, use it as a measure of distance traveled. Though he would have only twenty-four hours in Islamabad, not enough time to see enough, he would grind to Zero, pray, then go forth and learn the difference between nothing and something, absence and presence, meaning and chaos. From Zero Point, he told Khaled, he would skate forth to Islamabad's main drag, into the Blue and Green Areas, and cover ground quickly.

I hate to bust your bubble, Khaled said, but Zero Point is just a signpost that gives the mileage and kilometers to surrounding cities. You're overinvesting in it.

Khaled planned to spend a good part of his first twenty-four hours catching up on sleep. This will be the best accommodations we'll have for a year, he said. Definitely our last night with air-conditioning.

During his last visit to Pakistan, Khaled had signed on for a five-week retreat in the hills. After weeks of hard physical conditioning in a dusty camp, he said, I just wanted a hot shower and a real bed. My aunt picked me up. She claims I slept for thirty-six hours straight.

Barbara was paying for their night in Islamabad, and they were staying at the President, a three-star hotel popular for its all-night café, which John knew Khaled would enjoy.

If I'm up early, Khaled said, I'll pray at Faisal Mosque. It's huge. It can hold like fifteen thousand people.

John looked at a picture of the mosque in his guidebook. Though it was made of aluminum and heavy concrete, it looked as light and airy as a cluster of Bedouin tents, somehow afloat in the blue blue sky. The rooflines were white and taut as wind-filled sails. It's beautiful, John said. Poetic. He traced a path from Zero Point to the mosque. He would check it out on wheels.

He continued reading his guide all the way into Islamabad.

> Islamabad. The name of the capital means "the abode of Islam" and reflects the Islamic ideology in Pakistan. Islamabad is new, planned, spacious, leafy and green. The wide roads, detached houses and gardens contrast with Pakistan's older cities. . . . A skyline of high rises with posh offices is springing up in Islamabad's business district with the unusual name of Blue Area.

Armchair travel, Khaled called it. I'm going for real life. I don't need a guidebook written by an Englishman telling me what to see and do. We'll be residents, not tourists.

You know, John said. Not everything has to be so black and white, an either/or. Reading informs my experience. I want to be open to all of it, both the learning and adventure.

EARLY NEXT MORNING, showering, John discovered that Pakistani towels were strangely useless things, and he was glad he'd packed his own. He made a mental note to mention it to Barbara so she could pack a couple when she and Bill visited.

Outside, the sun was rising, with not a cloud anywhere. John stepped out and inhaled deeply. This was for real, he was here, in Pakistan, on the streets of Islamabad, on wheels. Finally. If only Barbara could see him.

The first call to prayer sounded, and suddenly the whole of Islamabad filled with it, from microphones everywhere. He turned his board toward Faisal Mosque, allowing sound and traffic to guide him, and came upon a scene in the courtyard that previously he'd seen only in pictures: thousands of rounded backs, backs of every color and stripe, prostrated in prayer. He found an unoccupied prayer mat, kneeled, dropped his center to his heels and his head to the ground into the jalsa which he still thought of as child's pose and gave his voice to the voices bearing witness: La illaha il'allah et Muhammed rasulu. La illaha il'allah et Muhammed rasulu. La illaha il'allah et Muhammed rasulu. And giving voice, he felt himself expand, grow larger on the inside. His skin stretched to accommodate this new self. He inhaled. He exhaled. His chest expanded, his ribs opened. He recited, a voice amid voices. He was alive. His voice hummed with the hum, and dissolved into the bluing air and brightening sky as one voice. And then, all together, all at once, he and these thousands, these thousands plus one, rocked back on their heels, and turned their heads to the right, turned their heads to the left, and acknowledged one another in their descent back to ordinary life: As salaamu aleykum, assaalamu aleykum, Allahu ak-bhar.

As quickly as the crowd had gathered, it dispersed. John remained on his mat, not yet wanting to move. He looked about him, at what was now a mostly vacant courtyard. Perhaps he'd only dreamed it. But it had been awesome, and he couldn't explain how or why. Not yet. His voice, a thousand voices. A wave of sound on which he'd been borne aloft. And he'd found himself wanting to stay aloft, with the sound, in the sound. Nothing he'd read had prepared him for this. He stayed where he was and repeated. Allahu ak-bhar. Allahu ak-bhar. He looked forward to the noon call. He would wait for the noon call. And the evening call. And the next day's call. To this experience of himself as a strangely enlarged I, a broom-swept, uncluttered I.

THEY TOOK THE TRAIN to Peshawar. The day had gone hazy, but still John could make out the landscape as his guidebook described it: long stretches of a huge gray bowl with a green bottom. He looked for the three chips in the bowl: the legendary Khyber, Kohat, and Malakand Passes. He read aloud to Khaled, who learned some new things about this country he already knew, proving he could benefit from guidebooks.

> North West Frontier Province is a British invention, an administrative convenience brought about by bureaucratic in-fighting in distant Punjab, on the border between Pakistan and Afghanistan. The predominant color of the landscape gave us a new word in English: khaki, derived from the local word for "dust." . . . Much of the North West Frontier is indeed very dusty. Areas are so dry, rocky and barren that the province has been described as a gigantic slagheap. This is a little unfair, for it does possess great beauty.
>
> . . . In Kipling's famous novel *Kim,* the Grand Trunk Road is described as "the backbone of all Hind." Grand Trunk Road connects Kabul with Calcutta. "All castes and kinds of men move here. Look! Brahmins and chamars, bankers and tinkers, barbers and bunnias, pilgrims and potters—all the world going and coming. To me it is a river from which I am withdrawn like

> a log after a flood. And truly the Grand Trunk Road is a wonderful spectacle. It runs straight, bearing without crowding India's traffic for fifteen hundred miles—such a river of life as nowhere else exists in the world."

That may have been true in Kipling's day, Khaled said, but the GT couldn't handle modern traffic. The new M2 motorway is three lanes wide and entirely computer controlled. Your guidebook is totally outdated.

John paused to absorb Khaled's update, decided he still wanted to know these stories, even if the information was ancient, and continued.

> . . . Continuing up the GT Road, Attock is 60 miles from Pindi. . . . Attock Fort sprawls across the hillside looking over the River Indus. The Indus here enters a gorge and continues through it for some miles down to Kalabagh. The Fort rises in steps reaching a great height above the river. The outer stone walls are nearly 1.5 miles in circumference. . . . Nearby, the muddy brown waters of the Kabul River join the blue waters of the Indus. The Indus is much tamer now since Alexander crossed it on his bridge of boats. Its flow is controlled and regulated all the way down to Sindh. Just upstream of Hund is the massive Tarbela Dam, completed in 1973, and the largest earth-filled dam in Asia, storing a peak of 14 million cubic metres of water and supplying 2.1 million kilowatts of electricity. Elders in rural Punjab, affected most by the building of dams, believe that dams "remove all the electricity" from the water leaving behind only "useless husk." This, they say, is why Punjabi youth is no longer what it once was.

Peshawar's streets were named for their functions—City Circular Road, Cinema Road, School Road, Railway Road, Hospital Road, Sunheri Masjid Road, Police Road, Jail Bridge Road—which ought to make getting to know the city easier, but unlike Islamabad's straight lines and hard corners, these were winding and circular and irrational. On his wheels John often came upon unexpected detours and dead ends: a crumbled ancient wall or tower, a sealed-up entrance. A sign in English usually explained the reason, always some age-old catastrophic flood or fire. An ancient city, Peshawar's history was made up of downfalls, ransackings, renaissances, downfalls, ransackings, renaissances. So Islamia College, John found, was not where he expected it, on Islamia Road, but in the cantonment on Jamrud off Khyber Road. In Old City, wide arches led to narrow blind byways while narrow one-person alleyways opened onto large open-air bazaars, each one renowned for its particulars. The Meena bazaar, with guards at every entrance to keep men out, sold pretty women's stuff: ribbon, lace, buttons, bows, beads, braiding, threads, embroidery, and printed fabric. To bring back gifts for the women in his life, he would have to rely on a woman, Khaled's aunt perhaps. The gypsy bazaar sold carved bone and wood, real and false hair, skin and hair dyes, and traditional gypsy cosmetics such as kajaal. Here, gypsies told fortunes, prescribed magical remedies, carved tattoos against the evil eye. Toward Chowk Yadgar was a bazaar for saddles and guns. At Pipal Mandi vendors sold wholesale grain. There were vegetable markets, fruit markets, cloth markets, bird bazaars; markets for pottery, copperware, salt, antiques. The tea shops were on Qissa Khwani, street of the storytellers, where travelers, John read, have been telling tales tall and short since time immemorial.

Khaled, who'd been to Peshawar more than once and had advised leaving the skateboard at home, now warned against exploring the bazaars on wheels.

You'll infuriate everyone, he said. Peshawar's crowded, more crowded than the six at rush hour. Besides, some of the roads aren't even paved.

John shrugged. He'd skated crowded streets in D.C., in New York City, in Brooklyn. He'd found concrete everywhere. CONCRETE CONQUERS EARTH was a headline in the summer issue of *Skate.* If fifth-grade geography hadn't changed and two-thirds of earth was still water and the remaining third still land, then two-thirds of this remaining third might now be concrete.

Khaled looked at him. That's the ugliest thing I've ever heard. But, listen, you've never experienced real crowds. D.C. and New York aren't crowded, not compared to what you'll see here. Seriously, it would be like trying to skate on a subway platform at rush hour.

Quit warning me, John said. I won't crash into anyone.

He was reading about the Pathan tribes, the Wazir, Mahsud, Khattak, Bangash, Afridi, Mohmand, Yusefzi, Shinwari. Even their names sounded more legendary than real. The Pathans themselves, he read, made all sorts of claims about their origins. The Wazirs thought they were the ten lost tribes of Israel.

Tell me about these tribes, John said.

Pathans, Khaled explained, follow a tribal code. First rule is hospitality, which is offered even to enemies. Revenge is the second rule. Tribal feuds usually begin over a woman. They're touchy about their women. The smallest gesture can lead to major retaliation. My mom says the Pathan word for cousin also means enemy.

Khaled's mother had lived in the hills above Peshawar until she was eight. But when John asked him to contact his Afridi relatives and wrangle an invitation, Khaled said no way.

You may think getting yourself killed's an adventure. I plan to live long enough to tell my life story, even if long life is very un-Pathan. But remember I'm half Brahmin.

But John wanted to meet these tribes, stay with them, learn their ways, know them. Into the twenty-first century, he wished to wrest a nineteenth-century-style adventure, complete with danger and deprivation, wounds and scars, immersion, scholarship, becoming. Though a twenty-first-century man, he wanted to insert himself into a medieval legend, a form of time travel, and he was prepared to go all the way.

If you worry too much about surviving to tell your stories you'll end up without any, John warned. Besides, I really can't do it without you. I need your contacts and your Pashto.

Khaled lifted an eyebrow. You could start by learning Pashto.

John agreed. Islamia College offered classes in Urdu, Pashto, and classical Arabic, and though he'd registered for the Arab-language sessions, he signed on to also audit a Pashto-based class on the Qur'an. With only a year in Pakistan, he would have to learn the way children do: he would jump in and flounder. To avoid falling back on English, on easy familiarity, he asked to be housed in a Pashto-speaking dorm, though it meant separation from Khaled.

Why do you always want to make life harder for yourself? Khaled asked.

To speed up my learning curve, John said.

HIS WHITEWASHED DORM looked like a Victorian orphanage: a large bare room with fifteen single white iron beds, each three feet apart, all facing the same way, headboards against the back wall.

His first night, after brief introductions in which he shook about ten hands and heard ten names, John felt an embarrassing lump in his throat. He missed Katie and the girls. He missed the surf, his large attic room at Southern Shores, his privacy. He'd asked for this, and now he had to live with ten strangers. Greeting him, they all spoke English, but they quickly dropped back to Pashto with one another. Pashto was the reason he'd moved into this dorm alone, but now he missed Khaled, both his teasing and guidance, and wondered whether he could still reverse his decision and move back to the international dorm. Then Zaadiq, who occupied the bed on John's right, noticed that John was too long for his bed, and laughed.

I'm hanging ten, John said, feeling better.

So you're a surfer, Zaadiq said in English. He was small and agile. And he'd grown up on the water—his father was a skipper on a fishing boat, he said. He shared with John a love of seafood, and they compared notes on crab feasts. Karachi crab, John learned, was stewed with potatoes, onions, and spices.

I'll show you where Peshawar's best fish kebabs are, he promised.

Zaadiq translated for John, as needed. A transfer student from the Aga Khan University in Karachi, he'd moved to Peshawar, he joked, to experience life higher up in the mountains, closer to the heavens.

MORNINGS BECAME BUSY with classes. John's first session was Arabic grammar, and though he was good at it, he was always glad when it was over. After a quick tea, he went on to his workshop on vocabulary and conversation, which was more fun. Then his Arabic poetry class. Afternoons, he audited the Pashto Qur'anic session.

Summer classes at Islamia were intended largely for students who were missing certain credits, needed a prerequisite or a language, and classical Arabic classes were most popular.

That's because Pakistanis already speak Pashto or Urdu or both, Khaled explained. Also English. Unlike Americans, Pakistanis grow up hearing many languages.

Between and after classes, grinding. On the smooth paved paths, his wheels rolled without a rumble. Islamia's campus was a giant white skate park, its concrete the smoothest and whitest he'd ever seen. Spotless white was Islam's color, its identity, it seemed to John. All the maulanas and scholars at the school wore spotless white, and since it was way too hot for jeans, he purchased several of these white sets of shalwar kameez, the Punjabi suit.

He was getting by on a combination of 65 percent English, 25 percent Arabic, 10 percent sign language, supplemented by the bits of Pashto he was picking up. Students, especially students from urban centers, spoke English well, often beautifully, and on wheels, he attracted attention. He became known as the Ahm-ree-kee Moos-leem, the traveling moo-seh-fer, and Mr. Skating. The younger kids in the bazaar crowded him. One kid named Mahmed presented himself as a skater and declared that he was better than John because he could fly. Oh yeah? John said.

Mahmed's friends formed a tight circle. Show, show show, they clapped.

John agreed to let Mahmed try, but it became clear in an instant that this grom had never been on wheels. He took a running start, as if headed for a soccer kick, leaped on, and flew indeed. The tight circle, which might have kept him safe, gave way, and the boy fell backward in a heap and howled. Frightened, John hovered over Mahmed, afraid to move him. Run, he commanded the boy's useless friends. Get a doctor.

The word was magic, because the howling immediately ceased. Mahmed stood. He held his scraped and bleeding arm away from himself as if it were a stranger.

No doctor, he said, and hobbled away.

Behind him, his friends closed rank to save him from the evil Ahm-ree-kee. After which, John was unwilling to take a chance on anyone, definitely no one under seventeen, he told himself. Though some of the older students at the college found his grinding disrespectful to the architecture, to the school, to scholarship, to Islam—Just see how it dirties your shalwar, one serious young man in spotless white stopped to complain—there were also students who dismissed the critics and wanted to try it, begged John to allow them. After repeated warnings that it was harder than it looked, that it required extreme self-balance, John let the persistent get on. One determined petitioner named Abel pushed off with too much confidence, flailed, and landed splayed, his shalwar ripped from his knees to his thighs, where he'd scraped on the concrete. For Pakistanis especially—there were also Indonesian, Bangladeshi, Balinese, Thai, and other Muslims at Islamia—balancing on wheels was a challenge, and John started recommending trying it on grass, but it often took a first fall before they agreed. And after a brief series of tries, of flailing and sprawling, although students continued watching him make it look easy, they lost interest in learning how. No one developed the kind of obsession getting good required. Perhaps it was the heat. High temperatures had a way of sapping intention.

JOHN MADE EVERY STUDENT he met his teacher. Over tea—drinking tea, it seemed, was Pakistan's national pastime—he asked questions and listened hard to the answers. Thus he learned fast.

Walking across campus with Zaadiq one morning, John felt his companion's hand slip into his own. He slowed down to see what Zaadiq wanted, but Zaadiq kept walking. Rafael caught up with them and held his other hand. Not wanting to hurt his new roommates, John allowed the handholding and soon found he liked it, though he was also afraid of liking it. It made him feel vulnerable somehow, younger. He wondered what Khaled would say.

Then one afternoon he met Khaled walking hand in hand with a student named Yusef.

Khaled high-fived John Brooklyn style, though in Brooklyn they'd rarely high-fived. You two have something in common, Khaled said, introducing Yusef. Wheels.

Yusef put his hand out to shake John's, and asked, So what poison's yours?

Khaled rolled his eyes.

Sorry, Yusef said. I mean what bike do you ride?

He had the dark skin of Pakistanis, but his eyes were strangely light, a pale hazel.

I'm just a skater, John explained, nothing fancy.

No engine, no engine trouble, Yusef said. You're a lucky man.

Except that he's really not, Khaled said. He was on crutches when I met him.

They were heading to the campus teahouse and invited John along. Seated on stools at the orange Formica counter, Khaled proceeded to tell Yusef the story of their first joint paper, on struggle versus submission.

A nice literary thesis, Yusef said, but incomplete. Historically, anyway. Submission to the angel was only the Prophet's first step. Without the struggle that followed, Islam wouldn't have become a nation. It was a long, terrible jihad. And he died young.

Yusef specialized in history at Islamia. Facts are necessary, he said. To inform your interpretations.

KHALED INTRODUCED HIM to the streets of old Peshawar. Walking, because Khaled refused to accompany John on wheels, John wondered aloud why so many street beggars and tramps and even merchants were missing an arm or a leg, an eye or an ear. Even eight- and nine-year-old boys were often damaged. Is it some sort of biblical eye for an eye thing?

Stupid accidents, Khaled said. Most kids experience their first camp retreat before the age of twelve. They're introduced to target practice and bomb making. Obviously some camps are totally reckless.

They let twelve-year-olds make bombs? John asked, incredulous.

Khaled clapped John on the shoulder. You've never been a Boy Scout. It's actually good for most kids. It toughens them up. They all come out convinced they want to become soldiers for Islam. Who do you think fights in Kashmir? Or Afghanistan?

After which John started seeing recruitment flyers everywhere. At the Internet café he visited, at the teahouses, in the bazaars, in his dorm.

ISHAMEL HAD A RADIO, which he kept tuned to Radio Shariat, a part Pashto–part English station out of Kabul. In bed, enjoying the lazy breeze of the uneven overhead fan, John listened to stories and statistics of rape and murder in Chechnya and Kashmir and Afghanistan. Every program ended with a call to Muslims to help Muslims.

It's every Muslim's duty, Ishmael explained, to help his brother and sister. This station's broadcast by the Taliban.

Ishmael was planning to volunteer again. This time in Afghanistan. In the fall, he said. After the summer heat.

One evening Mullah Omar was scheduled to deliver a special radio address, and students from the neighboring dorm crowded round to hear him.

Zaadiq translated for John when he lost the thread. Mullah Omar was reporting on the Taliban's successes in Afghanistan. They were in control of four of the largest cities, including Kabul. They were putting an end to corruption and bribery and usury. To the rape and murder of women and children. To the pornography and blasphemy and drugs and alcohol coming from the West. But they needed more soldiers. At every border, Mullah Omar said, the Northern Alliance armies encroach. In every small border village, corrupt warlords terrorize the local people, and we must come to their aid. We must preserve our borders. It is every Muslim's duty to join this jihad.

Rafael told John about Mullah Omar's rise to power. The corruption in Afghanistan infuriated him, and he acted. In one incident he freed young girls who were being held for sex and hanged the warlord.

He didn't just send an army, Ishmael added. He was already almost fifty, and missing an eye, and still he led the fight himself.

But John still didn't understand. Who are the rapists? Why aren't the mujahideen on the same side?

Ishmael grew exasperated with how much John didn't know. Read some history. Take a walk outside Peshawar, where the refugees are camped. See their misery. All because of Western occupations.

So John spent an afternoon at the library reading up on the area's history of foreign occupations, ending in 1834, with the Sikhs who burned most of old Peshawar to the ground, and the disastrous British occupation that followed. He also visited the Bala Hisar Fort's Regimental Museum near Kabuli Gate to learn the military history of Peshawar and the surrounding frontier. So he came to understand: Every tribe and people hankered for its own homeland. Every Pathan, Wazir, Afridi, and Kashmiri boy grew up with a sense of pride denied. For years, the Kashmiri had been fighting to the death, and thousands had been maimed or killed. Hindus wanted to destroy Muslims. Shia and Sunni Muslims were at each other's throats. India and Pakistan threatened each other with nuclear annihilation. The grievances and violence went on and on. He wondered how people grounded so deeply in ancient Buddhism and Sufism could fight for so many years over nothing or what seemed to him nothing. He asked Khaled.

Sectarianism is always just a cover-up, Khaled explained. It's how politicians excite the masses. They call it a holy war, but the fight is for political power, always. True in Kashmir. True everywhere. The Hindus really just want Kashmir's natural resources, and everyone knows it, but India continues playing its Hindu card and Pakistan its Muslim one, because that's the way they recruit soldiers. Both governments don't give a fig for religion. And in the meantime the people, like people everywhere, just want their freedom. Same in Afghanistan.

At the local bookstore, John picked up a book written by an award-winning expert on Afghanistan. *Travels with the Mujahideen.* A Lawrence of Arabia prizewinner with a foreword by Margaret Thatcher, the book raised questions about religion and culture and modern relativism. Which was cool, but the author's adventures with the mujahideen, whom Ronald Reagan had called freedom fighters, were the parts John most enjoyed, and he became impatient for his own real adventure.

GRINDING ON CAMPUS ONE DAY, John came across Yusef at work on his bike and hopped off his board to see what Yusef was doing.

This is the carburetor, he explained. Yusef traveled on a 1960s military model of the 350cc Enfield bullet motorcycle, an early British design specially manufactured for the border patrol in India.

Since the temperature and humidity have increased, the engine is running rich, and I must adjust the air-to-fuel ratio. For every gram of water, octane use decreases by .25 to .35.

John didn't fully get why humid air runs richer, but Yusef seemed to know such things. With precision, he adjusted the needle valve, then invited John for a ride.

You mean it? John asked.

Yusef strapped John's board to the back of his bike with a bungee cord, mounted, and instructed John to sit forward and snug behind him.

Hug me, Yusef said, revving the engine. Where to? he shouted to make himself heard.

To Kabul, John said.

Yusef turned to look at him. You're joking?

John pretended innocence. Is it too far?

They both knew that it was too far, the terrain too difficult and dangerous besides, and that a visa or day pass was necessary.

But I have an idea, Yusef said, allowing the engine to idle quietly. Today I have time only for a quick ride down Jamrud, up Charsadda, but tomorrow afternoon I'm going to Tangi. Want to come?

They arranged to meet at one.

AFTER PRAYERS THAT EVENING, John stopped at the Internet café just off campus on Jamrud.

Attar, our man of the hour, someone announced when he walked in. He was clapped on the shoulder, ushered to a screen whose connection had frozen, put to work. And he liked it: the warm welcome, the community. Muhammed, who worked behind the counter, brought John a limongaz on the house, since he was serving as the café's computer pro.

It's all right now, Muhammed announced, we've got the Ahm-ree-kee on the case, and the café returned to its usual working hum, the clicking of keyboards, the shifting of chairs, the quiet static of minds concentrating.

He was good at this, problem solving. He knew how to coax screens and connections back to life, how to download necessary software, retrieve lost files, unfreeze screens. And he performed with the calm authority of someone who knew he could. After rebooting and testing, he settled down to receive and send his own e-mail. He wrote, he realized, mostly to the women in his life: To Barbara, who of course reported to Bill. To Katie and Noor. Sometimes to Sylvie or Jilly. Since he'd moved to Peshawar, his only contact with women had been via e-mail, which was strange for someone whose friends, at least until now, had been largely female. In his e-mail to Noor, he mentioned the absence of women. Even here, he wrote, in this café designed for Internet use, girls are rare, though there must be plenty of Muslim women who want to go online. When one does stop in, usually at midday, and never in the evening, she keeps herself concealed in her headscarf, which means you hardly see her face. Or anything else, really.

WHAT'S IN TANGI? John shouted into Yusef's ear.

Wait and see, Yusef shouted back, picking up speed and leaning into the wind.

John hugged Yusef's back, holding tight. As soon as they were out of town, the tents and temporary settlements appeared, refugees from Kashmir and Afghanistan camped along the roads of northern Pakistan. You didn't live a day in Peshawar without hearing about their misery. Pakistanis didn't forgo a single opportunity to blame the West, including the United States. As a Westerner, John was beginning to agree, especially as a wealthy oil-guzzling American, he was awash in guilt, stood accused of swaths of shameful history, and not just guilt from the past, because it wasn't over.

But Yusef had something other than a misery tour in mind for this afternoon. They rode through the green Peshawar Valley, past miles of peaches and apricots, then long, wide fields of sugarcane, tobacco, and rice.

In Charsadda, they stopped at a petrol station to refill. Vendors everywhere displayed their produce, and John wanted peaches.

They're excellent, but try the apricots, too, Yusef said.

A few of both then, John said. Though he was paying, he let Yusef negotiate.

His first peach was just right; the sweet juice dripped down his chin, and without a napkin handy, he had to use the sleeve of his white shalwar. Yusef laughed. Somehow he'd managed to eat without a single drip.

After Charsadda, the road grew steep and steeper, and the bike climbed slowly. On their right, the Swat River. Up ahead, the mountain peaks were icebergs. In the summer. Though in the valleys the orchard trees were heavy with fruit, in the higher elevations pines were still covered with snow.

They approached the town of Tangi, passed the sign marking it as one of eight towns in the Hashtnagar of the Union Council of Charsadda District, altitude three hundred twenty-seven meters. Ahead, John saw, glinting in the sun, the green dome of a shrine, or it might be a museum, but Yusef turned off the main road, onto a dirt one, and detoured away from the town center. He took turns, doubled back onto obscure unpaved dusty byroads. The landscape grew browner with fewer signs of life, until finally they pulled up to a camp sited under the hard shadow of the Margalla peaks. John would later remember what he'd noticed first: the absence of color and smell. Traveling with Barbara and Bill, he'd formed what Bill called his unfortunate rating habit. He categorized and rated every city and country by its predominant color and underlying smell. Some smells were obvious: gray New York stank of bad bus smog, brown Brooklyn of the stinking drip from sanitation trucks. The surprises: Bangkok was orchid pink and smelled of fish sauce; Hong Kong was silver and briny. The places he'd visited. Islamabad, he'd found, was too white, too new, and too clean for smells. Peshawar, on the other hand, was a large overripe melon. On the outskirts of Peshawar, at roadside cafés, the spicy smoke of grilled goat mingled awfully with rotting fruit and even sewage. But this camp outside Tangi smelled of nothing live, or smelled of dust and gunpowder, unadulterated by odors of food or cooking or life or human waste. It was dusty; it was drab, a colorless monastic olive, a monk's camp but without the glory of ancient structures and stupas, without great old monasteries, without the tiers of distinguishing stonework, the phases of development. This camp was new and bare, a setting without history, with nothing cast in stone. It was new; it was modern; it had no history, though it was born of history.

Yusef propped the bike on its kickstand in front of a low white concrete structure. The only bright colors were on a clothesline, strung from a window to the tree. A gaggle of kids surrounded them, admiring the gauges and levers, the seat, the pedals, firing questions about speed and horsepower, which Yusef tried to answer. They knew him; they'd seen his bike before.

Someone their age approached. Yusef embraced him, and they kissed. My cousin Jalal, Yusef said, and they followed Jalal indoors.

Inside, John's eyes went straight to a stack of rifles in the corner, and he understood that this was a training camp.

For target practice, Jalal explained.

He busied himself making tea. He plugged an electric wand into what looked like a small generator, unrolled a small brown bag, and shook out a handful of loose black tea leaves.

Our students come from all over, Jalal explained in precisely articulated British English. From Pakistan, Afghanistan, sometimes England and Germany. We also get Americans, of Pakistani heritage.

Jalal's manner was both familiar and not. In appearance, he and Yusef could have been brothers, but Jalal was more reserved, or perhaps he was just older.

John asked Yusef if he'd trained here.

Of course, Jalal answered for Yusef with pride. More than once. He makes his annual taqahqur here.

The water boiled. Jalal unplugged the wand, poured three small decorative glasses, and John realized how thirsty he was. He could suck down the whole pot in one long gulp, though sipping slowly out of pretty glasses in this remote place was awesome. Civilized living but of an ancient variety. Roman or Greek. Would Jalal offer to wash their sandaled feet next? Here the biblical fetish for washing feet made sense, and John found himself wanting his feet washed, his unbearably dust-covered gritty feet. But Jalal only refilled his emptied glass.

Jalal told Yusef about a new aspect of training that was making him happy. We had an Iranian Shia mystic here. He led the boys in breathing and meditation and the results were impressive. Somehow he quiets even the most restless ones. I can't tell you how satisfying it is seeing the twitching and shifting and noisy breathing stop.

If I had more time here, John said, I'd sign up for that.

You should make time, Jalal said. Come, he said, taking John's hand, I'll show you around.

He led them through the main hall, then out through a back door. Our shooting range, Jalal said. Yusef stepped onto the small platform, picked up an SKS, sighted down the barrel, and fired.

John jumped.

Jalal walked up to the target and reported: Practically bull's eye.

Yusef's a good shot, Jalal said. One of our best. Would you like to try?

John hesitated.

Come on, Yusef said. You can't be Richard Burton without basic shooting skills. He placed the rifle in John's hands, guiding the butt into the soft spot of John's inner right shoulder, his left arm under the barrel, and his right hand on the trigger. Keep your elbows with your body, he advised, tucking them in. Like that, he said, and stepped away. Now, look down the barrel, and when your eye is on the target, exhale and pull.

John looked, adjusted his arm, his elbows.

Look through these two sights all the way to the target, Yusef advised. And pull the trigger.

John sighted, but the rifle moved; the target wavered.

Steady, Yusef said.

Breathe, Jalal reminded him.

So he inhaled. He exhaled. Inhaled. Exh—still the target danced. He squinted to keep it in place, but it shimmered. He exhaled again, and there it was, standing still, but when he went to move his finger, it disappeared again.

Ready, go, pull, Yusef commanded.

John felt the resistance of the trigger, and pulled. And though he'd braced himself, the rifle kicked back, the shot cracked loud, and the bullet—they didn't know where it went. It was nowhere on or near the paper.

On its way to Peshawar, Yusef joked. I can see you've never held a rifle.

The visit was over. It was time to go. Yusef had to pick up his sister. Jalal shook John's hand and finished with the triple kiss. Come back, he invited. Perhaps when your classes are finished you can stay with us for a few weeks. He brought his palms together, bowed his head. Im'sh'allah.

HOW MUCH DOES IT COST? John asked, when they were on the bike again.

It's free. Sometimes it's the only education local boys get.

The trip home was downhill and faster, and soon they were passing through the refugee camps again. This time Yusef pulled over, and kids surrounded them. John tried following the Pashto. The kids were asking Yusef whether he had brought them something.

What do they want? John asked.

They're hungry.

John took a Zone bar out of his backpack, broke it in half, and gave it to two children.

Candy? one asked.

John nodded. Close enough, he said, but better for you.

One boy broke his half in half and shared it with the little girl beside him. John reached into his backpack for two more bars, broke them into thirds, and passed them round. Nine skinny kids would have a small dose of protein and vitamins. But he worried about the others. He wished he'd brought more. He'd ask Barbara to ship packs of these, and he would deliver them. If she could commit to sending Power Bars on a regular basis, he could at least help feed these children.

More hopeful kids arrived, with younger siblings in tow. More kids needing nourishment. And he had nothing to offer. He promised to come back, to bring more. Next week, he said, feeling the inadequacy of such a promise. They were hungry now.

THEY RETURNED by way of Jamrud Road, but Yusef passed the main gates of the college and turned off into the Christian Cemetery through an entrance grown over with lichen. The gravestones were mossy, and covered in ivy. And the trees, mature apricots and plums, provided shade. Mishmish, Yusef said, reaching up to the nearest tree to pick a blushing apricot. He opened it with his fingers, removed the pit, and bit into it. Like honey, he said, and gave John the other half. With his toe, Yusef lifted thick green moss off the nearest gravestone and read: HERE LIES CAPTAIN ERNEST BLOOMFIELD, ACCIDENTALLY SHOT BY HIS ORDERLY, MARCH 2ND 1879. WELL DONE, GOOD AND FAITHFUL SERVANT.

They laughed.

When John got off the bike, he regretted it. Perhaps it was the physical proximity to another body or the engine's continuous rumble, or the heat, but now it was too late to hide the pogo stick of a fact. Yusef had noticed and he refused to avert his eyes.

Well done, John said, trying to make light of it.

Yusef smiled, stretched out on the ground between two gravestones, and patted the ground beside him, an invitation. Afraid, John found a spot between the next two stones, keeping a dividing headstone between them.

Yusef remained silent, eyes closed. What did silent Yusef want? John wondered. He hoped Yusef wasn't getting any wrong ideas about him, his sexuality, because he was definitely not homo, had never been sexually attracted to men, he'd always liked girls. Uncomfortable in Yusef's silence, John talked.

Burton, John said, used to compose such epitaphs for entertainment, and one day he made one up for his colonel: Here lieth the body of Captain Corsellis / The rest of the fellow, I fancy, in hell is. Needless to say, Corsellis hated it.

Yusef opened one eye. What do you think is your hero's best achievement?

If you mean most lasting, John said, then I'd say his translations. The *Kama Sutra* and *Arabian Nights.* But really his whole life was an achievement. He studied and lived hard. Spoke twenty-nine languages. Was initiated as a Sufi. Went to Mecca.

Pakistanis think of him as more playboy than hero, Yusef said. Some people say he was a British spy and blame him for Pakistan's problems.

Burton was a lot of things, John said. His arms itched. They felt sunburned. I'll remember this summer as one long thirst, he said.

Yusef smiled. Nice, he murmured. He found John's hand, slipped his own into it, and spoke dreamily. Baba Wali Kandhari lived on a hill nearby, and when Guru Nanak traveled here, he sent his disciple Mardana to ask for water. Baba Wali declined, but the guru sent Mardana back to ask again. Again Baba Wali declined. Again the guru sent his disciple back. Mardana climbed up and down the hill three times. When he returned without water a third time, Guru Nanak struck the ground with his staff and water began to spurt. In the meantime, up on the hill, Baba Wali found that his well had dried up. In anger, he pushed a huge boulder at the guru and Mardana, which the guru stopped with his outstretched arm. You can still see this boulder with Guru Nanak's handprint at Hasan Abdal on the road out of Islamabad.

But, Yusef finished, since I can't produce water with a stick, I'll take you to a tea shop on Qissa Khwani where your thirst will be quenched. Avoid sweet tea, and you'll feel better. Ready? He stood and offered John his hand.

On the bike again, they entered the old city by way of Jail Bridge Road, turned left at the first intersection, entered into the Khyber Bazaar, and slowed to a crawl. Only after-hours, at night, could you ride through the bazaars at a decent clip. In daytime, during business hours, shopkeepers, lawyers, accountants, artisans, doctors, dentists, and baskets and crates of glistening fruit and vegetables, alongside piles of rotting produce and the stench that rotting vegetation produced, all existed together in a maze of narrow winding alleyways. They arrived at Kabuli Gate and entered Qissa Khwani the back way. Yusef skillfully wound his way to the tea shop. He locked the bike in the alleyway between shops and asked for the small table at the back where it was darkest.

The dark was a relief from the sun if not the heat. It was too warm here, it was too warm everywhere, and John was beginning to adjust, but in combination, the heat, the sun, and the thirst were exhausting.

You must slow down, Yusef advised. You must slow your walking, breathing, eating, drinking, even your thinking and feeling, and you'll feel better.

John was beginning to understand. Indolence was a necessity here. Even Khaled's body, accustomed to Brooklyn, was taking time to adjust to the heat. It was an adjustment best felt, hard to explain. Though he wrote to Barbara about it, he knew she wouldn't get it. To make it through to the evening, he wrote, the midday siesta is absolutely necessary. In his room, he liked to throw himself spread-eagled on top of his bedcover and feel the warm breeze of the overhead fan on his skin. And soon his eyes closed, soon he slept. He was taking naps every afternoon. Barbara wrote back to ask if everything was okay, if he wasn't perhaps depressed. Even as an infant, he wouldn't nap.

Learning to nap is part of this adventure, John wrote back. There's a Pashto expression here, from colonial days: Only mad dogs and Englishmen are seen at noon.

On this day, though, he had not slept. On this day, he had baked on the bike in the sun, and now he felt it. Water blisters had formed on his upper arms. Rubbed, they let go thin rivulets of warm moisture. He dried himself with the front tail of his shirt.

I wonder how a doctor would explain that, Yusef said.

Probably as sunburn, John said. He brought the cup to his lips, watched Yusef over the rim. Since you've brought me to the street of storytellers, he said, tell me another story.

Yusef thought a moment. Okay. Here's "Sohni and Mahival: A Punjabi Romance." When Sohni, daughter of a potter, swam across the river to meet her lover, Mahival, she used a pot to help her float. One night her jealous sister-in-law exchanged Sohni's pot for an unbaked one, which dissolved as soon as it touched water. Mahival, hearing Sohni's cries, flung himself into the water, but he was too slow to save her. Unable to live without her, he let himself drown and joined her in death.

Jealousy can be fatal, John said.

He asked for another, but Yusef shook his head. Three stories a day is two too many. Drink up and I'll drop you off.

A story a day then. I'll hold you to it.

THE EXPERIENCE of prostrating himself and praying beside another person, and another, and another, and more beyond them, hundreds of men and boys prostrated and praying, was still awesome, though he'd been praying five times a day for months now. Like his roommates, he performed the midday, afternoon, early evening, and late-evening prayers privately, often in his dorm, but he liked starting his mornings with the crowd, where he was alone and not alone. Alone amid solitary hundreds. It was a contradiction, yet it worked. Afterward he felt strangely refreshed and newly expanded. Prayer set things right, made all love possible. He loved his roommates, his fellow classmates, even unknown colleagues at the library. He loved Khaled and Yusef. Noor, Katie, Jilly, and Sylvie. And Barbara and Bill. He loved the world. And he loved himself, too. He was an individual within a larger community, a one but not an only one. After prayer, with heart and mind exalted, in a community of exalted men and boys, he walked to his first class of the day.

Between noon and three, everyone knew to remain indoors or in the shade, out of the sun. John napped in his dorm under the fan, which he had come to think of as a luxury, the only luxury the dorms offered. By the time he awoke, the sun was lower, and it was possible to go out again. Refreshed, he went straight to the library to study. There he met others, Zaadiq or Khaled or Rafael, and they would push each other toward achievement: Work hard and well and we'll break in an hour. In two hours. After progress.

They frequented the cafeteria and the tea shops nearby, just off campus. Toward evening, when the temperature dropped, a longer walk was possible, and they would stroll, hand in hand, to the livelier tea shops and cafés in the bazaar.

Late one afternoon, leaving the library, John heard the rumble of Yusef's bike. Yusef waved and rumbled on.

Hey, what about my story? John shouted. You're way behind.

Not today, Yusef said. I promised my sister a ride. See you tomorrow, at the lecture.

A sister. Yusef had a sister. He would ask about her. Did she pray?

Do Muslim women pray? Do they attend classes? Do they even exist? He was living, it seemed to him, in an all-male world. In the bazaars and streets of Peshawar only the too-young and very old variety of females appeared. Barbara, he knew, would be appalled. Where were the women who would give birth to the next generation of students? Where were they hiding the beautiful women of Yusef's tales? How did Benazir Bhutto, a woman, become president of this country?

MAULANA SAMI AL HAQ of the Haqqania Madrassah system had a reputation as an inspiring speaker, and John looked forward to this outdoor event, his first. Morning classes were suspended so that students and faculty could attend, and Islamia's main field had been furnished with a stage, microphones, and rows of benches.

He was walking with Zaadiq to the al Haq event when Yusef rumbled up on his bike and handed John a folded piece of paper. Your story, he said.

The seats filled quickly. Sitting beside Zaadiq, John spotted Khaled on the east side of the field and waved. Then he read Yusef's two-line story, handwritten in English, all uppercase.

Anarkali was a favorite in the harem of Emperor Akbar, Yusef wrote. One day Akbar caught her exchanging a smile with his son. Jealous, he had Anarkali walled up alive.

John got out a pencil from his backpack. Why, he penciled at the bottom of the page, is illicit love the theme of all your stories? And why are the lovers always doomed? He passed his question to Yusef, who was sitting three rows back.

Because, Yusef wrote back, human love is only temporary anyway, unlike the love between God and the soul. Okay. Here's another story, minus the doom:

One day, before they were married, Jahangir handed his beloved Nur Jahan two of the royal pigeons to hold. When Jahangir returned for his birds, one had flown. He was surprised. But how did it fly? he asked. Like this! Nur Jahan laughed and let the second bird go. Jahangir was enchanted.

I like this one, John mouthed, giving it a thumbs-up.

SINCE THE LECTURE was open to the public, it was delivered in English. Al Haq opened with a quote from the Qur'an and translated: If you doubt what We have revealed to Our servant, produce one chapter comparable to it.

It has come to my attention, al Haq said, that a group of academics have sinfully allowed themselves to ask who wrote the Qur'an.

The unbelievers ask: Why was the Qur'an not revealed to the Prophet in a single revelation? The Sura answers, We have revealed it thus so that we may sustain your heart. We have imparted it to you by gradual revelation.

He was dressed in an all-white tunic and pants, with a long off-white vest over them. And he used his hands as he spoke, turning his palms up to ask a question, facedown to make his point.

Unlike the Jewish and Christian holy books, al Haq said, the Qur'an knows itself. It is self-aware and fully conscious. It recognizes itself as a book, as a holy text, as glorious and wise and clear and the book of truth; indeed, it knows itself as the Qur'an. It also knows that there will be interpretations and misinterpretations. It understands that it is sometimes clear, sometimes obscure. It knows and predicts that the unclear parts will attract the skeptics, those whose hearts are infected with unbelief, and it responds to these doubts and questions in advance: no one knows its meaning except God. According to some of our great moodar-ress, every verse can be understood in sixty thousand different ways.

The Qur'an speaks of its own origins, its source. Sura 32 opens with: This Book is beyond all doubt revealed by the Lord of the Universe. It goes on to tell its own origin story: Proclaim what has been revealed to you from the Book of your Lord. . . . You have received the Qur'an from Him who is wise and all-knowing.

Let no one convince you otherwise, al Haq concluded, coming round after a long series of digressions. Such holy all-knowingness cannot be said for the Hebrew books, nor the Christian, which have multiple authors and inherent contradictions. Their Bible does not and cannot know itself, therefore it has nothing to stand on, no firm grounding, no certainty.

But aren't all books based on books that came before them? John wondered. Even the Old Testament, the supposed first book, was made up of earlier ancient songs and texts.

THE FOLLOWING MONDAY, Yusef was waiting for him when he emerged from his last class of the morning, and John was relieved and anxious at the same time. Yusef's stories, arriving as they had as handwritten notes, had convinced him that he was no longer welcome on Yusef's bike, that his overeager penis, which stood erect at the least provocation, had embarassed or frightened Yusef.

Yusef slid forward on his seat, inviting John on, and even before he was on the bike, spooning Yusef's bum, John felt his peter stand up. It was this, he realized, this constant prickly unfulfilled desire, that was exhausting. And he was confused by this desire; he'd been unable to sort it out. His mind warned against it, held back, told him that he was not attracted to men, to Yusef, at least not that way, but still his body responded, celebrated the opportunity, another adventure. He hoped that with time, with familiarity to the experience of close proximity, his body would grow accustomed to the physical contact and become less responsive.

Where are we going today? John shouted into Yusef's ear.

A picnic, Yusef replied. He pulled into the petrol station to fill up.

You should get water, Yusef said.

John slid off the bike and entered the little market, a Pakistani-style 7-Eleven. He bought two tall bottles of purified water, a bag of banana chips, which Barbara had recommended as a source of potassium, and a bag of pepitas, a snack of the region. He paid for the items and slipped them into his backpack.

If we're going to have a picnic, let's pick up some chapli kebabs, John said.

My oom made sandwiches, Yusef said, and lifted the lid on the black leather case at the back to show him.

Y'allah, Yusef said. I'm taking you to Takht-e-Bahi, a Buddhist monastery on the Peshawar-Swat Road, just south of the Malakand Pass.

It was a long drive, through mostly flat plains, beautifully bare, green where they were irrigated, brown elsewhere. Riding behind Yusef in the open air, John felt enlarged by the long perspective the open countryside offered. In the final stretch, they climbed a rocky spur about five hundred feet above the plains, the site of Takht-e-Bahi.

Yusef locked his bike in the car park and, holding John's hand, led the way up the path to the Court of Many Stupas, named for the thirty-five votive shrines it once contained. They approached the main courtyard, surrounded by the silent stone walls twenty-five feet high with chapels built into the wall, their entrances facing inward. Corners and edges of cornices and pilasters were still traceable, beautifully broken in the way that ruins are. Yusef pulled John along to the steps that led the way inside, but a beggar stopped John at the first step, and another at the second, and John hung back, preventing advance. He'd reached into his pocket and come up with a handful of change. This foolish act produced twenty open palms, and with an indulgent smile on his face, John proceeded to put a coin into each hand. Which produced shouting. One beggar had gotten a five-cent piece, the other a ten, the next one a mere penny.

Yusef laughed. You have to place the same amount in each open palm.

But John had only a handful of change, in different denominations, and soon he ran out of change, and there were more steps, more beggars, more open palms, more shouting. He apologized, he shrugged, but the beggars wouldn't give up. They pinched his shirt. They grabbed at his pants, and John panicked.

Yusef stepped down and pressed the beggars back. Ik sal amir, ik sal fakir, he said. Ik sal amir, ik sal fakir, he repeated, and the hands that demanded fell away, the word got out, ik sal fakir, interest waned, and the beggars moved off to seek elsewhere.

John swallowed his panic and wiped his forehead. What does that mean exactly? he asked.

A rich man this year, and a beggar the next. In other words, you're like them now. And as a beggar, you're not useful. If you don't want to remain a beggar, don't reach into your pockets again. He led the way up the stairs and around the walls.

This court, he announced, taking charge, as if it were an architectural drawing and he the architect. This court, he said, consulting the brochure, measures thirty-six meters by fifteen meters, that is, one hundred twenty feet by fifty feet. The walls are about nine meters, or thirty feet high. Inside, against the walls, are thirty chapels. The chapels once contained huge statues of the Buddha, about four times his original size.

They walked the paved north-south path from the main stupa on the north end to the monastery on the south side, went up the five steps, and stood in the center counting the cells. Fifteen in all.

This is where the monks lived, Yusef said, and led the way into one of the two largest ones. They were bare and small, with high walls and one small window too high for even the tallest monk to see through.

Scary, John said. Kind of like jail.

Yusef led the way back to the fifteen steps that led up to the main stupa, now merely a square base. Not much left of it, he explained. Cleaned out by thieves. Originally it had three bases like this first one, each smaller than the previous one, stacked. At the top, the stupa rested on pillars.

He walked up the steps to the first and remaining base and turned to watch John stumble. He laughed.

The half step, he explained, is intended to surprise and awaken the pilgrim. Reaching up for the expected full step, he doesn't find it, and stumbles.

Nice idea, John said, but it probably works only once or twice.

Probably, Yusef agreed, but it wasn't intended for the monks who used them daily. It was the pilgrims who needed awakening.

They fell in line behind the other visitors—pilgrims dressed Punjabi style in shalwar kameez of all colors and stripes—keeping pace with those in front of them, remaining ahead of those behind.

After touring the Assembly Hall, the Low Level Chambers, which housed the granaries, meditation rooms, and study, they stopped at the Court of Three Stupas to admire the sculpture collection, the Wall of Colossi, where six pairs of giant feet were discovered at its base, along with remaining fragments of the six statues of the Buddha. Based on the size of the feet, the statues are calculated to have been about twenty feet high, Yusef read aloud.

They were hungry. Touring had given them an appetite. So they made their way back to the car park and rode west, to the modern town of Takht-e-Bahi, to a small park famous for its peepul tree.

You know the one at Pipal Mandi in old Peshawar? he said. It's said to be a descendant of the original peepul. These trees usually have legends attached to them, like the one in the Mahabharata. To prove himself as a warrior to Lord Krishna, Babreek offered to rope all the tree's leaves with one arrow. After Babreek's arrow had pierced every leaf, it hovered at Lord Krishna's foot, and Babreek warned Krishna that if he didn't move, the arrow would pierce it. It turned out that Lord Krishna had hidden a leaf under his foot.

Yusef withdrew a square of cloth, paper-wrapped sandwiches, and oranges. John unzipped his backpack and contributed the water and snacks.

Pepitas, Yusef said. To complete our meal.

We should give thanks, John said.

They folded their legs, Buddha pose, brought their palms together, and closed their eyes.

Yusef broke the silence. Let's break bread.

They took their first bites cautiously, tasting, then rushed into their next ones.

Your mom makes a mean sandwich, John said through a mouthful.

They're always better outside, Yusef said.

They ate in silence. John noted the blue horizon, the oily haze the burning sun made when it heated the molecules in the air. He was grateful for the reprieve of green shade.

Imagine, Yusef said, a monk's life, roaming during the day, returning to his monastery at Takht-e-Bahi for the night, meditating on nothingness.

I could have been a monk, John said. I was born in the wrong place and time.

Really? Yusef asked, pointedly dropping his eyes from John's face to his lower body.

John shifted, and waited for his blush to recede. He swallowed. Maybe that's why I would have made a good monk. I would have made the greater sacrifice.

Sacrifice, Yusef said, is hard, and fighting your own desire is self-destructive. I watch you, from free America, struggle against what you really want. So who do you think's freer?

Yusef stretched his legs to reveal his own aroused state. The mystics, he said, knew that indulgence is sometimes more effective than abstaining. Think Richard Burton. And don't think indulgence is easy. For example, I'm willing to give it to you, but are you prepared to submit, because that's the only way I'll have it?

John looked into the distance, the landscape stark in desert browns, sparsely vegetated, and the people, dressed as they were in their shalwar kameez, could, with a minimum of squinting, appear as classically draped Greeks. He imagined Yusef as Caligula, claiming every virgin, male and female, branding them as his own, because this was what Yusef proposed, and John found, shockingly, that he wanted to submit, or rather his body wanted it, ached for it, but it was also impossible to admit to wanting such a thing.

Yusef propped himself onto his elbows and reclined unashamedly, and John found himself both drawn and repulsed simultaneously. His body ached to stretch out beside Yusef, to give himself to Yusef; his mind, however, shouted against it. Submission. A word that had no place in Barbara's vocabulary, and she wouldn't welcome it in his. About his newly discovered bisexuality she wouldn't be critical, but she also wouldn't love it.

So I'm right, Yusef said. Your problem isn't sex, just submission. American men aren't used to that, but they can learn. They'll have to. Bismillah. You may not even know exactly why you're here, therefore I'll tell you that you've come to Islam in order to learn the grace and pleasure of submission.

I know, John said, that Islam doesn't approve of same-sex sex.

Actually, the Qur'an is silent on homosexual love, so it isn't haram. Our classical poetry is full of it. And most boys grow up doing it.

Yusef made submission more desirable with every uttered word, but John remained where he was, on his side of the blanket. Sex in America, at least with a woman, had never weighed so meaningfully, never seemed so political. With Yusef, or maybe this was true in all of Pakistan, nothing was casual. Pakistanis were blithe about nothing.

For the trip home, Yusef invited John to sit up front and steer, and with Yusef behind him, with insistent desire rumbling unashamedly against him all the way into Peshawar, the ride was both torment and delight, disabling, threatening, humiliating, and delicious.

When Yusef finally parked the bike in the narrow, dark alleyway of the tea shop on Qissa Khwani, John found he couldn't walk. And though his warning mind persisted, he found he could no longer hold back. He leaned his feverish forehead against the cool stone wall and untied his pants. Yusef's hand cupped and held his penis, and snugged his own penis between John's cheeks, and John dissolved. He was no longer John, he was something other that belonged to Yusef, who penetrated and fucked him, and it hurt and oh and but.

John finished first, and then Yusef came, touching off something somewhere deep, a chord, a resonance, and John discovered that he was bawling. Yusef remained with him against the wall, holding him up, and John came again.

SEATED AT A DARK SMALL TABLE, with a pot of cardamom tea between them, John felt weakened, vanquished, but also relieved.

Why? Yusef was amazed. This was your first time ever. You were a virgin.

No. John shook his head. I've had girlfriends.

What are you feeling then?

I don't know, John said. Weak. Confused. But not bad. You might call it submission, but this was not how I felt when I submitted to Islam.

Yusef touched John's brow with the tips of his fingers. Salty, he said, tasting it. Like the water of Kallar Kahar, a lake that was once sweet. According to legend. One day Baba Fariduddin asked the local women for a drink, but the women put him off claiming the water was salty. If you say so, so be it! replied the saint and went away. The water has been salty ever since.

Thirst. The theme of Pakistan, John said.

And love, Yusef said. Love makes life worth living. But—he sighed, and recited:

> And you still are so ravishing—what should I do?
> There are other sorrows in this world
> Comforts other than love.
> Don't ask me, my love, for that love again.

Whose is it? John asked.

Faiz Ahmed Faiz, a poet born in the Punjab, not far from here.

But John wanted that love again. They were in the alleyway, getting ready to leave, and Yusef turned away at first, held back, tormented, then satisfied him.

THE NEXT AFTERNOON, grinding on wheels across campus, feeling strong again, John saw Khaled on Yusef's bike, seated in front of Yusef, comfortably familiar in front of Yusef, and understood that he wasn't the only one.

They waved, but he turned away, refused to acknowledge them, refused really to accept what he felt. Furious, jealous, hating, and hateful, he ground down a set of concrete steps and kickflipped onto curbs, anger sharpening his skill, whittling it into pure form. What, he asked himself with fury, had gotten into him? Why had he submitted to gay sex? Why did his body ache for it? He wasn't a fag. He liked girls. His best friends were girls. Noor, Katie, Jilly, Sylvie. And Khaled had Samina. Even Yusef mentioned a girlfriend. Was everyone here bisexual?

He turned up Khyber Road, toward the bazaar, and traveled the back way to busy Qissa Khwani. He looked in the alleyway. The bike was there. He found them at the table in the back.

They made room for him, and the waiter brought another glass. Yusef poured.

Khaled quoted someone, John wasn't certain who, he wasn't concentrating well, something about the tree of life as not really a tree, but the best of man, his best virtues, his piety, his only chance at immortality.

Man is mortal, only mind can achieve immortality, Yusef countered.

No, John corrected. Nothing's immortal, but you can make yourself worthy of immortality. But still you die. Every day, every hour, every minute, you die a little, but if you make yourself unworthy, you can die a lot in one day.

You look alive enough to me, Khaled said.

John felt the pressure of Yusef's hand on his thigh and paused. It was possible he'd misread things. It was possible they were just friends who attended the same classes, drank tea after classes, as he did, as they all did. Jealousy and guilt might be misleading him.

Khaled was looking at him, with his one-sided smile. You should relax, he said. My mom has an expression about newcomers to Islam. She says they burn too hot and soon burn out. Muslims born into the fold understand that aspiring to an ideal is enough.

I've tried to tell him, Yusef said. He needs to slow down, respect the heat. His face is a ripe tomato.

Pour me some of that tea and shut up, John said.

Yusef and Khaled laughed and ordered a second pot of tea. John relaxed and sipped. They talked about the recent Hindu atrocities.

I read, John said, that this time the Kashmiri rebels incited the Hindus.

Of course they did, Yusef said. They're living under Hindu rule. History shows that wherever there's oppression, there's rebellion. In the end, the people always win. And the oppressor always knows this, fears it, but still he oppresses, stupidly trying to hold back what's coming anyway. During World War Two, prisoner workers sabotaged the Nazis by making faulty bombs. One such bomb fell into a home in London and never exploded. When the family unraveled it, they found a note: Dear English, Don't worry. We're with you. The Polish.

Good story, Khaled said.

Yusef looked at his watch. Y'allah. I must escort my sister home.

John perked up. He had been meaning to ask Yusef about this sister.

He has a date with his sister, Khaled teased.

Yeah, he keeps his women well hidden, John said. As everyone around here must because I never see any girls.

But Yusef remained unruffled. In Pakistan, he said, we protect the honor of our women.

THE REGULARS AT THE INTERNET CAFÉ greeted him when he came in, and after several repetitions of the handshake-hug-handshake greeting, John went to get himself a gaziz. He had to wait briefly for a computer to free up, chatted with Muhammed at the counter, then settled in.

He signed in. He had twelve messages. An urgent one from Barbara. News from Noor. Nothing from the girls. A p.s. from Barbara. A sale notice from Al-ma-Ha-laat.com. A note from Josiah. And, of course, spam, Hotmail's middle name. He opened Noor's e-mail first: She was working on the school newspaper, getting experience. They'd sent her to cover a film opening, and she asked Claire Danes to name the title of her favorite book of all time, and it was *Pride and Prejudice.* About the women in Pakistan, Noor wrote: They lead significant lives, I'm sure, but not in public, with the exception of a few, like Benazir Bhutto. As a male, and especially a foreign male, you probably won't be allowed anywhere near them. The women have contact only with male relatives. I'm sure, Noor wrote, if you stop at the fruit and vegetable bazaars late afternoon, you'll see women purchasing fresh produce for dinner, but they will be older, the married ones with families.

Noor sent love from Ali, who was beginning to jump curbs. He mentions you every day, Noor wrote. It's like you're his guru, and I think it's starting to annoy my dad. John smiled. And made a mental note to send Ali step-by-step instructions for a grind, but he had to consider which one. He opened Barbara's e-mail.

From: BarbDC672@adelphia.net
To: John_P47892@hotmail.com
Date: July 16, 2001
RE: Urgent

Honey,
Bad news. Jilly is missing, presumed dead————————————

————No! John shouted, slamming his head down on the keyboard. The screen filled quickly: ddeeeexxxxjjjjjjiiiiiiiiiiiiilllllllllllllkkkkkkkjjjjjjjssssssssaaaaaaddddddjjjjjjjjdsaaaaaaaassssssdddddddddddfffffffffffffrrrrrrrrrrrrrrffggggggggggggghhhhhhhhhhhhhhhhhhhhhhhhhhhhh—No he moaned and lifted his head, saw again the word dead, and stood and kicked his chair over, and the table, and, before he could destroy the screen, Muhammed jumped the counter and pushed him to the wall, to stop him. John crumpled.

The machine had to be rebooted, and a one-time warning was delivered: physical abuse of the equipment would not, could not, be tolerated.

Muhammed put his hand on his shoulder. You okay, man? He handed him water. John sipped, hesitated, rubbed his eyes, took another sip, took a deep breath, and waited for the machine to reboot.

We can't afford vandalism, Muhammed warned. Not even from you.

John sat staring, hearing nothing, shaking his head. It had never happened, he had not read it, not seen it, not true, it was not.

When the screen came up again, he reopened Barbara's e-mail.

From: BarbDC672@adelphia.net
To: John_P47892@hotmail.com
Date: July 16, 2001
RE: Urgent

Honey,
Bad news. Jilly is missing, presumed dead. For several days now. Her parents are in Hawaii, trying to learn what they can, hoping to find her body. She was with Katie and Sylvie, they were surfing, a storm was building, and the waves were high. Apparently she went too far. And disappeared. We're all grieving.

The funeral or memorial will be in Hawaii, on the beach, where she was last seen, which makes attendance difficult.

Dad and I are anxious about you. Write to tell us you're well and safe and being sensible.

Much much love from Dad and me, Mom

A p.s. e-mail followed because Barbara always had afterthoughts, but he was afraid to hear more. He opened it anyway.

From: BarbDC672@adelphia.net
To: John_P47892@hotmail.com
Date: July 17, 2001
RE: ps

Jilly's body turned up. Her family is relieved, that is, if one can be relieved in such a case. Your father wonders whether you really needed this information at this time, and I wonder whether I should have allowed myself to serve as the bearer of bad news.

Darling, I'm so sorry. I wish I could have prevented it. I wish there were something more I could do. I wish I could hug and hold you. If you need to talk, or even if you don't need to talk, please just call me collect. Or use your calling card. Best times these days: Mornings, before my 10 a.m. Evenings, after six. Tonight, I'm scheduled to go to dinner at 7:30, so call before 7:15 or after 10. Looking forward to hearing your voice,

Love, Mom

He pushed away from the shaky table and stood and found he couldn't stand, couldn't walk. His legs were buckling. Muhammed stepped up, put his hand under his arm, and led him back to his seat.

What happened? he asked. Bad news?

John nodded. He stared at his inbox and waited, wishing for an e-mail from Katie or Sylvie. Or Jilly. Telling him it wasn't true, it had never happened. He tried willing them to write one. He searched his inbox and found Jilly's last one, from back in February, from when they were packing for Hawaii, after which, once they'd gotten to Hawaii, they'd sent only an aloha postcard with only a wishyouwere-here, and sureyoudon'twannajoinus and always their bubble-letter sign-off:

THE WAHINES

He thrummed his fingertips, tapped his foot, wobbled his knee. The boy on the computer beside him frowned, asked him to stop, so he stopped. But he couldn't stop, couldn't stay still. So he stood. So he paced. Why Jilly? That's what's always asked. So he asked. Why Jilly? Why Donnie Soloman, who died at Waimea Bay? Why Mark Foo, lost at Mavericks? Why Tod Chessner? Mark Sainsbury? Jay Moriarty? Why Phil Shao? Why Jeff Phillips? Why Keenan Milton? Why Tristan Picot? Why Neil Edgeworth? Why Jeff Anderson? Why Craig Kelly? Why Vince Jorgenson? Why Jamil Khan? Why Jilly?

HE LOST HIS CONCENTRATION. The July heat was getting to him. In classes, stuffy and smelly with too many bodies, he grew irritable. And he wasn't sleeping well. Not asleep, he found himself in Jilly's head, thinking Jilly's last thoughts, experiencing the line and flow of her last wave, a warbly one, considering how to take it, at what speed, whether to ride or rip it, drop into the tunnel or stay on top. He wondered what she'd thought in her final moments, knowing she wouldn't make it. Was the experience worth the risk? Would she take that wave again? Finally asleep, he found himself pinned to the ocean floor, and he awoke drowning in his sheets. After which he lay awake under the fan, watching the fan, afraid to sleep. Awake, he listened to Zaadiq's even breathing and Ishmael's free snoring. They slept well because they weren't afraid to die. They'd confronted death and they'd lived. Therefore they were free. Which was what he needed. But it was dark and the world slept, so he counted sheep, counted backward, counted the hours and minutes to daylight.

He considered going home, but to what? He'd been doing well in his classes, making strides in Arabic. He could now write and speak in whole sentences that were grammatically correct if not super sophisticated, and he didn't want to regress. At the Sharia in Brooklyn, it was midsemester, so he'd be without classes. Besides, he'd given up the apartment in Brooklyn, and D.C. in July wasn't fun. The Outer Banks without the girls would be too sad.

Outside at dawn, the air was thick and still, not a leaf stirred, and figures shrouded in white moved silently toward the library, toward the mosque, to the tea shop for breakfast. In the silence, his wheels rolled soothingly on the smooth concrete. He rumbled toward Islamia's main entrance, hoped to meet Yusef, but Yusef wasn't an early riser; he rarely made it in time for first prayer. So John stopped for tea, met colleagues from his Pashto class who hailed him as the Ahm-ree-kee, and he waved but couldn't bear to stop. Tea in hand, he made his way to the open courtyard of the mosque. Prayer ought to help him, calm him. Prayer ought to tell him what to do. He kneeled on a mat, he rocked back on his heels, he whispered, and tears wet his face.

He meditated and reasoned. Jilly died, he told himself, in a moment of becoming, the highest moment. So she would never grow old, never get stuck at mere being. He heard her voice. I couldn't make a wrong move. My body sort of knew what to do on its own. The wave was a live thing, and somehow my body knew what to do.

He cut class and went to find Yusef, but Yusef was in a hurry. His class was just starting, he was running late. Anything wrong? he asked, but John held back. He couldn't talk about Jilly in a hurry. Besides, what did Jilly have to do with his desire for Yusef?

He tried a day's fast to take his mind off Jilly, and off Yusef, to make him think of something else, even if it was only food, but after breaking his fast, he still went looking for Yusef. But Yusef was becoming impatient. You have become insecure and needy, he said. Tell me. What's bothering you?

So John told Yusef about Jilly. I can't sleep, I can't study, I can't concentrate. And the heat doesn't help. At the library I read a paragraph three times and I have no idea what I've read.

I'm so sorry, Yusef said. You should have told me right away. Does Khaled know?

They had tea with Khaled.

Maybe you need a change, Khaled advised. A sort of time-out.

You should get out of the city for a while, Yusef agreed.

I can arrange a stay at my aunt's, Khaled offered.

What he needed, John thought, was physical activity to tire him out, so he could sleep. But it was the end of July, it was one hundred eight degrees, too hot for classes, too hot for the library, too hot to stay indoors, too hot to be outdoors, at least in Peshawar.

From: John_P47892@hotmail.com
To: BarbDC672@adelphia.net
Date: July 26, 2001
RE: <no subject>

mom,
it's about 110 degrees at 9 a.m. and i can't take it anymore. i want to take time off from classes and move into the hills with a friend, where it's cooler. i'll need money. love, john

ps you prob won't hear from me for a while since there's no internet or phone access in the hills. please don't worry. i'll be fine.

BARBARA UNDERSTOOD. One hundred ten degrees was indeed extreme, especially without air-conditioning.

I wish he'd just come home, she said to Bill. Even if only for August.

I'd like that, too, but would John? Bill asked. He seems determined to follow his own plan, his own curriculum. He deferred Brown a second time. I was surprised they let him.

But if he's taking a break, Barbara said, why not take it here? He could stay with us at Southern Shores. He could surf.

Yes, of course. If you can convince him.

But John had his own ideas. Moving back, he wrote, would mean falling into easy English. Here I learn even when I'm not in the classroom. I just need a short break.

Barring home, Barbara said, the hills with a friend might be best, and Bill wired money.

JOHN ARRANGED for a leave with college administration and rented a locker for his books, CDs, and duffel bag of clothes. He was taking only a small backpack. His wheels, useless in the hills, would remain in Yusef's care, Yusef rather than Khaled, because Yusef respected wheels.

After which he was ready. Yusef picked him up on his bike. Y'allah, he said, inviting John to steer.

So John climbed on the bike again, so he felt Yusef at his back, so he wanted Yusef, thus by the time they rumbled into the camp's dusty courtyard, he craved a last fuck, and though he said nothing, he knew Yusef knew.

Yusef mounted his bike, kicked back the kickstand, and paused in front of his cousin. Promise to take good care of my friend, he said.

Jalal nodded, and Yusef was satisfied.

WITH YUSEF GONE, the kids crowded around John, practicing their English on him, and Jalal, who was watching, had an idea.

How about giving English lessons while you're here?

The kids whooped. Then sat on their haunches to listen as Jalal composed John's daily schedule in the sand. He sketched with a stick. Your day will begin early, with physical conditioning. We'll train together.

After a quick bath at the stream, Jalal continued, we'll be in time for prayer and breakfast. Qur'anic study and meditation follow. At high noon, the midday meal is served, and we all retire for rest. In the afternoon, after a brief recitation session, classes in weapons and target practice. Early evenings, Jalal continued, I conduct a session in rhetoric, in which the children practice debating each other. These sessions will provide you with an opportunity to practice your Pashto.

We have a group of older students, all about your age, training higher up the mountain for the next weeks, Jalal explained. When you've become acclimated here, you'll want to join them there.

Picking up John's duffel bag, Jalal led the way to his own room. In the dorm, he explained, the kids would keep you awake with questions.

It was time for the noon meal. They stopped to wash their hands at the basin near the entrance and took their places at the back of the room. Inside, the kids passed large baskets of pita bread, then bowls of hummus. Even the youngest boys showed the elegance and motor skills of maturity. They scooped up the hummus with their pita, careful to keep their fingers out of the bowl. For dessert, small cups of mahlabiyya. Some of the groms, John noticed, took two.

In Jalal's room for siesta, two mats served as beds, folded towels as pillows, and Jalal lay on his back, one hand under his head. In the other, a book. He had stacks of books against the walls in what appeared to be a mix of English and Arabic titles.

You're welcome to them, he offered. Some are mine, others were left behind by former campers. Here, this one's an excellent history of the mujahideen movement. I also have Sufi books. And poetry of Arab Andalusia, which is my specialty. I like to read one poem before bed, sometimes only a line. So that beauty accompanies me into sleep. Listen to this one:

The tongue of dawn threatened to denounce us.

Whose is it?

Ibn Zaydun of Córdoba.

The tongue of dawn, John repeated.

How do you feel? Jalal asked.

The air is better here, John said.

Some of the younger boys get asthma in the summer, Jalal said. That's why their parents send them here.

Jalal's breathing grew even, and John closed his eyes, matched his own breaths to Jalal's, and slept. Finally.

He awoke to the sound of his name, and found Jalal at his side with a cup of tea.

Too long a siesta makes you more tired, he said. Best to keep it short.

They washed their faces in the basin of water at the door and slipped into their tunics. Jalal finger-combed his wavy hair.

We're due for Qur'anic recitation, he said, and parted the curtain that served as a door.

It wasn't exactly a classroom: there were no desks, no blackboard, no teacher. A large rug covered the concrete floor, and campers were seated in rows, two to a text. They sat with one knee tucked neatly under one buttock; the other knee supported the open book. Although John started in the same position, he couldn't keep it for long. He watched, listened, mouthed the verses, admired the kids their stillness, their ability to stay put. They were young, only eight or so, but without prompting, each took a turn reciting a verse aloud, and the group repeated after him. They moved fluently from boy to boy, row by row. When it was his turn, John tried for accuracy in the classical Arabic. He had been practicing the beat, complete with pauses and precise glottal work. He read sura 18:33, Kita aljannatayni atat okulaha walam tathlim minhu shayan wafajjarna khilalehuma naharan.

Well done, Jalal complimented him, and recited the next verse, complete with correct clicks and checks.

After the session, two boys offered to escort John to target practice. They slipped their small hands into his, and he walked with them, enjoying the contact, their quick friendship. Their names, they told him when he asked, were Ibrahim and Dawid.

He hadn't seen any adults besides Jalal and the cook. Who conducts classes? he asked.

When the older boys are in the hills for Ta'sisia, Ibrahim explained in Pashto, Uncle Jalal teaches.

What do we call you? Dawid asked.

Most people call me John, John offered. But my Arabic name is Attar.

Attar, Ibrahim said.

Attar, Dawid confirmed.

John nodded. Attar, then.

The session took place on the bare campgrounds beside the platform built for target practice. The carpet from indoors had been brought outdoors, and the kids sat in a ring. They made room for John and his escorts, and once again John had to tuck his legs.

His name got around. Attar, several kids said, by way of acknowledging him. Ahm-ree-kee? one boy asked.

John nodded. Yes, he said. When I'm not here, I live in Washington, D.C., the capital of the United States.

Washington, D.C., they repeated. Capital of the United States.

They'll learn quickly, John thought, but he would have to figure out how to organize the material, both alphabet and vocabulary.

Jalal arrived, and the kids transferred their attention to him. He started by asking for some moments of silence and breathing. The kids closed their eyes and breathed noisily, inhaling deeply, forcing the exhale.

Smooth, silent breathing, Jalal announced, will make your shooting more accurate. If you breathe smoothly, your arms will relax, the rifle won't move, and the target won't disappear. And we have a new pupil with us today. Let's see if we can both impress him and help him become a sharpshooter.

They were required to lie on their stomachs. Jalal lowered the target, and three kids got into position. The others were reminded to remain behind the platform at all times.

Breathe, Jalal reminded them. Sight down the barrel, keeping your eye on the target. He corrected hand and head positions, straightened fidgety legs.

Elbows tucked in at your sides, Jalal said.

Two bullets hit the paper target. The third went awry. Then the next three kids moved into position. When it was John's turn, he looked at Jalal.

Yes, Jalal confirmed. On your stomach. It will aid your steadiness.

John reminded himself to breathe, to sight, to keep his eye on the target, which should have been easy, but it wasn't. The target moved. He closed one eye, which helped. He exhaled, he pulled the trigger, and the bullet hit an outer corner of the paper target.

The boys cheered, though they were better at it.

Better than your first time, Jalal said. Next time, when you squeeze the trigger, try doing it in one slow continuous motion.

John went to the back of the line, impatient now for his next turn. Slow and continuous, he told himself. One motion. He was eager to achieve a bull's eye. He was eager, he discovered, for the boys' admiration and applause.

Spicy smoke drifted from the dusty courtyard, and John found that he was hungry. He stopped at the stream with the others to wash his dusty hands and face before dinner. After prayers, with the sun lower in the sky, they dined outside.

Again baskets of pita made the rounds, followed this time by a tray of skewered cubes of beef with onions. With their pita, the kids picked off a cube at a time, catching the juices with the bread. John soon got the hang of it, and enjoyed the outdoor, no-utensils camp style.

FOR HIS FIRST ENGLISH-LANGUAGE SESSION, John decided on basic introductions. He started with himself: My name is Attar. My oom's name is Barbara. My ahb's name is William. I have no ahk or ohkt. I am from Washington, D.C., in the United States of America, and I am visiting Pakistan. My favorite food is pizza.

The boys were good at it and challenged each other to reach deeper and farther into the vocabulary of family relations. Arabic, which had no word for cousin, used phrases to describe extended family relationships: ahm ibn for son of a paternal uncle; khaal ibn for son of a maternal uncle; ahk ibn for son of brother; and so on. Pashto was similar, and it was soon clear to John that Pakistani families were multitudinously branched; not a few of the kids in the group were related one way or another. By the time the forty-five-minute session was over, he'd heard the names of immediate and extended families of the twenty-two groms in his class and, he noted ruefully, remembered none. Even the names of his students would take some effort to remember. He resolved to know them all within a day or two.

THEY WENT TO BED with poetry—

> until darkness smiled
> showing the white teeth of dawn—

and woke before the camp stirred. John sipped the weak tea Jalal made, rolled up his mat, folded his blanket, tied his sneakers, and was ready.

They started with an easy warm-up run around the campsite, then Jalal took a footpath up the mountain. When John could no longer keep the pace, they switched to a quick walk down and a fifty-yard sprint up. And again, until John's legs were aching. At the end of every sprint, Jalal dropped down on the path and delivered something extra, twenty push-ups or twenty sit-ups, and though John tried, he couldn't keep up. He might have been in good enough shape for surfing, but Jalal was in better physical shape than anyone he'd known.

The air is thinner here, Jalal pointed out, so your lungs have to work harder.

After, they washed beside the stream. Hearing John groan because his arms were too sore to reach his back, Jalal offered to do it for him. In his room, he offered Bengay, and John massaged his arms and legs,

Jalal did his back, and John felt his stupid penis respond. But if Jalal noticed, he didn't say anything, for which John was grateful.

When the wind blows
I make sure it blows in my face:
the breeze might bring me news of you

THE EARLY WORKOUT became his favorite part of the day. He loved the thin morning air, crisp, fresh, clean. He looked forward to this quiet time with Jalal, to Jalal's attention, and pushed himself to deliver an extra sprint or extra push-ups and earn Jalal's compliments. He wondered about Jalal's ability to live out here away from the city without colleagues his own age. But Jalal seemed to welcome the quiet, meditative life, with time for poetry, alongside the physical rigor.

Who's your hero? he asked Jalal one night. I mean like your mentor.

Jalal thought about it. The early mujahideen, he said. Of the seventies. If you're asking about someone more contemporary, then Mullah Omar. He's a scholar, not just a warrior, Jalal said, and I like that.

Yusef and I served two tours together, Jalal said. Both in Kashmir. I volunteered for a third tour in Afghanistan because of Mullah Omar.

I saw dawn come
shaking dew from her clear brow

THE WEEK FLEW BY. The lorry came down the mountain to load up on food and ammunition.

When you're ready, Jalal said, as they worked side by side, loading the lorry. When your lungs are accustomed to the thinner air, you'll want to train up there.

Soon, John said. In the meantime, he'd enjoyed his first week here. He was sleeping well. He liked Jalal. He liked the boys whose names he'd come to know. Also the teaching and target practice and Qur'anic recitation. His Pashto was improving. And he looked forward to his morning workouts. He felt his heart expand in his narrow chest. His throat and nostrils opened wider. His long arms ached, his long legs burned, he groaned, but when Jalal traced the developing sinews and tendons on his limbs—maturing muscles, he called them, your reward—John was proud.

> captured
> as wine drinks the reason
> of those that drink it.

AND ALWAYS his penis threatened to embarrass him, though Jalal revealed nothing. He massaged, he soothed, then capped the tube of Bengay, and set it down beside John. Some nights John found himself awake and wanting Jalal. He wondered at himself, at his fickleness in love. This wasn't the first time his fickle heart had shifted from one love to another, and he rebuked himself for mistaking lust for love.

> she provides better cover
> than the night itself

THEY TALKED over slow pots of watery tea. He told Jalal about riding a wave, about waiting for the right one, knowing it, knowing yourself as a mere humble drop in its wake, and going back for more. He told him about Jilly, who went and didn't return. He explained: Wiping out in an extreme wave could take you twenty to fifty feet under water, and if another wave breaks before you've had a chance to surface, you could be held down for too long. A triple wave hold-down is near impossible to survive. Therefore the name: extreme wave surfing.

Walking on water, Jalal called it.

I keep thinking about her final moments. About what she knew. About what there is to know.

> white moons
> amid the night of black braids

HE TOLD JALAL about Katie and Sylvie, who were now incomplete without Jilly. He couldn't explain very well. About what was lost. About what he felt. It wasn't only the loss of Jilly, since she remained within him forever as Jilly. It was something more basic: they'd been perfect as three, and now the circle was broken, and he found himself aching for its repair, for the number three. He couldn't explain very well.

> oh, fateful night!
> hold back the hour of sundering!

IN BED, on their separate mats, Jalal on his back, always with one hand under his head, and John on his stomach looking into Jalal's face, they talked about sacrifice, about submerging the individual self for the greater good.

It's an old mystical ideal, but it's also a military one, what every soldier in every army in the world must do, Jalal said. Self-surrender. In the Prophet's day, this experience was expected of every man. Today's jihad extends this tradition.

But I keep thinking, John said, that maybe there's a better way to free Kashmir and unite Afghanistan. Without violence. Like Gandhi.

I wish, Jalal said. But Gandhi's pacifism worked because of Gandhi. Some say Gandhi was the Buddha's gift to India.

> love was kept awake by her reed-waist, dune-hips
> face as beautiful as the moon

JALAL QUOTED HERACLEITUS, of whom John hadn't heard though he considered himself well read.

Well read compared with whom? Jalal asked. Americans? He was your first philosopher, Greek. Most famous for his idea that all things are in a state of flux.

John nodded. He already knew about the significance of life in flux, eternally becoming. He told Jalal about his paper on Jacob's struggle with his ego, his inner enemy.

Exactly, Jalal said. That's how he became a powerful nation. Struggling with himself. Knowing himself. Of course, it helps when it's for a good cause, and Islam provides one. For two hundred years, our umma has been under attack. First the French invaded Egypt. Then the British took Egypt from the French. Then the Italians went for Libya. Then after World War One, when it suited them, the French and English agreed to carve, divide, and subdivide our land.

Jalal knew his history. They were beside the stream, soaping each other's backs. As a Westerner, Jalal said, you are as wet with colonial guilt as you stand here slick with soap.

Go ahead. Rinse off, Jalal said, and pushed John toward the water.

But John wouldn't let go of Jalal's hand and pulled him along, and together they flung themselves in, splashing, and still John held on, though they were both slippery with soap. The stream was too shallow for vertical immersion, so they went under horizontally, nose to nose, mouth to mouth, chest to chest, and then they floated to their sides and spooned, with Jalal holding John snug against himself, hardening against him, and John wanted nothing but this hardened flesh within him. Now, he begged.

So facedown in the water, he gets what he asks for. Jalal stands, and thrusts, and more, holding on, holding out, for what John wants, long enough to wonder for how long John can take it, underwater, a receptacle without breath. He seems suddenly limp, he is only taking, offering no arching response, and Jalal becomes afraid, and afraid, he reaches to lift John's shoulders and sees the arc of cum in the air, continuous cum arcing, his own cum which is entering John, flowing through John, emerging from John, into blue air, and into clear water. And as if from a distance he hears the noise of John's ragged choking breaths, a body catching up on life.

After they floated as one, bobbing up and under, up and under, allowing the intervals underwater to grow longer, stretching their lungs to accommodate their desire to submit.

You're actually pretty good at this, Jalal said. Do you know about the concept of wu-wei? To live as if you're already dead. Have you been to Hyderabad, to the shrine of Shah Abdul Latif, the uncrowned king of Sind? They stage sunset performances of Sufi music there. Latif wrote:

Try to be dead from now on / Everyone's dead in the end.

He called it the greatest freedom, the only freedom available to man.

THEY SCHEDULED EXTRA SESSIONS of target practice. Jalal stood behind John, helped him line up the rifle along his left arm, tucked his elbows in. Though he'd gotten good at hitting the target from a prone position, elbows supported by the floor beneath him, he was all over the place once he stood. His arm wavered; he lost the target, lost control.

Breathe, Jalal said. Relax.

But the target shimmered; the target danced.

Listen to your breath, Jalal said. Count the exhales. And keep sighting down the barrel.

John inhaled, looked up, exhaled, tried sighting again, pulled the trigger and sent another bullet nowhere.

Jalal suggested dropping down on one knee, and John felt he was regressing.

You're tall, which puts you farther from your center. That's why you're unsteady. Dropping down gets you closer to your core.

So John practiced on one knee. Some days now he hit a bull's eye, but when he couldn't repeat it on demand, he called it beginner's luck. He was inconsistent. He still couldn't qualify as a marksman, though he was getting better.

He went from practicing with one knee on the ground to standing up. He learned to breathe. He learned to relax. He learned to squeeze the trigger, to think of it as a slow consistent squeeze rather than a pull.

Like other challenges, Jalal said, achievement takes time. And practice. But you've gotten really fit.

It was the end of his third week of training. Jalal was administering the daily Bengay, and he took his time, massaging and soothing.

You're ready, Jalal said, tracing John's newly hardened muscles, ligaments, and sinews. And this is an opportunity for you because this group is heading into Afghanistan. The Taliban has been calling for help.

But the lorry came. The lorry went. John stayed a fourth week until Jalal reminded him of his duty, of what he wanted, and why he'd come: He must think wu-wei, give himself over to the chance of death, become. His reward: greater spiritual life. The great spiritual men of this world escape biology, become immortal.

Do you know the "Tale of the Sands"? Jalal asked.

From the *Mystic Rose*?

Think of yourself as the stream that allows the wind to carry it across the desert sands, then falls like rain and becomes a river. You, too, will return as the higher essence of yourself.

Will you still recognize me? John joked.

Listen, Jalal said. It's your duty. And it's an experience you've been wanting. You owe it both to yourself and to Islam. You must go to the mountains. You must struggle to become.

But why must it be violently? Why not with love? Like Ibn 'Arabi's. Like the Beatles'. Like ours. He was asking the questions Barbara would ask.

Don't speak like a foolish naïf, Jalal said. Violence is life. You were born in violence, tearing away from your mother, hurting your mother in the process, and you live by violence, fighting to survive. If you do anything worthwhile with your life, you'll die violently, as most men do, even your namesake, John Lennon, singing for love and peace, even Mahatma Gandhi. Read the Bible, read the Qur'an, read the daily papers. Life's violent. Preaching love, Jesus Christ died violently.

LATE ONE NIGHT, they were under netting to avoid the fidget of flies, and beside him, Jalal was breathing with deep sleep, but John remained awake, thinking:

It will be an adventure and he's been wanting adventure. He has learned much from Jalal, received much, and he wants to give back, to Jalal, to the people, to Islam. He is Muslim, and he wants to fulfill his duty to Islam. More than anything else, he wants to become. He is here to know and become the age-old way, the way the Buddha became the Buddha, the way Abraham became father to a nation, the way Jacob became Israel, the way Christ became the Savior God, the way Jilly became Jilly. And though their achievements were impossibly difficult to understand, impossible to explain, he has come to understand what they've done, and he knows what he has to do.

He thinks of Richard Burton dancing with the dervishes, cutting himself. He thinks of Jacob struggling with the angel and walking away with a limp. He thinks of Muhammed reciting as commanded. He thinks of Jilly giving herself to the wave, her last one. He would do as they had. He would give himself to becoming.

So he swears allegiance to formative struggle. So Jalal packs his backpack. So he is packed, so he is strong and muscular, so he is ready for the lorry to take him up the mountain. He is the only passenger in this vehicle loaded with supplies of food and ammunition. So the lorry grinds up the steep incline on a road designed for old switchback train tracks. The lorry grinds to steep right, steep left, and right again, inching forward, inching back, and forward again, in ever smaller degrees. The mountain grows steeper, narrower, steeper, the switchbacks become more frequent. So he gives his body to its rhythm, this forward and back, this inch up, and inch back, and understands this as life, the rise and drop, the up and down, with no stop at peak, a wave, which comes in, collects itself, gathering meaning, then heaves over and disperses back to nonmeaning. An eternal attraction and withdrawal, progress and regress, with the reach toward crest already showing the drop down and away. This, he thinks, is what Jilly knew. That all experience is like this. That this is life, with meaning and nonmeaning side by side, touching. Before meaning, chaos. After meaning, chaos. Before life, senselessness. After life, senselessness. He must embrace the before and after, the forward and away, the switch there and back, the becoming, because only becoming is eternal. Because being doesn't exist.

It is summer, it is brown, with only a patch of green here. Another one there, the driver says, pointing toward a corner of the dusty windshield. They are headed to the makeshift camp pitched beside a stream. He hopes the camp will be in the shade, though shade up here is rare. The hills, he knows, cool off at night, it is already cool, and he rubs his brown, goosebumped arms. It is only late afternoon and already he's chilled or perhaps it's his body adapting to the mountain climate, to extreme heat followed by extreme cold, to the large round flat cardboard cutout sun dropping fast off the Margalla Hills, reddening the ridge in the east as it drops west. So he feels cold already, though he shouldn't, having grown rugged. So he is on his way to becoming a soldier. Four weeks of predawn workouts; four weeks of unsweetened diluted mint tea and target practice; four weeks and he is strong and he is proud of his new strength. So he rubs the new knots on his biceps. So he is beginning to feel like a soldier. So he will spend the next weeks in Ta'sisia. Ta'sisia: the making of a Muslim foot soldier. He will fight corruption and bribery and tribal violence. He will unite the tribes under the banner of Islam. He will do what the Prophet had done.

THE LORRY FINALLY PULLED UP to what appeared to John as a makeshift camp in the process of decamping. He counted ten, no eleven, young men about his age, and they all seemed in a hurry, breaking down tents, pulling stakes, packing bags, strapping bags.

John looked at the driver, Faqir, who served as camp teacher, driver, cook, adviser, whatever was needed.

You won't need to unpack. Faqir shrugged and got out of the lorry.

Someone approached. Amin, Faqir said, and they shook hands.

Amin raised one thick eyebrow in John's direction. So this is Jalal's American protégé? he asked.

Attar, John said, shaking Amin's outstretched hand.

Jalal got you up here just in time, Amin said.

In time for what?

For our journey to Kabul.

John swallowed. He'd wanted to see Kabul, and now he was somehow really headed there. Which should please him. He'd finally have his adventure, his experience of becoming, but he found he was a little afraid. He knew no one here, he'd be traveling with total strangers, fighting a stranger's war. But Richard Burton was also a stranger, he reminded himself. So he worked alongside Amin and Faqir, unloading supplies, which they then broke up into smaller parcels. Every soldier carries his own supplies, Amin explained.

John asked about passes and visas. His passport was at the bottom of his backpack, but he'd never applied for a pass.

No problem, Amin said. We travel during the night, dar tariki, tariquat. In darkness, the path. Once we cross the Khyber, we'll make our way to Hadda.

Where all the Buddhist stupas are?

Were, Amin said. Bombed by the Soviets in the seventies. It's all rubble now.

Someone sounded the early evening call to prayer, and they paused, washed their hands and faces at the nearby stream, and, with rounded backs and bowed heads, prayed. And prayer, it turned out, was precisely what John needed. Though he welcomed every opportunity to perform the salaat, he found himself especially eager for it here and now, in this far-flung place among strangers. He prayed for the success of his journey to becoming. He prayed for Barbara and Bill. He prayed for Katie and Sylvie. He prayed for Jilly. And Noor. He whispered the la illaha with extra fervency, rocked back on his heels, turned his head right, turned his head left, and ended on the as salaamu. And beside him and in front of him the others greeted him: as salaamu aleykum, aleykum as salaam. Though strangers, though he'd never met them before, they wished him peace.

They finished packing and loading, then stopped for a dinner of spicy tandoori chicken with minted chickpeas and naan.

Eat plenty, Amin advised, because you won't get another hot meal for a while.

JOHN HIKED beside Amin, who introduced him to some of the others: Jamal, Ishmael, Kamel, Abdul, Sayed.

Attar, they said in greeting, and shook hands.

Welcome to our unit, someone named Tameel said. He introduced himself as their leader, though he could not be more than twenty-three, John thought.

Tameel suggested John spend some hours walking beside each of the others, getting to know them, allowing them to know him. This way, by the time we arrive at Hadda, you'll be one of us.

John wondered how long a hike it was. According to his guidebook, you could go from Peshawar to Kabul by car in eight hours, but they weren't going all the way to Kabul.

From the mouth of the pass at Jamrud, the road's about forty-eight kilometers long, Amin said, but we're on the footpath, which is somewhat shorter. We'll keep moving through the night, rest at dawn, then continue on. At Torkham we'll find transportation to Hadda. Im'sh'allah.

About thirty miles, John calculated. All on foot. Good thing he'd brought very little.

We don't want to attract notice, Amin explained. Without horses or donkeys, we can move quickly, enter and leave villages easily, make no impression.

John wondered whom they were trying to avoid.

Everyone and no one in particular, Amin said. As foreigners we have no right to fight in Afghanistan's civil war. And the Northern Alliance generals like to murder captured foreign fighters rather than trade them for their own soldiers. So we'll avoid the official highway and all its checkpoints. Which also means no fees and bribes and paperwork. Anyway, the highway is for vehicles. It's easier to cross on foot.

IN THE FIRST HOURS of their hike, in the day's waning light, the jagged mountain peaks grew dark and darker, and when the path narrowed to single file, he came to think of them as watchful ancient elders looking over his shoulder, ushering him forward into this journey.

They began their climb as a talkative group, and he was glad they all spoke some English. He learned details about each of the hikers' lives, about where in Pakistan they were from, which madrassah they'd attended, how long they'd trained. And the training exercises.

Kamel teased Abdul about the time he got lost, and then Abdul got Kamel back with a story about one exercise in which he forgot which side he was on.

Just be sure you don't end up fighting for the Alliance, Abdul warned, or I'll have to shoot you.

Jamal reminded Abdul of his own early deficiencies. He couldn't hit the target for weeks, Jamal revealed.

Jamal and Amin had already fulfilled one tour of duty. Tameel was the most experienced of the group, having served three times.

Keep Khyber Road always in sight and on your left, Tameel advised. If for some reason we're separated, continue forward, keeping the road on your left, and you'll be moving in the right direction.

This turned out to be easy enough while they had light, but then it grew dark, and it was difficult staying on the narrow, winding path. John found himself stumbling over outcroppings, stones, shrubs—he didn't always know what they were. He found it impossible to see Khyber Road and was glad to have Amin behind him and Tameel ahead, glad not to be at the end of the line, where, if delayed, he might lose sight of the others.

They walked in silence for what seemed hours. And then finally a sliver of moon rose and he could once again see where he was going.

Traveling with a full moon's foolhardy, Tameel explained. Anyone could shoot us from miles away.

Toward dawn, John felt a blister on his left heel, but they were stopping soon. They would rest in a cave through the morning hours. Tameel informed them they were more than halfway there.

IT WAS MIDMORNING when he awoke. After prayers and a bite—they found pita and olives and water in their packs—they gathered for instructions.

We have to walk this final stretch in daylight, Tameel explained, because the footpath into the valley is narrow and steep, too difficult to navigate in the dark. Split up in groups of three, and we'll meet on the Afghan side of Torkham.

Now, listen closely. Loti Kotal's about five kilometers from the border. Before you get there, begin traveling alone with enough distance between each other so that no one on the path has reason to think you are companions. Exchange pleasantries with any Afridi merchant you meet, and if he welcomes conversation, stay with him, give him a hand if he needs it, so that at the pass itself you'll appear as a father and son traveling together. Attar, you should probably not try conversation. Get by with a smile and a helping hand.

Tameel made certain that everyone had enough change for tea and something to eat. John was glad he'd packed protein bars for emergencies.

He teamed up with Amin and Iksander, named, Iksander said, for Alexander the Great.

Cool, John said. I read somewhere that the year he died, children all over the world were named for him. Alexander, Alexandrine, Alexandra.

They were the second team to get going, having given the first team a twenty-minute head start. Before they left, Tameel advised John to darken his face and the back of his hands with dirt to avoid standing out. Though he was tanned and had something of a beard—he'd stopped shaving his second week at Tangi—he was still paler than most Pakistanis.

They walked single file on a well-trodden footpath that led steeply up the face of the mountain. They would have to make their way up before finally descending into Torkham. Deep below to his left was the pass, which looked like a gap in a wall of mountains, but he had to avoid looking that way because the steep incline made him dizzy, and he felt himself falling.

It's vertigo, Amin explained. Keep your eyes straight ahead, on the path. The valley below is known as the Zorzai, but look up ahead rather than down. See, up there is an Afridi village with its high walls and watchtowers. And there, thirty-five hundred feet above the pass, is the village of Loti Kotal. It has a smugglers' bazaar, where you can get everything illegal: from opium to DVDs.

They soon shared the footpath with Afridi villagers leading donkeys and camels laden with fruit and vegetables, and with no signs anywhere of the twenty-first or even the twentieth century, John felt himself transported to ancient days. Surrounded by this bare brown landscape, by the sounds of Pashto and Dari, by the hardships of premodern life, he felt as far from the English language and the West as Alexander the Great must have been from George W. Bush.

Where are they going? John asked.

They sell their produce in Torkham or on the road to Jalalabad, Amin explained. For them, this walk is a daily journey.

It was slow going, and then they saw Loti Kotal ahead, which, at least from where he was, didn't look like much. They split up. John kept an eye out for someone friendly. Rather than hurry ahead and attract notice, he slowed down and dropped behind. And then up ahead, he saw what he thought might be a slender young woman. She was riding sidesaddle for one thing. And she kept her hair covered. Her feet were bare and brown, slender ankles exposed. For an adventure with her, he knew, he'd give up this journey. For now at least.

He caught up to her. Her donkey was loaded with sacks of peaches and plums. As salaam, he greeted. Today, at least, he joked in Pashto, you won't go hungry.

As salaamu aleykum, a voice replied, but it was definitely not a girl's voice.

Ta la kuom hiwad na raghelay yi? the boy asked.

John paused. He'd done what Tameel had told him not to do. He'd given himself away in one breath. Za la deyr lirey na raghelay yem, he answered. Za la gharb lirey.

Gharb? the boy echoed, gesturing west.

Hoo. John nodded. Wa u? he asked, hoping to distract him.

Te pe angrezai pohegy? the boy persisted.

John nodded.

Then welcome to my country, he said in impressive English, after which he went on to tell John in a mix of English and Pashto that he lived with his mother and sisters and uncles and cousins in the hills, where they had orchards and goats. My name, the boy said, is for my father, Sayeed al Kuchi. He mimed a cut throat. When I am grown tall—the boy indicated a foot above his head—I must make badal, and John understood that this boy's father had been murdered. They were making their way down a steep grade with difficulty. The donkey worked hard to keep its weight on its hind legs, and Sayeed helped by sitting farther behind the vertical, throwing his shoulders back, and he did it intuitively, without much thinking or planning. John, too, found himself leaning away from the incline, to keep from tumbling down. And throughout their three-mile descent, Sayeed kept up an English-Pashto-mime conversation. John worried at first that they might attract notice, but the terrain was difficult and narrow, and people kept a good distance, seven to ten donkey lengths. After they passed what turned out to be Fort Maude and then the Ali Masjid, the canyon narrowed to only about nineteen yards wide, and their walking path ran right alongside the road, which was heavily trafficked with steaming, hissing, spitting vehicles, shifting down and down and down all the way to the gate at Torkham. Walking these three miles, John came to appreciate Tameel's strategy. Beside Sayeed and his donkey, he appeared as just another villager on his way to sell his daily crop, and though the cars stopped to unload, he walked through the gates with Sayeed chattering all the way.

I to Jalalabad, Sayeed said, pointing.

But before he took off, John wanted to give him something, but what? Money might not be appropriate. He reached into his backpack and pulled out a Zone bar.

Candy? Sayeed asked.

John nodded. He wished he could do more for the kid, but Sayeed was all business. As salaam, he shouted, and kicked his donkey toward Jalalabad.

TORKHAM WAS A RUNDOWN OUTDOOR VERSION of airport customs, with money changers, bus depots, and shabby teahouses in what amounted to a giant dusty parking lot. Lines of travelers with packs and sacks waited to show their papers, answer questions, pay fees. Customs officials and armed guards moved stiffly between the lines. A lorry pulled up and spilled forth more guards in uniform. Afternoon was turning toward early evening, and everywhere minibuses, vans, and taxis hawked rides: Jalalabad, Kabul, Kandahar, Wazir, Hadda, Pahshad, drivers shouted.

Beyond the stone gates, clusters of businessmen, travelers, and families gathered with their luggage. Keeping a low profile, John looked for the others and found them farther ahead on the road toward Jalalabad, under what might have been the only tree. They were sipping fresh mango juice and directed him to a cart across the road. John went to get himself a juice and a chapli kebab, a burger made of lamb and spices. He sat and ate and watched.

Boys pushing wheelbarrows served as luggage porters. From where he sat, John followed the strange procedure. The boys unloaded packs and sacks off the taxis and minivans on the Pakistani side of the gate, wheeled the heavily heaped wheelbarrows through the gates while the travelers walked through and hired a taxi on the Afghan side. Then the boys loaded the luggage into the trunk and received some change for their service.

It took another hour for the unit to regroup. Tameel, traveling with two of the youngest recruits, who were not yet seventeen, arrived last. They were hungry, and John recommended the chapli kebabs from the cart across the way.

They're the best I've ever had, he said.

Amin laughed. That's probably because you were the hungriest you've ever been. Believe me, there's better. Much better.

But he complimented John's stamina. You're strong, Attar. Despite the thinner air, you weren't out of breath, not even on the steepest climbs.

Dusk descended. The mountaintops went from bright to dull orange, their outlines grew darker and more defined, and Tameel thought it best to get out of Torkham before nightfall. He went to find a willing driver.

By the time they were on the road, it was too dark to see, and John regretted that so much of this journey was traveled at night.

Don't fret, Tameel assured him. You'll see a good part of Afghanistan before you're through.

Hadda was quiet. They got out on a sort of main square crowded with shabby small guesthouses that looked as if they'd been built in a hurry, with no time for trim work or even complete paint jobs. The street had a transient appearance, a place no one stayed long enough to care for. Whatever grass grew was trodden down. If there were once trees, they'd been lost to construction and neglect. The front walks were dusty, the entrances unremarkable, with only a bare lightbulb dangling above each one.

Where's everyone? Iksander wondered, and Tameel went to find out.

He returned with Yakub, who introduced himself as the man in charge of new recruits. He directed them up the street, toward a small white guesthouse that was no different than the others, and John wondered how Yakub differentiated between them. He unlocked the front door, led the way into a small kitchen, and, from a cabinet, produced a tin of biscuits. He filled a kettle and put up water for tea.

We served dinner early today, he said, because we had an important lecture by a visiting dignitary scheduled. He's just finishing. Why don't you wash up, get some sleep, and I'll see you at breakfast.

IN THE MORNING, after prayers and a breakfast of tea and mahalabiyya, the new arrivals were ushered into a room to wait for their interviews. Tameel went first and stayed. Yakub came to escort Amin. After Amin, Jamal went, and John understood that they were interviewing the more experienced volunteers first. They'll ask where you're from, Amin said when he got back. Who your father is, where you went to school, where you trained. Questions you'd expect.

When John's turn came, Yakub blindfolded him with a black strip of cloth. For security, he explained. They walked down an echoing corridor into what felt like a room. When the blindfold came off and John could see again, he found himself momentarily confused, facing three men in full dress, white shalwar kameez, white vests, and white turbans. In the dim light, the white of their clothes and the whites of their eyes glowed. All three were seated on cushions, legs crossed in front of them. To avoid their hard eyes, John looked around at the craggy cave walls. This was not a dream. He was really about to be interviewed in a Hadda cave. By mujahideen fighters. Had their experiences as fighters, he wondered, turned them into finer essences?

Tameel, who sat to the left of the men, also on a cushion, cleared his throat and started introductions. John concentrated on their faces, largely camouflaged by bushy beards. Though they were all probably only in their early thirties, their beards belonged to older men. One of them—his name, Tameel said, was Qari Ziaur Rehman, a cleric's son from Kunar Province—had a way of keeping his head lowered while still maintaining hard eye contact. Which was scary. No one in his right mind, John thought, would ever disagree with him. Darim Sedgai had a rounder face and redder beard, and he wore his turban wrapped wider somehow, to suit him. The third man was introduced as Noor Islam, and John wondered briefly whether this was his real name. He had a long scar on his face, sort of like Burton's, but why would a fighter take a woman's name? John nodded to acknowledge the man, each of the men.

Attar, Tameel said. These men want to hear your biography. They want to know what brought you to Islam and Pakistan. And how and why you started training at Tangi. They're concerned about your ability to train with a Pashto unit. Speak in English. I'll translate as needed.

John swallowed. This wasn't going to be easy. He didn't know where to begin. He took a deep breath and introduced himself as the only son in an American family living in D.C. My parents, he said, read philosophy, psychology, science, and law, but not much religion. At school, I signed up for a class in world religion, and I became interested in Sufism and the Prophet Muhammed. I began reading Arab history and Muslim poetry, but if I wanted to really understand what I was reading, I needed some knowledge of classical Arabic. John paused. Did they really want to know all this?

Darim Sedgai signaled for him to continue, and John went on. And finished: From surfing and skating and Walt Whitman, I learned how to lean and loaf. Islam invited my soul.

Well done, Tameel mouthed, when John was finished.

Noor Islam addressed him directly, in Pakistani English. Why shouldn't we believe you're a spy and slice your head off right now?

John imagined a long jeweled knife in Noor Islam's hand. This man, he thought, might be capable of doing exactly that. And he was waiting for an answer.

If I were a spy, John said, I'd have arrived speaking perfect Pashto.

Darim Sedgai nodded, and John hoped that was a smile behind Noor Islam's beard.

WASHINGTON, D.C.—OCTOBER 2001

BARBARA WAS ANXIOUS. She'd had no e-mail from John, no call, which wasn't what they'd agreed on, wasn't like him. Even if a connection was hard to come by, after September 11 he would've and should've gotten himself to one. He should've written. He should've called.

He must have found what he needed in the hills, Bill said to calm her, but at his desk in the evening, he e-mailed Khaled, with apologies up front for the intrusion. We haven't heard from him, he wrote. Please let us know what you know, anything you know.

Twenty-four hours later, Khaled informed Bill that John had signed on for meditation at a camp outside Tangi, stayed there for three weeks, then took a trip higher into the mountains. He probably has no access to e-mail or a phone, and he might not even know about 9/11, Khaled wrote. He's missed his first few weeks of fall classes. I hope he gets back soon.

Your son, Bill told Barbara, is becoming a yogi, and yogis aren't known for staying in touch with their mothers.

His report hardly served to calm Barbara's fears. The country was on high alert, and second and third attacks were expected. On the subways, planes, in cities. Nuclear plants and water supplies were reported vulnerable. Even regular first-class mail wasn't safe.

You know what, one of Barbara's oldest friends suggested. Right now, John might actually be safer overseas.

They were dining out, and Barbara was agitated. Maybe so, Bill agreed, hoping to calm her, though he knew better.

The U.S. Army, he knew, was gearing up for war in Afghanistan, and the mountains above Peshawar were no place for an American. He engaged a law firm in Islamabad to file a missing person claim.

The North-West Frontier Province, the head of the law firm informed him, is an ideal place for an adventure. Unfortunately, it's also where people disappear. Without telling Barbara what he'd heard, Bill e-mailed all John's friends, asking them to forward their most recent correspondence with his son.

From: khaled102@islamia.edu
To: BillParish@ParishWalkerBrown.com
Date: October 2, 2001
RE: John Parish

Dear Mr. Parish,
Here's John's last email to me. We didn't email much. We met in classes. Went for tea.

I asked his friend Yusef who took him up there to find out more. I'll let you know as soon as I hear.

Yours,
Khaled

———————Forwarded Message

From: Attar attar75@islamia.edu
To: khaled102@islamia.edu
Date: July 29, 2001
FW: locker key

khaled,
i'm giving my locker key to yusef to give to you to keep with your own. will get it from you when i get back, allah willing. since my pig aka my board is too long to fit in the locker, i'm leaving it with yusef.

jjp, also known as attar

———————End of Forwarded Message

From: Noor Bint-Khan NoorK@earthlink.net
To: BillParish@ParishWalkerBrown.com
Date: October 3, 2001
RE: John Parish

Dear Mr. Parish,
I hope this helps.

Best,
Noor

———————Forwarded Message

From: Attar attar75@islamia.edu
To: Noor Bint-Khan NoorK@earthlink.net
Date: July 30, 2001
FW: board slide

dear (princess) noor,
i'm taking time out from classes to live in the cool or cooler hills above peshawar and might not have internet access for some time. but i'll do what i can to stay in touch. i never did meet the female half of peshawar's population, but perhaps in the hills i'll come across a shepherdess, though according to the stories merely looking at a tribal girl can start a feud. right now, i know, you're thinking he's jinned, and i might agree, but i might also ask what's wrong with a jinned life.

here's a maneuver that ali might be ready for. instruct him to practice it first on the lowest rail or curb he can find. it's called a board slide, combines two 180 ollies, one to get up on the curb, the second to get off. executing the slide in between requires momentum and balance. the trick is to land your board right between the front and back trucks, which means it will really test his balance. so here goes:

begin by rolling parallel to the rail, do a 180 onto the rail, use your knees and hips to push into the slide, then heel into your ollie down and land buttery. in the slide, you want about 20% more weight on your front foot so your board is tipped somewhat forward. this will also help you get some height. ali, have fun and don't hurt yourself.

noor, i miss you, ka-thee-ran. thank you for taking me inside, allowing me to learn and understand as an insider.

as salaamu + love,
john

ps do you know about rabia, a female sufi saint whose teachings emphasize love?

———————End of Forwarded Message

From: Naim Naim24@optonline.net
To: BillParish@ParishWalkerBrown.com
Date: October 4, 2001
RE: John Parish

Mr. Parish,
Here's what I got. I hope he's okay.

Naim

———————Forwarded Message

From: Attar attar75@islamia.edu
To: Naim Naim24@optonline.net
Date: July 30, 2001
FW: immersion

naim,
before i move on for further, deeper immersion, i want to thank you for your advice way back last year. you were right: this is the only way to truly learn and know. immersion as a kind of submission, really. to islam, to the culture, to the crowds, the heat, the tales, the small and larger cruelties, the poverty, the smells of rotting fruit, the food, the water, to the strangely non-absorbent towels, and more. and it's true i'm learning much about islam and its culture, and finding it very beautiful, but i'm writing to also tell you that my learning confirms something i said all along: that the choice of religion finally doesn't matter; only the ideals they teach are important. which means it really doesn't matter which religion you follow so long as you understand the goal. the prophet learned from the gnostics. the sufis wear wool because john the baptist wore a wool shirt. walt whitman got his transcendentalist ideas from buddhist texts. as one

sufi wrote: different grapes offer variations on the taste of grapes, but their essence which is wine is the same.

so, as i take off for my next adventure, shook-rahn for helping to inspire it,

attar

-----End of Forwarded Message

From: Katie katie101@optonline.net
To: BillParish@ParishWalkerBrown.com
Date: October 3, 2001
RE: John Parish

Dear Mr. and Mrs. Parish,
Sylvie and I are sick with worry, but still we believe, no we know that John will turn up. Just like that, just like John. He will arrive and he will be home again. Thinking of you both with lots of love,
Katie

ps Sylvie sends her love too.

pps My Mom says to send her love too and hopes to see you here soon.

ppps Everyone at OBX sends their love.

——————-Forwarded Message

From: Attar attar75@islamia.edu
To: Katie katie101@optonline.net
Date: July 30, 2001
FW: Jilly

dear katie,
i wish i could be with you, because then i wouldn't have to try to say what i feel. i'm glad you made the difficult decision to stay on in hawaii despite what happened. it's the right way to honor jilly. in my own way, on land rather than sea, i'm planning to honor jilly by immersing myself further and deeper than i have until now. i am moving to the hills for a couple of months, which

means i won't have internet access for a while, so i want to say i think of you often and with much much love and miss you. stay safe. here, in this brown brown country, i look up at the sky to see your forget-me-not blue eyes. so i'm not forgetting. i remain yours, xxxooojohn

ps give my love to sylvie too.

——————End of Forwarded Message

ON OCTOBER 7, Operation Enduring Freedom began with air strikes against military and terrorist camps, and Barbara, who had a map of the area on her desk, grew ever more anxious. John was somewhere in northern Pakistan, much too close to the war zone. Though on September 11 it had helped her to know that John was far from Brooklyn, now she wished he were living there again.

He might not even know that we're at war, she said.

That's what I worried about, Bill said. At first. But now, if he's anywhere in the area, if he's not far away in India, he's hearing the bombs.

In newspaper headlines and lead stories on every television and radio station, Donald Rumsfeld announced the initial strikes successful. Not knowing what else to do, Bill e-mailed Noor to arrange a meeting, and instead of going to his office one day, he took the Metroliner to Penn Station, and then a taxi to the café on Mott.

It was early, the café was quiet, and she brought two coffees to the small corner table.

Business has been slow since 9/11, she said.

She took a vial from her backpack and sprinkled some into her coffee.

Cinnamon? Bill asked.

It's called havaj, Noor explained. It's a mix of several spices. John liked it. Would you like to try it?

I'll pass, Bill said.

Have you heard anything? Noor asked but didn't wait for Bill's response.

It's unusual for him to let so much time pass between e-mails. Before his final e-mail, he was writing every week, and he always remembered everyone, especially Ali, that's my little brother. He would include detailed instructions for a new skating maneuver, and then Ali would practice hard until the next one arrived. He's gotten really good. John's a good teacher.

He impressed me in the beginning, and then he started scaring me, Noor continued. I worried that he was doing things for me, but I was mistaken. It had nothing to do with me. He was just going for full immersion, for the experience, for some kind of adventure. He had a sort of fantasy about becoming a great adventurer in the grand style of the nineteenth century. That's how he explained it, anyway. And I think that's what he's doing. He's disappeared into an adventure.

I hope you're right, Bill said. Then he asked a series of questions. I don't need an immediate answer, he said. I want you to take time to think about them: Did John ever mention training camps? Did he mention someone named Yusef? Did he say anything about fighting on the Kashmir border? About traveling to Afghanistan? About the Taliban? Had she been in touch with Khaled?

Noor answered the questions in the order they were asked. No and no and no and no and no and no, but Samina is probably in touch with Khaled. Khaled's girlfriend, Noor explained. I'll e-mail her. She's in Paris this year.

Bill hadn't heard of a Samina, but knowing that Khaled had a girlfriend, that he was a kid with the passions of other kids, was comforting. Do you know, Bill followed up, whether there were discussions of Islamic politics at the Sharia School?

I never attended classes, but I've heard Sharia students talk politics, though I don't know whether you could call that Islamic politics. The students at the Sharia are from everywhere—Indonesia, Yemen, India, Egypt, Iran, Pakistan—so they talk about all these places.

Ten minutes later, Bill left money plus a tip on the table. If you hear anything, he said, you know how to reach me.

They shook hands, but then Noor surprised Bill and stepped forward for a hug. I'll pray to Allah that he comes home soon.

He flagged a cab, gave the driver the address in Brooklyn, and leaned back to think. He hadn't notified the school of his visit because he didn't want to give them time to consider any particular position, though by now, since 9/11, no Arab institution anywhere in the world was without a position. He planned to walk into the main office, present himself as father of a former student, and ask permission to observe a class.

The school's administrator directed Bill to Brother Sami, John's former teacher.

Your son, Sami offered, wasn't here long, but he made himself noticed. An excellent student, his reading was varied and esoteric. He provoked the conservative mind.

In that, Bill said, he takes after his mother.

May Allah guide him back to safety, Sami offered.

The session Bill audited focused on the grammar of Arabic, and after half an hour of it, he left. Unlike his son, he had no interest in or facility for foreign languages. Of the school itself, he could say nothing damaging. They offered the instruction they promised. His son, he knew, could be trusted to find trouble on his own, but if he'd stayed in Brooklyn, he would have been all right. Now, too late, Bill wished he had taken a firmer stand against study in Pakistan. And he hoped that Noor was right, that John was having the adventure of his life, and that he would emerge alive to tell about it. He rubbed his forehead and eyes. This time, with his cracked cocktail of curiosity, bravado, misguided empathies, and taste for the strange, John might have gotten in over his head. But what more could Bill do? At a dead end, not knowing what else to do, he found himself wishing that he, too, could place his trust in Allah.

Crossing the Brooklyn Bridge back to Manhattan, Bill looked up at the skyline and saw only what wasn't there.

AT HOME THAT EVENING, Bill told Barbara where he'd been and what he'd learned. I'm waiting for more from Khaled, who's getting in touch with a Yusef, John's last contact. I also told the lawyer in Islamabad about this Yusef. And now I'm wondering what else to do.

Let's go there, Barbara said. Right away. Instead of waiting for the holidays.

I thought about it, Bill said, but I want to wait a week or two. Here, John and his friends know where to find us. I also wonder what we could do there that we can't do better from here. It's not as if we know our way around Pakistan. It's not as if we can go hiking into the mountains looking for him.

In two weeks then. Maybe we'll hear from him in the meantime. He'll want to come home for Thanksgiving.

He won't want to miss your turkey, Bill agreed.

NOVEMBER 22, 2001. It wasn't yet dawn, and already Barbara was awake. So over sweatpants and T-shirt, she pulled on John's high school hoodie. She'd put the turkey into the oven early, swim at the Y, return home to attend the fixin's, John's word. She would be home most of the day. She would be near the phone. She had become a woman who waits by the phone, addicted to the news, no matter how unpleasant. She went nowhere without her laptop, she checked her inbox too many times a day. She woke up to the papers, ended her day with the evening updates, and spent the night with Google, in search of the latest postings, while half the world was in bed, even if not sleeping. Sleep, a recent study reported, had become a commodity. More than half of Americans were losing sleep. Bin Ladin had murdered sleep. Knowing that even after hours, death and destruction didn't stop, not for the night, not for women and children, not for pity, justice, belief, Americans were having trouble sleeping. This country was at war, and even when there were no reports of anything particularly significant, there was death. Somewhere overseas someone's son was dying. Somewhere in the world a mother would grieve. This kept her awake. She checked for e-mail. Thanksgiving was John's favorite holiday, he had never missed a single one, and if he could, if he were anywhere near an Internet connection, he would send turkey tidings. Or he was on his way home to surprise them. He would walk through the door in time for turkey and stuffing and pie. She wanted nothing so much as to see John demolish the turkey, leave no leftovers, eat the way only a hungry nineteen-year-old can. She made a pot of coffee. She checked for e-mail. If he could he would send holiday wishes. He would surprise them, arrive in time for turkey, overstuff himself with pie. He was perhaps the only person in the world who ate his pumpkin pie with chocolate-fudge-brownie ice cream. She checked for e-mail. They wanted nothing so much as to see John demolish this turkey. She checked for e-mail. She rinsed and dried the turkey. She checked for e-mail. She rubbed salt into the cavity. She mixed paprika, cayenne, and sage in a small bowl. She poured in olive oil. She stirred. With bare clean hands, she thoroughly basted the turkey. She soaped and washed her hands again, dried them, checked for e-mail. She fiddled with the dial on the kitchen radio, found what she wanted. Reports of an imminent Taliban surrender in Konduz. She turned up the volume. Advancing Northern Alliance troops were hit with a sustained volley of Taliban artillery shells, the announcer said. The Alliance responded with a barrage of long-range rockets. U.S. forces continued to bomb Taliban front-line positions in Konduz. Contradictions were multiplying fast as Alliance and Taliban commanders, meeting in Mazar-e-Sharif, both claimed that the fighters would lay down their arms. Amid the turmoil and confusion, as winter drew near, aid agencies in Afghanistan were attempting to move in supplies for millions of war-weary civilians.

She chopped onions, celery, mushrooms, went to check—no, she stopped herself, it was too soon. She peeled carrots and sweet potatoes, couldn't help herself, and checked for e-mail, but the headlines were the same: Alliance and Taliban commanders, meeting in Mazar-e-Sharif, continued promising that their fighters would lay down their arms. Surrender, she thinks, is good news if it means an end to senseless fighting and killing, an end to untimely deaths, on both sides, all sides. The fighters were only kids, John's age. And then the bars of Alice's Restaurant opened, too early in the day, she thought, which meant she'd hear it too many times that day, all day, though hearing it too many times on Thanksgiving Day was practically a family tradition, would be an American tradition if America could be said to have any.

You can get anything you want, at Alice's Restaurant

With this song as their anthem, wearing bells and flower power and tie-dye, she and Bill and their friends had boarded the bus that took them from Boston to D.C. to march on the Pentagon and demand love not war.

You can get anything you want, at Alice's Restaurant

With aching bellies, exhausted and undernourished, hundreds of foreign Taliban fighters boarded trucks destined for Mazar-e-Sharif, for surrender to the Northern Alliance. The agreement, brokered by generals, required the foreign fighters to offer themselves up as prisoners in exchange for the lives of Afghan Taliban. The agreement demanded that the fighters drive into enemy territory and surrender themselves and their weapons into the hands of General Dostum's men, who would transport them for imprisonment in Qala-i-jangi. The agreement, Taliban leaders rationalized, would give these crazy foreign fighters what they'd come for, a chance to fulfill themselves in martyrdom. Sick with dysentery, thirst, and the hundred-mile trek to Tahkt, they climbed into the waiting Toyotas and stretched their useless legs, and hardly noticed when the next exhausted fighter climbed in and stretched out beside them, and the next one stretched out on top of them, all of them packed and layered and marinated in Toyota sardine cans, paid for by oily Soviet and U.S. greed. Relieved to be off their rubbery legs, relieved the terms of surrender were finally agreed upon, that the wait was over, the exhausted fighters hoped this jihad would soon be finished, that they would soon be delivered to their deaths or their homes, either one.

You can get anything you want, at Alice's Restaurant

With flower power and flares, Barbara and Bill had marched on the Pentagon. With placards and chants and love, they protested the war and the draft, and still the senseless killing continued for years. Even after veterans spoke in front of Congress, condemned what they'd been sent to do, condemned having been implicated in the murder of civilians, even then, politicians in Washington insisted on staying the course, if only for appearances' sake, so that the United States of America could continue to believe in its strength, could continue to prove itself a superpower. And so we didn't get out without more bloodletting, and when we finally did get out, we were quite certain that we'd never go to war again.

> It's the Alice's Restaurant Anti-Massacre Movement

She chopped, she peeled, she washed, she cooked. The U.S. military, she read, was flying in hundreds of turkeys, and six hundred pounds of stuffing, and a thousand pies, and eleven flavors of ice cream. Our troops in Afghanistan will eat well. But where would John eat? In the basement, the deep freezer was stocked with Ben & Jerry's chocolate-fudge-brownie ice cream. She dressed and stuffed the turkey, put it in the oven, and hoped and willed John onto a plane, into a bus, into a taxi destined toward home.

> You can get anything you want, at Alice's Restaurant
> You can get anything you want, at Alice's Restaurant

Downtown New York City, in the rubble that was once the World Trade Center, ashes smoldered; sniffing dogs unearthed shoes, bones, teeth, arms, legs, fire-retardant items of clothing; fathers dug for sons and daughters; sons dug for fathers and mothers. For those who weren't going home, didn't want to go home, couldn't think for what or to whom to give thanks, local restaurants announced that they'd be cooking and serving turkey, stuffing, and pie through the day. John would be returning to a changed world, a different America, and Barbara wondered what he knew. She worried about his judgment, about his misguided ideas, about his new friends and where they might have led him. She prayed against what she was afraid to put into words, that John had signed on to fight for what he thought was right, for someone else's cause that he didn't begin to understand. She turned to the television for more news.

THE TURKEY WENT INTO THE OVEN at noon, roasted for three and a half hours, rested on the counter for half an hour. Between the hours, every hour, Barbara went to the door, opened the door, looked up and down the street. After four in the afternoon, she and Bill sat down to eat. And ate little. There were only the two of them. They'd invited no one. Anxious and heartsick and sleep deprived, they'd declined invitations to give thanks with others and hoped only for the joy of John's last-minute arrival.

How about a movie? Bill asked, sorting through the rented movies.

Barbara found the remote, turned the TV on, heard again about the prison uprising that left an American CIA agent dead, the first American casualty of the Afghan war. And then a commercial break. U.S. military fighter planes, they heard, were sent in to help the Northern Alliance regain control of the prison compound. And again a commercial break. This is awful, she said. How can they?

Turn it off, Bill said. That's all the information they have, and they're going to make it last all night.

I'll get more details on the Internet, Barbara said.

Let's watch the movie, Bill said. He pressed PLAY and the black-and-white lion roared. Paper curtains parted. Hollywood starlets wrapped in ermine materialized. And with darkened eyes and stained lips lived. And two hours later died. And again the news offered no news: On

CNN, a rerun of Larry King interviewing the widowed and the suffering. On CNN2, a rerun of Larry King interviewing a fatherless son. On CNN3, a rerun of Flight 11 flying toward the first tower, in slow motion. On CNN4, a rerun of the tower collapsing, in slow motion, and again the towers fell, again people jumped and died. On CNN5, a rerun of Larry King interviewing a motherless daughter, a daughterless father, interviewing the motherless, fatherless, wifeless, husbandless, childless, shameless—disgusted, Bill pressed POWER and beheaded King, exiled CNN, and the world went dark. They sat relieved in the silence and dark. Not much road traffic now, but somewhere in the distant overhead the honk and flap of southbound geese, instinct bound, in vees for victory. The turkey was still on the table; the sides were still out. Let all who are hungry come and eat. Let all who are tired come home.

Bill tied on his red Coca-Cola apron and cleared the table and washed up. Barbara pulled the laptop into her lap and read:

> In the bloodiest engagement of the war in Afghanistan, imprisoned foreign Taliban soldiers, in a mud-brick fort outside of Mazar-e-Sharif, are all killed. The death toll includes scores of Northern Alliance soldiers and a CIA operative, who was questioning the Taliban at the time of the prison uprising. Speaking at an Air Force Base in Tampa, Florida, Defense Secretary Rumsfeld said the U.S. military bombed a compound near Kandahar used by Osama bin Laden's Al-Qaeda network. It clearly was a leadership area. Whoever was in there is going to wish they weren't, said Rumsfeld. The CIA identifies Michael Spann as the operative killed in the Mazar-e-Sharif prison uprising. Spann officially becomes the first American combat death in the Afghan war. The Pentagon says the Taliban leadership has lost control of its troops.

She went to tell Bill. She loaded the dishwasher and told.

We're at war, Bill said, which means this is only one story. There are surely ten unreported variations on this one.

He sliced the rest of the turkey, and Barbara filled a collection of leftover refrigerator containers with food that only John could demolish.

They washed up, they went to bed, but sleep, elusive sleep, stayed away. Awake, Barbara opened her laptop and read:

American warplanes fired into the compound, burning and shredding humans and horses, Dostum's stable of prized Arabian horses. At the end of day two, rockets blasted the armory, which exploded and smoldered for days. On the third day, when no more Taliban appeared, Red Cross officials entered the compound to collect bodies, but when two workers went down to the basement, they were fired on and killed. There were armed Taliban rebels still down there, still alive, alive enough to fight and kill, and no one would risk going in to get them. The Northern Alliance poured in water to drown them. They poured in gasoline to burn them. They threw in grenades to bomb them. Unable to hold out any longer, the remaining prisoners emerged from hell and surrendered to purgatory, or emerged from purgatory and surrendered to hell, they couldn't know which.

ON DECEMBER 3, early morning, Barbara opened the door and retrieved the daily bundle of newspapers, set it down on the counter, and went to make coffee. She separated the *Post* from the *Times,* the *Times* from the *Herald Tribune,* the coffee dripped, she unfolded the papers, slowed by sleep, by the need for sleep. She smoothed and straightened the papers, stared at the covers. But who was this? John? She was asleep, she was dreaming. She poured coffee. She swallowed coffee. She was afraid to look. She looked and read. An American. Named John. Naked. All bones. And bleeding. But why were his hands twisted and bound between his legs? And why had he arrived on the front pages, under this banner, this headline, AMERICAN TALIBAN?

Bill, she wailed. And ran to the bedroom trailing the front page. Bill sat up, groped for his glasses. What? What's wrong?

But the paper was crushed in her hand and had to be uncrushed.

American, he read. Taliban?

Look, Barbara keened. Look.

Bill swung his legs off the bed, found ground, the cold floor on his sleepy feet. He snatched the newspaper from Barbara's hand and looked, shook his head.

This isn't John, he said.

Read it, Barbara heaved. It's John.

Yes, but not our John, not John Jude.

It could be, she sputtered.

But it's not.

It might be.

What do you mean? Bill asked. What are you talking about?

I don't know, Barbara sobbed. Call it a mother's intuition. I feel that John's there, alive, somewhere, that somehow he's gotten himself caught up in this mess. And I must go to Pakistan. Today. We waited. He didn't show up for Thanksgiving. He probably couldn't. So we have to go there. We have to help him.

Bill promised to make the necessary calls.

AT SIX THAT EVENING, Barbara and Bill and the people of the United States sat stunned in front of their television sets tuned to CNN:

> I was a student in Pakistan studying Islam. And I came into contact with many people who were connected with the Taliban. I lived in a region in the northwestern province—the people there in general have a great love for the Taliban, so I started to read some of the literature of the scholars and the history of the movement. And my heart became attached to them. I wanted to help them in one way or another . . . [Yes] it's the goal of every Muslim to be shahid . . . I tell you, to be honest, every single one of us, without any exaggeration, every single one of us was one hundred percent sure that we would all be shahid . . . all be martyred. But you know, Allah chooses to take a person's life when he chooses. And we have no control.

Barbara wept. If only this were John Jude. It would be enough. To know her son was alive. To hear him talking. Smartassing. Like this John. If only our John like this John were in the hands of the United States Army, a prisoner of the United States Army. Mouthing off. Badassing. They probably know each other with their same smartass talk.

They watched the replays. Late night, after replays and tears and repeated replays, and after seeing Barbara to bed with a Demerol, Bill sent another e-mail to Khaled asking him if he'd found Yusef and demanding all available information about Yusef. Then he dialed the best criminal defense lawyer he knew. They would need him. If and when John Jude turned up, if he turned up in the hands of the United States Army, they would need the best.

EARLY THE NEXT MORNING, better rested and calmer than she'd been in weeks, Barbara scanned the headlines of the *Times,* the *Washington Post.* She paged through Glenn Reynolds' Instapundit, Gunzberger's Politics1.com, the Kausfiles, and Andrew Sullivan's blog. She went to the Israeli intelligence conspiracy site, Debka.com, to see what they might be revealing about yesterday's headline: American Taliban. Homegrown. She and every American, probably every citizen of the world with access to CNN, had watched and listened, repelled, attracted, and afraid all at once, and had gone to bed profoundly disturbed.

To be an American and speak so calmly of your own death, to offer yourself up as a martyr for Islam, to make martyrdom your goal, it was incomprehensible, especially for a contemporary American, unaccustomed to such sacrifice. But she needed to understand. She'd read Hegel, Hegel for whom overcoming one's fear of death was the only way to achieve true freedom. How else to understand the martyr's impulse? Self-consciousness, she knew, comes with beginnings. This was true for societies and nations as well as individuals. When the Middle East freed itself from its colonizers and came into independence, it became self-conscious about itself, its nationality. It was this long ongoing struggle toward self-realization that drove its politics now.

She looked again at the cover of the *Times,* the photo of this long-haired, bush-bearded American Taliban who, with his wounds and his nakedness and the bindings that nailed him to the stretcher, resembled Jesus Christ, resembled her own John. And it was a photo-op for jihad. That was what was so disturbing. In other words, the White House should not have permitted its dissemination. If she were working PR for the White House, she would have censored this image for evoking what every child knows as Christ on the cross, what every child comes to understand: that Christ fulfills himself in his crucifixion, becomes distinguished in death. Without his death, he could not have become Christ. In one of his papers for World Religion, John had argued for Judas as enabler rather than betrayer. Judas, his thesis stated, sacrificed himself and not Christ as the church has claimed. If Judas had refused Jesus this service, if he had put self-interest first, Christ would not have become the Savior God. Therefore without Judas, no God. Therefore without Judas, no Jew to blame and hate. But Christianity needed an enemy, a religion against which to fulfill itself, and found what it needed in Judas.

And this kid, Barbara wondered, this John Walker Lindh, with his wild hair and beard, resembling Jesus, Jeremiah, John Brown, resembling all martyrs, proving himself their descendant, what does he know? He has created himself in the image of martyrdom, with features in symmetry, eyes well paired with nose, nose with mouth, a harmonious face good to look at. The White House should have censored this photo, would surely have censored it given half a chance.

And John Jude? She hoped, she prayed, that their John, wherever he was, had made better decisions than this kid. If only he would call or write. If only he would come home.

THE STATE DEPARTMENT strongly advised against travel in northern Pakistan. It's where the Taliban is hiding. It's where Osama bin Ladin's friends are. It's where the CIA thinks he might be hiding.

We're at war in Afghanistan, someone at the office of Richard Armitage informed Bill, but the North-West Frontier of Pakistan qualifies as within the theater of war.

Over Barbara's protestations, over her accusations of coldheartedness and unfatherly unconcern, Bill canceled plans for their trip to Pakistan.

Getting ourselves trapped in a war zone, he snapped, possibly the same war zone John's trapped in, would be completely stupidly ludicrous. He's my son, too, and I want to find him as much as you do, but hysterical irrational behavior will get us nowhere. Careful thinking and planning will. For example, this: I'm debating whether to file a missing person report for an American abroad with the State Department's Office of American Citizens Services and Crisis Management. On the one hand, given Ashcroft's decision to try Lindh as an enemy of the state, filing could leave John similarly charged. That is if he too foolishly took up arms against Americans. But then I think no matter what, I'd rather have John in the custody of the U.S. Army than anywhere else.

I don't know how you can even hesitate about this, Barbara exploded. I'd rather have my son incarcerated anywhere in the U.S. than leave him rotting in some tribal prison.

Bill went ahead and filed.

BARBARA AWOKE, heaved her Demerol-deadened limbs out of bed and onto the cold dead floor, and lurched down the hard hall into her study, to her laptop, where she hoped an envelope hovered telling her she had mail, an e-mail from John Jude, or at the very least, a Red Cross letter, which would mean secondhand word from John. It was now four months since she'd heard from him. She was a mother who hadn't heard from her son, who didn't know whether he was still alive, and not knowing, she was stuck marking minutes, hours, and days, with only the daily papers, the news, and the postings, stuck in chronology, not life:

> On December 9, at Camp Rhino, on a marine base near Kandahar, an FBI agent interviewed John Walker Lindh and walked away with a nine-page report that would become the basis for the criminal case against him.
>
> On December 11, Zacarias Moussaoui, a French citizen of Moroccan descent, was charged with conspiring with Osama bin ladin and al Qaeda to murder Americans.
>
> On December 22, Richard Reid, a British citizen, was apprehended for trying to blow up a Miami-bound jet with explosives hidden in his shoe.
>
> On January 9, the White House declared that the Guantanamo detainees were not entitled to the protections accorded prisoners of war under the Geneva Conventions.
>
> On January 11, the first twenty detainees arrived at Guantanamo's Camp X-Ray.
>
> On January 16, Defense Secretary Donald Rumsfeld announced that he did not feel the slightest concern regarding the treatment of Guantanamo prisoners. They're being treated vastly better than they treated anybody else, he said.
>
> On January 17, the official detainee count at Guantanamo was one hundred ten.

JOHN WALKER LINDH was scheduled to arrive at the correctional facility in Alexandria, Virginia, and Barbara wanted to be there.

Bill tried discouraging her. Her obsession with the Lindhs was getting to him. Her irrational persistence in somehow identifying the Lindhs' John with their John made him think she might be losing it.

Pray, he said, that our John is safe elsewhere, far from the Taliban. Pray that he had better sense. Should have better sense.

He was still waiting for information from Yusef, for the law firm's findings, for the State Department's response to his missing person report, but answers were slow in coming, and Barbara was losing patience.

I think these kids don't know anything or they know and won't tell. Before September 11, before Lindh's capture, they might have been forthcoming. After, telling is like a confession of guilt. That's what I feel intuitively, and in the absence of facts, I'm placing my trust in intuition.

Without facts, we'll get nowhere, Bill warned. Therefore I'm engaged in fact gathering.

That might be fine for trial preparation, Barbara criticized. When you're working for a client. But in an emergency, especially an emergency that involves your son, it's not enough.

You know, Bill said, looking at her. Maybe, just maybe, if you hadn't encouraged John in his crackpot ideas and readings, he'd be at Brown now and we wouldn't be in this emergency.

Upon which Barbara broke down and refused to say anything. She wouldn't eat dinner, wouldn't answer questions, wouldn't share a bed with Bill. She moved into John's room, but halfway through the night, Bill joined her in John's bed.

ON JANUARY 24, Barbara canceled her morning appointments in order to get to the facility early and position herself near an entrance. She wanted to see the boy and hoped to have a word with his mother. She hoped Mrs. Lindh would agree to ask her son whether he'd met John Jude. Mrs. Lindh, she thought, would understand. A suffering mothers' group might be just what was needed. An international suffering mothers of the world group. They could band together and effect change, eradicate war.

She drove south to Virginia, found the facility, found a place to park with some difficulty and at some distance. She wasn't the only one who wanted to see the boy, it turned out. There were others, and by the time she arrived at the gates of the compound a large crowd had gathered. People jostled for position, but Barbara pushed toward the entrance and then had to make an effort to hold her ground. If she didn't get near enough, she wouldn't be able to make contact.

A helicopter droned overhead. The crowd looked up and watched it circle and land inside the prison compound. It was difficult to see what was going on on the ground, but when Barbara looked up, she saw sharpshooters on the rooftops of every structure. Motorcycles rumbled, radios and CBs crackled, the propeller spun, the door opened, and men with guns clustered and huddled and completely obscured the nineteen-year-old boy who had somehow provoked this scene out of—it has been years since she's watched anything like this—out of ludicrous *Starsky and*

Hutch. For a nineteen-year-old. What were these people thinking? That he was Bruce Lee? What were they afraid of? Barbara turned to say something to someone beside or behind her and noticed for the first time that the crowd was angry. The rumble started low, but quickly grew in pitch. Traitor. Shame. Hanging. These people had taken time off from work to be here, to see with their own eyes the boy who'd betrayed his country. They'd come to accuse him, to judge him without a trial. They were mothers and fathers and brothers and sisters, but they were unforgiving. Of a nineteen-year-old's misadventure. Of a self-seeking journey. Did they know he was only nineteen? Did they understand—

A black limousine pulled up to the gates, and Barbara felt a huge weight forcing her forward, toward the car, as if to crush it, crush her. She panicked. She needed air. She raised her arms, reaching for air and sky. Help, she called.

Traitors, people shouted. Hot-tubbers. Murderers.

Hang him, someone shouted. By his balls.

This crowd hated the boy and his parents. This crowd hated her. They were wrong. She wanted to tell them they were wrong, they didn't understand. She wanted—she was unable to tell them.

Security officers surrounded the vehicle, pushed the crowd back, and Barbara felt herself falling backward. She grabbed someone's jacket and held on. She steadied herself. She breathed. And then the gates opened, the car pulled through, and the gates shut. The Lindhs had gotten through safely, and the crowd didn't like it. They protested. They shouted. Hot-tubbers. Latte sippers. Liberals.

WHAT DID YOU THINK would happen? Bill asked.

But he's only nineteen, Barbara protested.

Your son, our son, is nineteen. Walker will be twenty-one in two weeks and the 9/11 terrorists were not much older than that. This boy fought in a war against Americans, on the side of the enemy. Worse, he witnessed the murder of a CIA man, and did nothing to help him. Do you have any idea how America feels right now? Do you have any idea how much hate mail the Lindhs must be getting? Probably death threats too. I hope to God that our John didn't do anything this stupid. Pray that he didn't.

If he did, Barbara said, he didn't know what he was doing.

That night when, with the help of an Ativan, Barbara finally slept, she relived the scene. Traitor. Shame. Murderers. Hot-tubbers. Hang them. She tried running and couldn't. She was surrounded. She shouted for help. Someone was calling her name.

Barbara. Wake up. Barbara. It's okay.

They turned on CNN and heard that John Walker Lindh had arrived in Alexandria to be tried in a civilian criminal court, that he'd made his first appearance before a U.S. district court and heard the criminal complaint against him, which listed four charges, including conspiring to kill fellow Americans in Afghanistan, providing support to terrorist groups, and aiding the Taliban. Though CNN had been allowed into the compound to film, they showed very little, the helicopter in the air, the landing, a glimpse of Walker in his orange prison clothes, then moved on to other news, non-news really.

Barbara sat, astounded. They were giving hours of coverage to daily nonsense, and mere seconds to this.

The arrival, Bill said, was handled pretty well actually. No one wants this kid to attract a cult following. Ashcroft screwed up the first half of this case by allowing the interview to take place without a lawyer. Which means it will never go to trial. Heads are expected to roll at the Justice Department. Rumors are already emerging. There's a story of a Jesselyn Radack, a young attorney in the Justice Department's internal ethics office, who is said to have advised against interviewing Lindh without an attorney present.

Radack? Barbara said. Radack. I know that name. From somewhere.

She Googled it. Jesselyn Radack, she read, was the activist student at Brown who'd appeared on *Phil Donahue.* Then Barbara remembered. She'd come across her writing somewhere. In the Brown alumni magazine? That's why the name was familiar. What an odd connection. Mere coincidence, Bill would say, as she would have said only a few months ago, but these days, anxious and afraid, Barbara found everything relevant.

THE STORY OF JESSELYN RADACK

December 7, 2001. Justice Department attorney Jesselyn Radack received an inquiry from John De Pue, Terrorism and Violent Crime Section. Would it be okay, he asked, for the FBI to interview Lindh in Afghanistan without the presence of his lawyer? Radack researched the question and consulted with a senior legal adviser before replying: We don't think you can have the FBI agent question Walker. Lindh's father had retained an attorney, Radack noted, so interrogation outside of the presence of counsel would be improper.

December 10, 2001. In a follow-up, De Pue informed Radack that the agent had conducted the interview anyway. The interview, Radack wrote back, will probably have to be sealed or used for national security purposes only. Ashcroft disregarded this advice and insisted on using the interview as a confession.

February 4, 2002. Jesselyn Radack received an unscheduled scathing performance review. Her boss, Claudia Flynn, who had not signed the review, offered to keep it out of her file if Radack found another job.

March 7, 2002. Randy Bellows, a prosecutor in *United States of America v. John Philip Walker Lindh,* e-mailed Radack, asking whether there'd been only two e-mails in her exchange with the terrorism unit. Bellows had sought all of Radack's e-mails on the Lindh interrogation and received only two. Radack knew there had been a dozen or more, but when she pulled the file now, she found only three e-mails and some cover sheets. Working with a computer technician, Radack retrieved fourteen archived e-mails. These she printed the same day and addressed, with cover memo, to Claudia Flynn.

April 8, 2002. Jesselyn Radack began working at the Hawkins law firm.

DESPERATE FOR WORD, for answers to queries and questions she hardly dared voice, Barbara couldn't help herself and looked for connections and meaning everywhere. Everything connects. Jilly's death was also somehow connected. She worried that the loss of Jilly had somehow engaged John's instinct for risk and destruction, his death drive, what Freud called the Todestrieb, and now she blamed herself for telling him. She should've known better. She should've waited until he got back, until he was safe, or safer, at home, where love could counteract this destructive impulse. At the time she'd worried that not telling him was wrong. Now she spent long nights thinking, arguing, agreeing, resolving, compromising, begging, negotiating, conceding, seething, settling, fighting, negotiating again, compromising.

But with whom are you reasoning and cooperating and compromising? Bill wanted to know.

I don't know, Barbara sobbed. With whatever power's keeping John from us. I know he's alive. I know he's being held. Somewhere. Against his will.

Bill attempted to hold her still so she would sleep. You've got to keep it together, he whispered. I agree with you. He's alive. And he will need our help when he shows up. You can only help him if you keep it together.

She was convinced there was someone who knew John Jude's whereabouts and wasn't telling. She was convinced the U.S. military knew or had the capacity to know. They might have him at Guantanamo and they weren't telling. Or they'd already killed him and weren't telling. Or it was possible he'd been left behind as Dostum's prisoner, and he was now without arms and legs or minus his tongue so that he couldn't write and couldn't talk. Or he was one of the many dead in the compound at Qala-i-jangi. Or. Or. Or. Something convinced her he'd been there, a prisoner at the fort, along with Lindh. If only she could talk to Lindh. As long as she didn't know anything with any certainty, as long as she was without answers, she was stuck in a loop, going from step to step and back again, with only the news to inform her, with only what was revealed on any given day, with chronology. She was stuck in this story without an ending.

FEBRUARY 13, 2002. John Walker Lindh pleaded not guilty to a ten-count federal indictment that charged him with conspiring to kill Americans. His attorney notified the court that he will argue against the use of forced statements his client made in Afghanistan.

February 21, 2002. A federal judge dismissed the legal challenge to the Guantanamo detentions in which Barbara had placed hope.

February 21, 2002. A jihad website leaked a video titled *The Slaughter of the Spy-Journalist, the Jew Daniel Pearl.* The video showed Pearl's body naked from the waist up with his throat slit. Then a man decapitated him.

Barbara and Bill watched the short clip of the video made available for airing. Beside herself, in despair, Barbara called out to her nonexistent God: If you exist, she cried, prove yourself and bring on the Apocalypse NOW.

Perhaps this is the Apocalypse, Bill said, rubbing his exhausted eyes.

Though he doubted that John Jude was in Guantanamo—his American citizenship would have forced the military to bring his case to a civil court—Bill contacted one of the attorneys scheduled to visit there and asked him to be on the lookout for John Jude.

A thin man, Bill had lost too much weight and was now fragile looking. He was keeping long hours, working his usual fifty-hour week, and then working evenings to learn what he could. At work, colleagues stopped by his office to discuss the situation, to sympathize and advise.

Your boy can't be represented by a lawyer until he shows up, somewhere, anywhere, Chip Brown, one of Bill's partners, said, pointing out the obvious. We'll go to work as soon as he shows up.

John, the John I know, has an instinct for life, Brad Walker said. I agree with Barbara. He's alive, and he will turn up. In a while. He put his hand on Bill's shoulder. You and Barbara just have to sit tight, you have to find some way to get through this. After the Lindh fiasco, Ashcroft will hold back embarrassing information of other captured Americans for as long as he can manage it.

But Barbara wouldn't or couldn't live with mere waiting. She closed the door to her office, opened her Rolodex, and started at *A*. She would call in every favor from every politician who had ever attended her fund-raisers and parties, anyone with any clout in this White House. And she did get people on the phone, and though the conversations would begin convincingly enough, when she met with inaction, or what she thought of as stonewalling, she raised her voice. She ranted. She shouted. And when the other party hung up, she ate. Between A and B on her Rolodex, and between B and C and C and D and D and E, she ate. She'd gained twenty pounds since Thanksgiving. She'd demolished the leftovers they'd saved for John. She'd become a fearsome figure, a major matriarch in appearance.

When people stopped coming to the phone, she determined to go where they went. Mornings she scanned the day's lists of events, circled the ones likely to attract the most powerful, and attended. She made herself available to bloggers and gossip columnists for the most outrageous quotes. At a book party for a young dot.com editor noted for her witty political discourse interspersed with frequent references to gin and anal sex, Barbara offered an explanation for the prevalence of sex abuse in Washington: *Caligula* is the politician's guide to D.C. They watch the film so often, they come to know it as their gospel. Remarking on the number of politicians at the party who were either losing or had lost their voices and therefore couldn't comment on her questions about the American Taliban, she offered a Freudian analysis:

their penises were rising up into their throats. On the phone with a young intern who refused to connect her to his boss, she suggested he imagine himself in Nazi Germany. They weren't all evil, she ranted, just weak in character and dignity, like you, people unwilling to do what's right, afraid to pursue justice. You would have been one of the millions who performed their jobs and asked no questions; in essence, you would have been, as you are now, a collaborator.

At home, she continued scanning postings and blogs, both the reliable and ridiculous, and staying close to online rumor mills and postings and blogs, she learned about another American Taliban, a young man named Yasir Hamdi, born in Texas to Saudi Arabian parents. Hamdi, she reported to Bill, was captured alongside Lindh, but he didn't make headlines or even the news.

It's possible there are others, Bill said. It's entirely possible, he thought, that John had kept his wits about him and remained silent. A lawyer's son, he knew not to talk without a lawyer, not to the military or the press.

ON APRIL 5, Yasir Hamdi was scheduled for transfer from Guantanamo to a naval brig in Norfolk, Virginia. This headline served Barbara as the burning bush served Moses, and the angel Muhammed, illuminating the unknowing dark. She suddenly KNEW. John is going by a different name, as he has before. He might be Attar or Ishmael or Abdul. He might even be going as Yasir Hamdi. He might BE Yasir Hamdi. How could she not have thought of that: he wouldn't use his real name. She canceled her appointments for the day and drove down to Norfolk, riding and deriding Bill all the way down, Bill and his paper attempts at finding their son. Then she turned on herself: how could she have overlooked something this obvious? She worried about what else she might be missing. She tried thinking John's thoughts. What did he want her to know, say, think, do?

This was his adventure of becoming. But what was the use of becoming, if you ended in annihilation?

You're not fully alive unless you're risking death, he'd say.

And what would you say we're doing, Dad and I? she'd ask.

She arrived early this time, prepared for the tight security, expecting the angry crowd. This time, she would get in. Wearing a smart dress and sensible heels and dark Chanel sunglasses, and carrying a journalist's bag, flap open just enough to reveal a journalist's props, the notebook, the recording device, and authentic-looking ID, she stepped up to the pier gates with as much official know-how as she could muster. She smiled at the guard, reached for the flap to show her pass.

Reporting for whom? the guard asked without looking.

Washington Times, Barbara said, with authority.

And miraculously, the gate opened, miraculously she was waved through. It'd worked. She'd managed it. She walked toward the group of reporters gathered under an awning. She nodded greeting and inserted herself into the side flank of the huddle, mindful of the others, careful not to attract much notice.

He's expected to arrive in an armored vehicle, one journalist offered. And we are not to expect to speak with him.

Any family members present? Barbara asked.

Only an uncle, with a lawyer.

A limousine pulled up to the gate, and a suited man stepped out to speak with the guard, but the vehicle would not be allowed through. The lawyer opened the door and escorted a thin wiry man out. The uncle, presumably. Which meant there was a Yasir Hamdi. Which meant he wasn't John.

Desperate, Barbara moved quickly. This was her only chance. She had to know whether this kid had met John, knew John. She had to ask him. She separated herself from the journalists and walked toward the two men, stepping between them. She kept her eye on the young straight-backed marine leading the way toward the gangplank that led onto the brig. He didn't turn around.

Who are you? the lawyer asked, taking her arm.

A journalist who wants to bring this story to the public, Barbara murmured. A mother suffering the absence of her son. Mr. Hamdi? she asked, bending her head to bring it closer to him. Is there a Mrs. Hamdi? she asked, but got no response.

I need to talk to your nephew, she persisted.

A-hem, the lawyer said, taking her elbow, though he kept walking. For whom are you covering this story?

That remains to be seen, Barbara said. The more access, the better the story; the better the story, the higher the odds of selling it. Publicity could be useful to your case.

The lawyer nodded. He'd already thought of that. FYI, he said. We haven't been guaranteed access to the boy ourselves. Decisions—or perhaps I should say indecisions—are made case by case, which means they're taking their time. In the meantime, the boy remains in lockup.

In the meantime, his parents are losing sleep, losing their health, losing everything they have. And this is taking place in the United States of America.

I know all about it, Barbara said.

The young marine stood aside and ushered them onto the brig and into a bare inner chamber. Wait here, he said and left.

She was in. She'd made it in. She waited. They waited. They were made to wait long enough for Barbara to have second and third thoughts.

Half an hour later, the marine returned to say not today, and Barbara exploded. What do you mean, not today?

The navy isn't prepared, the marine said. They need time to set it up. The meeting might be rescheduled to take place off-site.

It means, the lawyer translated, that they're not allowing a face-to-face. They want some kind of screen, the standard prison setup.

She'd gotten so close, she was inside, standing with those closest to the prisoner, and inside, close as she was, she had missed Yasir Hamdi's arrival outside. As a journalist huddled outside, she would have at least seen the boy. Even the crowd outside the gate had seen more. Somewhere in her stomach a strange rumble gathered and came up her throat and emerged hysterically. She laughed. She cried. She laughed and cried.

Hamdi's uncle backed away. The lawyer escorted her. Get ahold of yourself, he said.

He directed her down the plank, onto the pier, and onward, through the gates. The familiar clack of her heels on metal comforted and calmed her. Reminded her of who she was. She'd gotten in once; she could do it again. The limousine pulled up and the lawyer handed her in, not so gently.

Now, he said, tell me who you are.

Barbara reached into her bag for a tissue and noted that her hands were shaking. She couldn't talk. This strange hysteria was still in her throat, choking her. She'd come so close. Hamdi must have met John Jude. Of this she was certain.

My son, she hiccuped, is missing. I'm doing everything I can to find him.

She heard Hamdi's uncle exhale. He seemed to have been holding his breath. She turned to speak with him, but he turned away. He has nothing to say to a fellow sufferer, a hysterical woman, Barbara thought.

Where's your car? the lawyer asked. We'll drop you off.

BARBARA CAME ACROSS a story reporting on the interrogation of John Walker Lindh. Included in the story were a number of Radack's e-mails. Phone calls and e-mails to and from the reporter were traced to the Hawkins law firm, and the Department put Radack under investigation.

This is good for us, Bill said. And good for this country. There are also rumors of illegal detentions. These stories will start turning public opinion against Ashcroft and the Bush administration. Which could help us. Now we just have to wait for John to turn up.

He will turn up, Bill said, for which Barbara kissed him.

OUTER BANKS (OBX), NORTH CAROLINA—MAY 2002

MAY 1, 2002. Every age, the Hegelian theory of history goes, is a progression toward better, an improvement over what came before. This is May 1, of A.D. 2002. This is the age of oil, the age of the corporation, the age of terrorism, the age of martyrdom. It is surely not an accident that I am describing one and the same age. This is the Virginia Correctional Facility of Alexandria City, VA, 1212 Alexandria Station, cell block P. On a cot in his cell, John Walker Lindh awoke at dawn without the muezzin call, without an alarm, with only his inner clock borne of faith and passion, and washed his hands and face at his urinal of a sink and kneeled on number two of two towels provided by prison housekeeping. He knows the way to Mecca and prays toward it. Twenty years minus six months already served minus three years for good behavior, that is, sixteen and a half years from now, in the year 2019, perhaps he will make the pilgrimage in person, in body as well as mind. That is, if his lawyers get what they hope for. He will be thirty-eight years old. By then it might be the Muslim era: M.E. 2019.

From another cell down the hall, and another cell around the bend, and from the next hall, and the next cell the voices of other Muslims in prayer echo, altogether twenty Muslims praying, giving voice to belief, la illaha il'allah, no god but god, et Muhammed rasulu, twenty Muslim men bearing witness to the God of the prophet of Islam in, lalalalala, an American facility—

Prison Guard: Where do you think you are? Where DO they think they are? This is no mosque in Medina, this is an American prison goddammit paid for by the American people, so keep it down, shutthefuckup—

in an American facility nine miles from the White House, where our president worships his own God.

IT IS MAY 1, 2002, early morning on visitor's day at the prison in Alexandria, and Barbara is already in line, hoping to meet Lindh's mother, hoping to one day be a mother waiting to see her son, knowing he is alive. She is preparing herself for this future, for this false incarnation of her baby, her John Jude, in baggy prison jumpsuit and shuffling slippers, ears made prominent by a close prison shave, and in the extreme bareness of his head and face, temples overwide and eyes too close, LYING FACTS. They will remake him in the common image of the common criminal housed in a maximum-security facility, though he is her beautiful, her gentle son. His crime: an ability to immerse himself in the new and other and become, a selfless ability to *other* himself, though he'd started life as her baby, though he was her scholarly John Jude, her Goofy-Foot John, summa cum laude graduate of John Harlan High. By the time he turned sixteen, he'd already been collector of various things collectible, rapster, songwriter, skater, and honor student of world cultures. At eighteen, he was a surfer, mystic, student of Arabic, and more. He was known online as Sun-T for Ice T, as Attar for the Sufi poet Fariduddin Attar, as Ibrahim for the father of Ishmael, as Abdul for—she couldn't remember for whom. He was perhaps unduly influenced by books. Reading, he became hero, narrator, adventurer, and walked and talked the parts. In Psych 101, this is known as role-playing; in literature, empathy. Also the source of Shakespeare's genius. But in the twenty-first century, genius has become a crime, and for this crime he will be sentenced just as he is coming of age as a man, a danger to non-man, the system.

It seems to Barbara now that John had been thrust into this mode of becoming through no fault of his own when she and Bill named him for their favorite Beatle. On December 8, 1981, the first anniversary of Lennon's death, the day she learned she was one month pregnant. She was on her way home from the doctor in her old orange Datsun 510 with only AM radio, because Bill had an afternoon meeting at his firm's Baltimore office and needed the Toyota to get there. She was driving and praying that this Datsun on last legs would give her another year, though it had always been something of a lemon and she'd long suspected that its first owner, her long-haired professor of economics, had replaced the Japanese parts on this car with cheaper American ones which were constantly cracking and breaking; she had broken down on every street and street corner in the area, and she and this orange lemon were notorious for toxic spillages of every kind, motor oil, gas, fatally sweet green radiator fluid. You don't need this heartache, the mechanic advised. Get yourself a reliable little Honda and dump this bad job somewhere. But they had put all their savings on the house in Adams Morgan and taken out a mortgage and now they were bringing a child into the world, and she wanted not to work its first three years. On the radio Hey Jude came on just as the car stalled at the light on California and Eighteenth Streets, and the honking behind her threatened to drown the music, and she turned up the volume and placed her hand on her soon-to-be-kicked belly and didn't care that she was draining the battery. After which she might just get out and abandon this orange turncoat. In college she'd played the song over and over and over again until Caitlin her roommate threatened to smash the LP. So they'd middle-named John for it, Hey Jude . . . Take a sad song and make it better. MAKE THIS SONG BETTER INDEED. Better better better better—

MAY 1, 2002. Border skirmishes between India and Kashmir have resulted in a breakdown of diplomacy, and the threat of nuclear war is high. Pakistan plans to start testing missiles and is preparing to shift troops from the border with Afghanistan to the front in Kashmir, where tensions with India are quickly rising. Prime Minister Atal Bihari Vajpayee told Indian soldiers along the tense frontier in Kashmir to prepare for a decisive battle against terrorism.

IT IS STILL MAY 1, and still more than 2 million are starving to death in South Africa. May Day. May Day. MAYDAY—

Also today, in what will become the largest bankruptcy case ever, WorldCom prepares to file for Chapter 11.

Also today, the president reminds us, that is, as of last Thursday, no suicide bombers managed to blow themselves up on buses, subways, in markets, or in front of falafel stands. We are doing something right, he says. God loves America, he says.

UNABLE TO SIT STILL, desperate to do something, to act, to move mountains, Barbara packs a change of clothes and drives down to the Outer Banks. And all the way down, she listens to John's music. She begins with the Ensemble Ibn 'Arabi, a meditative set of songs, moves on to Shankar, to Nusrat Fateh Ali Khan. She is surprised by some of the CDs in her son's collection: Steve Reich's *Music for 18 Musicians,* which she didn't know John liked. The Kronos Quartet, and of course Dylan.

Dylan chants. Barbara drives. And sobs. She turns left on Wright Memorial Bridge and remembers last night's dream. She'd been flying. She'd been airborne and exuberant, and now she can't remember why or where, whether she'd flown over anywhere in particular, seen anything. She is here now, crossing the Wright Brothers Memorial Bridge, to the Outer Banks, where man first flew, and she knows. That the Outer Banks has been expecting her. That the house has been waiting. She opens the windows and inhales the saline air. She feels John in the air. The Saab is in the driveway. His long board leans in its place in the garage; his short board clutters the front hall. So she changes into a swimsuit and a pair of aloha board pants, an old gift from John. She finds and slips into one of his rash guards, and though too long, it's snug. She loads his short board into the Saab and drives up Byrd to the surfers' stretch of beach. She finds a spot on the corner of Byrd and Lindbergh, beside a blue jalopy she recognizes. Sylvie's car. She unloads. She walks to the beach. She looks. She watches the waves.

So she sees the waves collect themselves, gather meaning, heave over, and disperse to nonmeaning. Two sides of the same thing, rising, dropping. What John wants her to know.

She looks up, sees the girls bobbing in the water. So she waves. So the girls see her and ride toward her. So she walks toward them, enters the water, with Katie and Sylvie at her sides. She does as they do. Rushes the water, surfboard in front of her, and then with the board supporting her, keeping her afloat, with the girls encouraging her, giving her a hand, she paddles with them toward the depths. They paddle past the third breaker and move toward the fourth. They duck under and come out past the fifth. They keep paddling, past the sixth and the seventh, where it's finally quiet. They are beyond the crashing waves, beyond the noise. She pulls her knees up under her as they do. She waits.

Thus three boards bob in the water, thus three wahines wait for a wave. They pass on the first one. They duck under the second. And then the third one begins to build, and Katie signals. Sylvie gives the sign. This is yours, a good beginner's wave. They push her board into it. So she crouches on her toes, hands on the sides of her board, balancing. She breathes and waits, feels the water build under her, heave and lift her. So she unbends her knees halfway, stands, and gives herself to the wave, to the pleasure of giving herself, a surrender. Her weight shifts to match the water's weight. Her knees bend and unbend. One and two. One and then two, left shift, right shift, left shift, right. She moves with the wave, with the rhythm of the wave. And she understands. It's all continuous movement, no standing still, no holding on. There is only becoming. Being doesn't exist. So she keeps moving, shifting her weight right, shifting her weight left, right left right left right. And the wave lifts her, the wave carries her, and she rides. It is awesome, it is extraordinary, it is absurd, and, yes, glorious. She feels Jilly with her, holding her up. She feels John beside her, keeping the rhythm: left, right, left, right—she is a fifty-two-year-old mother on her son's board. She is fifty-two years old and becoming. She rides for a long half minute, the fullest thirty seconds of her life.

ACKNOWLEDGMENTS

This work is indebted, as all books are, to the many texts that informed it. First and foremost, Henry Corbin's astounding *Alone with the Alone: Creative Imagination in the Sūfism of Ibn 'Arabī* escorted me into Sufism. Harold Bloom's introductory essay on Corbin showed me how the mystical ideas and myths of the Kabbalah expand into this wider system of thought. Idries Shah's *The Sufis* introduced me to the founding Sufis and their work.

Several books and articles offered insight into the education and psychology of martyrs, among them *Whistleblowers* by C. Fred Alford; *Kamikaze Diaries* by Emiko Ohnuki-Tierney; Jane Mayer's "Lost in the Jihad," for *The New Yorker*; Laurie Abraham's "Anatomy of a Whistle-blower" for *Mother Jones*; Mark Kukis's *"My Heart Became Attached"*; and William Dalrymple's "Inside the Madrasas," for *The New York Review of Books.* The notion of Islamabad as D.C. dropped into the foothills of the Himalayas is from Dalrymple's "Days of Rage," published in *The New Yorker.* From Charles Seife's *Zero* came the idea of Zero Point as a cosmic/spiritual starting point. The translation of the *Tao* is by Ron Hogan, editor of Beatrice.com. The lines of poetry at the end of part three are from *Poems of Arab Andalusia*, translated by Cola Franzen and published by City Lights. Edward Rice's biography *Captain Sir Richard Francis Burton* provided me with an example of a scholar-adventurer and the mixed motivations that inspired him.

Several publishers generously allowed me to excerpt from published work, and I am grateful for their permission. Special thanks to Eddie Hirsch for his "I Am Going to Start Living Like a Mystic" from *Lay Back the Darkness*, published by Knopf. The translation of the 'Arabi poem "My Heart Is Capable of Every Form" is from Corbin's *Alone with the Alone*, published by Princeton University Press. Faiz Ahmed Faiz's "Don't Ask for That Love Again," from *The Rebel's Silhouette: Selected Poems,* was translated by Agha Shahid Ali and published by University of Massachusetts Press. APA Publications GmbH & Co. Verlag KG, Singapore Branch, provided permission for the excerpts from its *Insight Guide to Pakistan, 3rd Edition.* And Appleseed Music, Inc., allowed the reprinting of the lines from Arlo Guthrie's "Alice's Restaurant."

I'm deeply grateful to the following people: my first reader, Stephanie Grant, whose close readings and nuanced comments made this a better book, and whose friendship serves me as a rock; Patricia Chao and Jonathan Freedman, who read early, sketchy beginnings; my luminous agent, Mary Evans, whose capacity for optimism and desire for transcendent life shaped this story. David Ebershoff's tireless editing helped sculpt the book into its final form.

Finally, I'm indebted to Stephen Spewock, who continues to tolerate the tortuous writing process, the long years from happy conception through to the torment of publication.

ABOUT THE AUTHOR

PEARL ABRAHAM is the author of three novels, *The Seventh Beggar, Giving Up America,* and *The Romance Reader,* and the editor of the anthology *Een sterke vrouw, wie zal haar vinden?* Her stories and essays have appeared in literary quarterlies and anthologies. Abraham teaches literature and creative writing at Western New England College.